ACES WILDE

Immortal Vegas, Book 5

JENN STARK

ISBN-13: 978-1-943768-16-5

Cover design and Photography Gene Mollica

Formatting by Bemis Promotions

This book is a work of fiction. References to real people, events, establishments, organizations, or locations are intended only to provide a sense of authenticity, and are used fictitiously. All other characters, and all incidents and dialogue, are drawn from the author's imagination and are not to be construed as real.

Other Books by Jenn Stark

Getting Wilde
Wilde Card
Born To Be Wilde
Wicked And Wilde
One Wilde Night (prequel novella)

For You

IV
II
III

Chapter One

In life, it is said, each of us must play the Fool.

Simon had the part down perfectly.

"Take it easy," I muttered as he bumped into me for the third time. "You don't want to draw attention."

"Then move it already." The Fool of the Arcana Council squeezed past me, squinting in the predawn gloom. Ahead of us, a recently unearthed Roman gate beckoned from its cordoned-off place of honor at the Hippos dig site, the spot still carefully brushed free of sand and gravel. "I've got places to go, my doppelgänger to see."

Not this again. "You know that mask has *barely* a passing resemblance to you, right?"

He grinned. "I know that I'm famous, is what I know. So let's move before my fans get here."

Ignoring Simon's grin, I stared hard at the Roman gate, arguably the most intriguing find of the Hippos excavation site since the discovery of the mask of Pan several months earlier. Despite my comment, the ancient mask did have a decidedly Simon-esque look about it. That artifact had put Hippos on the Arcana Council's radar, but now, with the discovery of the

Roman-era gate, the Council was in full damage-control mode. Enough to send me in with trumped-up credentials, a trowel, and my trusty Tarot deck.

And Simon.

"They found the mask right over there," he whispered now, pointing to the left. "Did you see that? Did you see the marker? Right in that exact spot. That close to the surface, in such good shape—it wanted to be found, you ask me. You ever feel like that's the case? Like the artifacts you're searching for want to be found?"

"Not as often as I'd like." I moved past the gate excavation and deeper into the remains of the fallen city. Another mound of rubble gave way to a cleared rectangular space, with columns forming a few long lines. "Here," I said. "This is what I think this morning's cards were trying to show us. It's the only thing that looks close to a set of swords lined up together."

"Totally," Simon agreed, his awed tone evocative of the mid 1980s…which made sense, given that was when he'd taken his seat on the Council. As the Arcana Council's youngest member, Simon might look like a shiftless twenty-something hipster in his Chucks and skinny jeans, skullcap and T-shirt, but he was a bona fide master of digital everything. Now he angled his magic-enhanced LIDAR ground-penetrating scanner between the pillars of the ancient forum.

"Yeah—something's hollow under there," he said. "Gotta be the chamber where the locals stashed Eshe's platter of doom. She's going to owe us so large."

He wasn't wrong. The Arcana Council's High Priestess had apparently lost a scrying shield in Hippos during what had been a Pan party for the ages. While the ancient Pan mask discovered a few months ago had lost its mojo, however, the shield could still potentially rock the nonmagical, non-Connected world. Eshe needed that like a fourth eye.

Now Simon was buzzing with energy, his gaze sweeping the ground. "Four of Swords, you said, that's the first of the two cards you pulled, Four of Swords." He spoke the words like a benediction. "We got this. Four pillars, four swords." He glanced back to me. "There's no way down below, though. That's a problem."

I shook my head. "The entry's not supposed to be obvious. Otherwise they'd have found it already." I scanned the rest of the forum site. There were multiple collections of pillars in the wide space, lined up neatly. "Keep going."

The voice behind us brought us up short. "Ms. Wilde, Mr. Pew. You're up early."

The small man's rich Greek accent rolled over us. I pivoted as Simon stifled a giggle, the Fool's amusement at his trumped-up surname knowing no bounds.

"Well, there are so many people once the day gets started," I said with a guileless smile. "It's tough to get a perspective on what this place looked like."

Andrico Fonti's brows lifted, white tufts of straw on his weathered face. "It's the forum that holds your interest, though? That surprises me. We've gone through it piece by piece. The excavation has moved on to more interesting possibilities." He waved at the piles of rock forming the broken-down walls. "I expected to find you at the gate. We resume digging there today."

I didn't buy Fonti's casual good cheer. This international excavation was the brainchild of Israel's University of Haifa, allowing them to move thousands of years of dirt a year from the earthquake-buried city for relatively little cost. Fonti, the dig's communications coordinator, had stuck to us like frosting on an Oreo since we'd shown up at the site earlier this week, tracking our every move. Supposedly, we were representatives of ultra-private, ultra-rich donors to the Haifa University cause...which wasn't exactly untrue. But there were scores of such donors from all over the world tramping these grounds. We shouldn't have attracted our own parasite.

Simon remained blithely unconcerned. His gaze was on the forum's pillars, and I could practically hear gears churning as his brain kicked into overdrive. To him, the world appeared as an ever-widening matrix of angles and connections and probabilities, but right now I needed him focused on the Four of Swords—three upright pillars or rocks of some kind, one horizontal. Never mind the sleeping guy the card also depicted, I suspected he wouldn't figure into this reading. One bit of crazy at a time.

"You'll be here for another week, your manifest says," Fonti continued. "So much longer than most of our donors."

"Israel is a long way from Las Vegas." I shrugged. "We figured we might as well see as much as we could."

"See it," Simon blurted, then he swung his gaze to me. "See it. Right. We wanted to see it." His grin was wide and eager, and I shot him a quelling glance that had no impact at all. "And there's a *lot* to see, really. Four times more than I would have expected."

Fonti blinked at him, clearly startled, and for once I didn't mind Simon's silliness. It seemed to puncture the Greek's concern that we were a threat to anything but his patience.

Still, the coordinator tilted his head. "You look familiar, Mr. Pew. Is this your first visit to Hippos?"

It was the third time the Fool had been asked such a question, and Simon's delighted laugh was only slightly manic. "I have that kind of face," he said.

"I suppose…" As Fonti hesitated, Simon put a little more effort into his smile until the man's face cleared. "I'll leave you to your morning walk," Fonti said. "If you have any questions, I am, of course, at your service."

He moved on, and it was my turn to scowl at Simon. "Did you put some kind of go-away whammy on him?"

"Nothing permanent." Simon laid a modest hand on his chest. "Still, see? You're so wrong about that mask—*everyone* can see the resemblance. It's like Pan's my long-lost grandpa."

"Well, do me a favor, don't stand next to it anytime soon. We don't need a family portrait posted on Facebook."

"Not a problem." Simon lifted up his handheld device again. "More importantly, I found our four swords. Last set by the wall, down on the left."

I swung my gaze that way even as we ambled down the long, open space of the forum. "There's only two upright pillars."

"Nope, three," he said, gesturing. "The third one's broken off but still standing. Right next to one that's completely on its side."

We approached the large stone columns, and I paused, looking up. He was right. From this angle, the ancient pillars formed the exact perspective of the Four of Swords—three up, one down. A thick knot of rock jutted out in an aggressive overhang beyond the tableau, where it appeared that the digging had stopped after the trowels had met solid stone.

Simon began circling the pillars, muttering nonstop. "Two of Pents was the next card, right? Two of Pents. A man holding two objects, balancing, balancing…" A second later, he shook his head. "There aren't any pentacles here."

"Keep your pants on." I continued staring at the overhang. "Fonti still watching us?"

Simon glanced over my shoulder. "He's on the ridge now. Facing us, yep, but talking to someone else."

"Watch him." I turned as if to study the columns while edging backward toward the overhang. The cards were apparently going to be a literal interpretation after all. "The Four of Swords shows a reclining man, a sleeper. Someone injured, whatever. He's on his back."

"His *back*." Rather than continuing to watch Fonti, Simon swung toward me, his attention squarely on the overhang as well. "Of *course*."

Before I could stop him, he dashed past me and hit the dirt, scurrying under the rock. If Fonti noticed, he didn't give any indication. I stepped back, pivoting slowly. "Simon…"

"Sara!" The urgency in the Fool's voice was unmistakable, but not as strong as the tremor that rumbled through the ground beneath my feet.

"Whatever you're doing, quit it," I said through my teeth. Simon had an eerie electrical connection with anything he touched. I hadn't expected that to be a problem in a place where the only electricity for miles was the result of what looked like Soviet-era generators. Up on the ridge, Fonti scanned the forum, clearly looking for Simon.

"There are two carvings," Simon said from under the rock. "I can almost reach them with my hands. Like handles or seals, but pressed into the stone here. *Two,* Sara." His words were gleeful. "Just like your cards said. Two!"

I'd been hunting artifacts for long enough to recognize disaster when I saw it. It was one thing for me to hurtle myself over the abyss, but the Fool was a member of the Council. An important member. He wasn't supposed to end up broken. "Don't touch anything, Simon," I snapped. "Fonti's coming, and we don't want to—"

Simon's gleeful cackle overrode my words. "This is so cool!"

There was a loud crack. Another tremor zipped through the ground and rolled the entire length of the forum. By some miracle, all the pillars stayed standing. Up by the newest excavation site, however, a blowhole of water suddenly burst into the sky, showering Fonti and the archaeologists next to him with mud and debris.

"Simon!" Giving up all pretext of subtlety, I flattened myself to the ground and peered beneath the overhang. "What did you…?"

But Simon was gone. The overhang now sheltered a slender crevice into the earth, as if the entire wall had lifted up at the touch of the Fool's hands. Scrambling forward, I peered into the darkness, but there was no Simon, only dust-filled black.

"Simon?" I called again. No response.

I shoved myself over the edge.

The fall wasn't far, and I had the advantage of hitting a relatively soft body at the end of it.

"Oof!" Simon groaned, shoving me off him and onto the rough stone floor. "You're heavy."

"And you're an idiot." I rolled to my feet, crouching in the darkness and letting my eyes and ears adjust. I could hear water churning beyond the far wall, but this chamber was still and shrouded in gloom, barely illuminated by the skylight we'd opened. "Don't ever rush in like that. It's dangerous."

"Yeah, well, it's what I do. And look." He lifted a penlight to illuminate the near wall. Two more disks. "Easy peasy," he said, standing.

"Don't—"

Simon didn't listen. Instead, he placed his hands on the wall. More debris clattered to the ground as the gaping hole leading up to the forum floor sealed shut. The Fool flipped his penlight to his face. "How cool was that, right?"

I stared at him. "Cool as in we have no way out, Simon. Pretty much exactly that cool."

"You worry too much." He sent his beam bouncing around the room. "Look at this place. How did it survive the quake thousands of years ago? There were two tremblers that leveled the city, right? Yet it all looks totally chill in here. Has to be some powerful magic, wouldn't you say?"

"It…" I looked around. The room we were standing in was pristine—but beyond the chamber's arches were layers of fallen rock that'd clearly been there a long time. I pulled out my own penlight to avoid Simon's overcaffeinated wobble.

"That must have been the main temple chamber, through there, next to some kind of aquifer," I said, flicking the beam toward the biggest archway. The light picked out the carved edge of an ornate table or stone chest, almost indistinguishable in the rubble except for its deep port-wine stains. "That looks like the edge of an altar, maybe used as a makeshift bar." I moved the penlight beam slowly, scanning the small, four-cornered space. "This room seems more like storage."

"Storage of awesome, maybe," Simon said. He darted forward, then pried open a box and peered inside. "Cups and flagons. A lot of them. Homies liked to party."

"Well, you know. Pan."

"Right." He sighed. "I kind of thought there'd be a statue or something of him down here, though. Maybe a note. I'm not feeling any of that." He moved to another crate. "How long d'you think we have?"

"Until they notice we're missing or until we die of starvation?"

"I have Twix bars."

"I'm so relieved. But this place isn't big. I don't think we'll be here long."

I was wrong, of course. Two more storage crates yielded nothing but intricately worked ruby and gold jewelry. Pretty but ultimately useless, though Simon pawed through them with unfettered delight.

"Eshe's shield is how big?" I asked.

"She couldn't remember. The size of her face, she said. That's not so big."

"Better than her ego, which wouldn't fit in this room." Was it me or was the air getting a little stuffy down here?

Gritting my teeth, I looked again at the room. Really looked this time. I didn't have magic, but I did have a strong sense of intuition, and right now it was picking up on the energy radiating from the chamber's walls and surfaces. This was different from the rushing water that Simon's initial jolt of magic had sent raging to the surface. There was something here, something that—the Fool was correct—*wanted* to be found.

Following the pull of that energy, I moved to another storage box carved out of the rock. I put the penlight in my teeth, then heaved the container's lid free. "Mmph."

The tenor of my grunt caught Simon's attention. "What?" he asked, before realizing I couldn't speak around the light. He abandoned his own crate and joined me, adding his wiry strength to mine. We didn't get the lid pushed far, but we got it far enough.

Score one for instinct.

Simon whistled low. "This looks promising," he said as rich silk fabric pooled beneath the dust motes. "Eshe is going to flip."

He reached in and pulled out a thin, cloth-wrapped package, straining with the effort as he shimmied it out of the narrow space. The moment he cleared the lid, I dropped it, the resulting boom bouncing off the walls. Simon laid the package on the closed box. "This is the coolest."

"Yo, wait. Keep it—" I broke off.

Ignoring me, Simon reached up and tugged the fabric free. It fell apart in his hands, revealing what lay beneath—a perfectly round shield. The Fool's penlight beam illuminated the shield's dull gray surface, but instead of reflecting back, it seemed to pull the light in, concentrate it.

"Holy shit," Simon breathed.

I understood the sentiment. The image on the shield's surface started as little more than Simon's blinding light, but then it cleared. A weird sort of mist bubbled over the edges, and in the center of that mist, an image flickered and rolled—a fight, a battle. No, not a battle.

An attack.

Men swarmed over a house like beetles, pouring through windows and doors. Different figures streamed out the back, as if fleeing in terror. The beetles ravaged the house completely, leaving nothing but a gleaming skull, then they too rushed on. A moment later, the skull house disintegrated into tiny swords of bone, scattered by the wind.

The image cleared.

"What the hell was that?" Simon squeaked.

I didn't want to think about it. "Cover that up," I said. "We need to get out of here."

"Affirmative." Leaning down to pick up the ragged cloth, Simon quirked his head to the side. "Ya know, that geyser is still rushing along at a pretty good clip," he said. "We get to the aquifer, we could get out."

I squinted toward the unforgiving rock ceiling where we'd fallen to the temple floor. "Well, we're not getting out the way we came in, that's for sure."

Fishing into my hoodie pocket, I pulled out a card. Only one this time. I didn't have time to screw around.

My heart sank as I ran my penlight over the image.

"What is it?" Simon stepped toward me, also angling his light down. He paused. "Three of Swords? That means you're going to do surgery or break my heart or something, right?"

"Sometimes," I said. "Or it's grief, dismay, disappointment."

"None of those sound good. What else?"

"Recognition of your limitations, necessary cutting—" I pursed my lips, thinking about that, then glanced his way. "Simon, how did you get the two disks to work? The ones in the rock."

"I grabbed them." He shrugged. "Flattened my palms against them, actually." He paused, screwing up his face toward me as he swept the light my way. "Why?"

"No reason." I looked at my hands, the shiny gold band on the third finger of my left hand, mocking me in the thin beam. The thing looked exactly like a wedding ring, a fact I was sure hadn't been missed by Armaeus Bertrand, the Magician of the Arcana Council, when he'd clamped it on me days earlier. Only, the band wasn't a wedding ring; it was a tracking device. And apparently, the only way I could remove it was to chop my finger off—or invoke stronger magic than Armaeus's.

Irritation riffled through me anew. *Stronger magic.* I was an artifact hunter, hard stop. Sure, I used Tarot cards to find what I needed. Sure, if the money was right, I was a willing assistant to those who possessed their own power. I was even getting pretty good at astral travel, at least when a Council member boosted me along.

But I *didn't generate magic.* Armaeus knew that. The entire Council knew that. So this smug attempt to test me was seriously cheddaring my cheese.

I grimaced. If what I suspected about the Three of Swords was right, it looked like I was about to possibly kill two birds with one stone. Still, I'd kind of grown attached to my fingers. I wanted to keep it that way.

"Hey, what're you doing?" Simon's penlight followed me as I strode across the room to where the altar peeked out of the rubble. The stains that smeared over it seemed much more malevolent now, and I sighed, staring down for a long moment.

"You got the shield wrapped tight?" I asked over my shoulder. "I don't know if this will work, but if it does, we probably won't have a lot of time."

"Sure...whoa, really?" Simon stopped short while I reached down to free the knife from my boot. "I know you hate that ring Armaeus gave you, but you really think this is the—"

"Shut up, Simon."

I slashed the blade deep into my palm and slapped my hand to the stone altar.

A fiery river of agony blasted through me, the regular pain of the knife cut mingling with something far greater. A temblor rumbled through the ground and sent a sizzling jolt up my legs. I wondered for a moment exactly what *had* triggered the devastating earthquakes in ancient times that had buried this city not once, but twice. Behind me, Simon staggered to the right, his scope swinging crazily.

"Nothing's happening," he said, the tiniest bit of panic creeping into his voice. "Shouldn't have something happened? Because I'm looking around, and nothing's happened. Whatever you did, it isn't enough."

"Son of a—" Stowing my penlight, I put the hilt of the knife between my teeth and bit down. Then I lifted my other palm and slid it along the blade, slicing open a deep flap of skin. I bit out a curse as I smacked that palm also down on the stone altar, my blood mingling with the blood and wine of the ancients. Of all the times to leave the hand sanitizer back in the hotel—

A second tremor rocked the room, then a deluge of debris showered from the ceiling, rocks clattering around us.

"There—there!" Simon shouted as a portion of the nearest column swung inward. "Come on."

Not waiting for me to react, he dashed forward. Queasiness swamped me despite the adrenaline surge, but I yanked my hands back from the altar, then ripped the blade out of my mouth. I pounded across the open room as chunks of dirt and stone rained down.

"C'mon, Sara, pick it up—" Simon's call sounded strained, but I didn't need the extra motivation to lean into my run. I dove through the opening even as the door started rolling shut. The force of my progress pushed Simon forward, and we splashed into shallow puddles lining a narrow, tall tunnel. The floor of the tunnel angled sharply up.

"Shouldn't there be more water?" I gasped. I shoved the knife back into its boot sheath. My hands stung with pain as I clenched them into fists.

"You'd think." Simon had tucked the shield under one arm and was now pointing his LIDAR scanner down the corridor. "That's no good," he said, squinting at the screens. "Something's coming—fast. Water and rock, and a whole lot of it." He shoved his gadget in his pocket and pulled something else out.

Another rumble through the ground sent us both reeling. With no further need for conversation, we started climbing up the steep incline of the aquifer, scrambling over chunks of fallen rock that served as unintended stairs. Water swelled behind us, and Simon pivoted, emptying his pockets even as I stumbled past him. I squinted at him, but he was dropping what looked like rocks into the corridor—fistfuls of them.

"What're you doing? I demanded. "The passage splits off here, and I need your scope."

"Gimme a second—"

"Dude, now." I turned and stumbled forward, wincing as my hands shredded further against the rough rock.

"Go, go, go!" Simon barreled into me right as the upswell reached us. We dove into a side passage, drenched but not drowning, while the water continued its race to the surface along the main aquifer.

"There!" Simon urged—forcing me toward a hole that looked no larger than his penlight. "Readings say its thin, maybe only a foot, and mostly shale."

Another temblor ground through the stone. Earth fell away from the hole, opening up a patch of daylight the size of my head. Muttering an apology to my bleeding hands, I scrabbled at the disintegrating dirt. Simon worked beside me, pummeling the gap until the walls gave way. We tumbled through the cavity, Simon's lanky body somersaulting beside me until we both landed in a heap.

Above us on the ridge, another mini geyser burst through the blowhole. We'd somehow landed below and to the south of the dig site by a good fifty feet, nowhere near the forum.

"Careful," I muttered, scraping the mud out of my eyes as Simon popped upright. "We need them to think we've gotten showered by the same mud they have, so Fonti doesn't blame us for whatever's going on up there. Let's get close enough to be seen by one of the lower-level interns, then clear out."

"Sounds like a plan." Still, Simon seemed in unusually good spirits as we made our way along the ridge. A final burst of water shot high in the air. He stared upward, grinning ear to ear. "I don't think anyone will be paying too much attention to us, though."

The screams of the diggers drowned out Simon's quiet words, their cries escalating into whoops and yelps of delight. I flashed back to the image of the Fool emptying his pockets in the middle of the rushing water of the underground aquifer…

As priceless treasures of rubies and gold rained down over the Hippos dig.

Chapter Two

"Armaeus will want you on this flight, Sara." Simon peered at me worriedly as we walked through the Tel Aviv airport five hours later. "He thinks you're coming right back to Vegas."

"Uh-huh." I eyed him. "What did you tell him?"

"Mission accomplished, and we were heading for the airport, that's it" he said. "But he'll figure it out soon enough. Why piss him off?"

I grimaced. So many reasons, so little time. "I'm flying commercial, and my manifest isn't a secret. You're going back with the shield. It's already on the plane, right?" Simon nodded and I pushed on. "So I'm going to spend a few days in Paris, visit some old friends I haven't seen in far too long. No big deal. I'll be back to Vegas after that."

His steps slowed to a trudge, like a kid brother I couldn't shake. "Yeah, but—when?"

"A few days, Simon. A week. Nothing's going to blow up in the next week that I can't handle when I get back."

"Hey." He brightened. "I've already packed the shield onto the jet. Maybe it can fly back on its own, and

I could come with you. I haven't been to Paris in a while. I could kick back, take in a few museums—"

I halted in my tracks. "What's your deal? You got your field trip to test out your new tech, and you got Eshe's shield. You did everything Armaeus asked you to do." My own words echoed back to me, and I narrowed my eyes at him. "Unless I'm missing something?"

He shrugged. "He's the head of the Council, and you're the most powerful mortal we know right now. He wants to keep an eye on you."

"Keep an eye?" I held up my left hand, bandaged edge to edge. "Not even that blasted altar of doom could pry that stupid ring off my hand. That's plenty of tracking for one person. You can tell Armaeus to go spin in small circles, and I'll get home when I get home."

If anything, the Fool looked even more morose. "*What*?" I demanded. "I can't read your mind, Simon. No matter what you people think of me."

"It's just... There're too many changes in the Connected community." He rocked back on his heels. "Too quick. Too many people coming out of the woodwork and throwing shade, when it's been excessively boring for decades."

"Forgive me if I think you have a skewed perspective on boring."

"You don't understand." He shook his head. "I've been doing this for three decades. Thirty years of bumping along without anything much more interesting than watching the stock markets go big then go bust then go big again. When Armaeus found you, things started to move faster. We were collecting artifacts again. Not like we needed more of those, but still. Stuff was happening. The Council actually convened meetings. It was cool. Then the veil between the worlds started to wobble."

I lifted my brows. "It can do that?"

"Fray, split, whatever." He waved a hand. "And now there's this talk of Houses. Like, real live Houses of the Minor Arcana—giving mortals actual standing right alongside the Council. No one even *told* me about Houses, and I've been kicking around for thirty years. The orientation manual absolutely sucks for this job."

I tried to process everything Simon was saying, but he was talking way too fast. I glanced at the monitors. My flight wasn't for another hour, and his was whenever his bony ass got on the Council's private jet.

We had time. And I wanted answers.

I steered Simon into a bar, never mind that it was ten in the morning. He'd done worse to me. "So what's the real story with the Houses?" I asked, casual as all hell. It was a reasonable question. Annika Soo, head of one of the most powerful syndicates on the Connected black market, had also, it turned out, fronted one of these mythical Houses. Right up until she'd conferred that leadership position to me not two weeks earlier. So it'd be handy for me to know some details.

Simon lifted his hands in defeat as he slumped further on his stool. "That's the problem. I don't know anything more than you do. I don't even think Armaeus does anymore."

The bartender cruised over. I pointed at the bottle of vodka on the middle shelf. "Neat," I said.

"That's why Armaeus is all freaked," Simon continued as the bartender busied himself with our drinks. "The four Houses of the Minor Arcana haven't been in play since the Middle Ages. There's no history, no hint of them—other than Soo's House of Swords—

and we didn't know about that until these past several months. As to the rest..." He shrugged. "The Council stopped looking a long time ago for evidence of House activity. We couldn't poke our noses too far into what wasn't our business."

I'd heard this song before. "Because you didn't want to interfere."

"Bingo." He smiled wearily. "The number one rule of Arcana Council: there is no Arcana Council. We don't mess with mortal magic, other than making sure it stays balanced. Since the Houses are for mortals, when we lost track of them, we simply had to accept that."

Simon picked up his glass. "Except, we couldn't believe they'd simply disappeared. Armaeus was convinced they'd gone underground, and was furious he couldn't do more, learn more. And there weren't any mortals who could get him deep enough into the Connected community to draw out the truth."

Slow understanding dawned. "Until me."

"Yep." Simon squinted at me. "You were the first mercenary we'd hired who didn't...well, die. In a hurry. The others didn't last."

I stopped in the process of lifting my own vodka, then put the glass down again. "There were other artifact hunters?" Of course there would have been others. The Council's need for toys hadn't simply erupted out of nowhere a little over a year ago. But I'd never questioned Armaeus needing me for such work. I'd simply done it. "They died?"

The last question was more rhetorical, but Simon answered it anyway. "Not so much died as burned out. Literally, zzzzzt." He made a gesture with his fingers as if pulling a string taut. "They couldn't function after a few jobs." He rolled his empty vodka glass. "You're different."

I was different, yeah. I'd run more than thirty jobs for the Council in the past year and change, and so far, no zzzzzt. But Armaeus couldn't have known I'd be so hardy at the outset. He'd simply kept pushing me. And apparently, I hadn't been the first mercenary he'd ever pushed.

The wreckage to my body was one thing. He'd done a good job healing that so far. But what about the wreckage to my mind?

I scowled. "Where are they now? The others?"

"No clue," Simon shrugged. "Maybe they're dead now. Armaeus stopped hiring for a while, maybe ten years before he found you. But in all the time he'd been working with hunters, the Houses never came up. When he realized Annika Soo was more than the head of a criminal syndicate, that was the first I'd heard about the possibility of the Houses still existing. I don't think he knew she ruled Swords, though."

"Oh, right." I quirked him a glance. "Reading minds is kind of his thing."

"I know. But it's like there's some sort of shield between the House leaders and the Council. He's not used to being shielded…except from you, of course, and you surprised him from the start. Which means maybe there's more out there like you, and that's kind of a problem."

I signaled to the bartender to pour us another round of drinks, and pushed my glass toward Simon. I hadn't had a chance to drink from it yet, but this information was enough of a high.

"A problem for who?" I asked. "If the Houses stay hidden, how does that hurt anyone?"

"No one can stay hidden anymore," Simon said, lifting my glass. "It's all hands on deck. Magic hasn't been moving this fast in hundreds of years. The Council thinks maybe we'll have an arcane renaissance that hasn't happened since the Dark Ages. Why do you think the Magician went all the way to Hell to find the Hierophant? This war that's coming, it's mortal on mortal and mortal on magic, yeah. But there's something else stirring, some deeper shift, and we don't know if it's good or bad. We have to be ready." He grinned wryly. "Which means we have to keep tabs on you."

"Uh-huh." I narrowed my eyes at him as he drained his drink. "Well, you're not coming with me to Paris. I'm not on the Council, no matter how much work I do for you guys. I'm a free agent."

He tipped his glass my way, looking more relaxed than I'd seen him in ages. "You *were* a free agent. When I met you, anyway. You were getting us, what, some bowl from Crete? I think that was what Armaeus had sent you for. You got it too, and all you wanted was money and to get the hell out of Vegas as fast as you could."

"Yeah, well. I wasn't a fan."

"But now you're in it up to your neck, aren't you? So important that Armaeus needed to put a ring on it." Simon snickered, setting down his drink. His smile got a little looser—too loose, and he pointed a wobbly finger at me. "You keep surprising him every time he turns around, blowing things up and—"

"Use your inside voice, buddy." I reached out to stabilize Simon as he lurched toward me, his arms windmilling. When I caught him, heavily, his face was right at my ear.

"Poison, Sara," the Fool said succinctly. "High grade. Fast acting. Didn't track it at first but it's going to incapacitate me pretty quickly, starting with my extremities. Not going to be worth shit to you here, but I can ah, make myself scarce."

I blinked at him. I knew Simon had some teleporting capabilities—something about bending electrons—but… "You can teleport while poisoned?"

He pulled back and met my gaze. "I'm sure going to try. This is seriously high-grade dope, and I don't want any part of someone who knows this particular blend. Sorry to bail on you." He stared hard into my eyes, and I felt the hum of his desperation. "You got about eight seconds till you're on. Lead guy is short and he's coming up fast."

"Right." I opened my mind and with Simon in my arms like this, my vision expanded broadly. I saw not only Simon in front of me, not only the bar, but the bar, the building, the rushing workers outside, the tarmac, the hangar, the plane—Armaeus's plane.

With a jaunty grin, Simon dissolved in my arms, leaving me with an armful of cotton shirt, cargo shorts, and a skullcap.

A sudden rush of steps closing in was my only warning. Without rising, I thrust my elbow back as the first assailant reached the bar, up and to the right at about throat level for a size-challenged assailant. I was rewarded with a gargling sound as some tourist across the bar shouted in alarm.

I spun off my stool, grabbed my empty vodka tumbler, then swung it wide. It connected with another face, but that didn't stop assailant number two. Something bright flashed toward me and I dropped, boneless. A syringe missed my neck and impaled itself in the chairback. I scrabbled away on my backside as a pair of flashy loafers and impeccably tailored trousers leaped over me, clearing my head...

Then it was my turn to stare.

A well-muscled, highly trained blond in a fantastic suit cracked one of the assailant's heads on the counter and shoved him back toward the guy now wielding a second needle, then flipped the man's hand around to bury the syringe in the assailant's own neck. A fourth attacker raced in and whipped out a gun. This was the Tel Aviv airport we were in, however, and by this time, the crowd had dispersed and security with guns were coming fast, booming orders in multiple tongues as my protector whipped around and located me on the floor.

If I had any doubts before, the impossibly perfect shaving job would have clued me in.

"You can run?" asked Nigel Friedman in his crisp British accent.

Without waiting for me to respond, he scattered a few metallic spheres on the ground, then helped me up.

"Move out," he ordered, even as the first officer noticed me staggering to my feet and shouted for us to stop.

Then the bombs went off.

They were flashbangs, not meant for anything but the most superficial of damage, but the effect was impressive. Travelers and workers screamed, bolting away in all directions. Nigel gripped my arm hard enough to bruise as he hustled me out of the bar area and into the main line of scrambling tourists. Rather than heading for the exit off the main concourse, he banked hard to the right, following signs that led to the smaller terminal set up alongside the large commercial carrier gates.

"What—how—" I managed, but not much else, as Nigel's long strides took up two to three of mine.

"You never choose to do things the easy way." Nigel scanned the monitors as he walked, but every new step brought more modulation to his voice and pace, both of them tempering the farther we got away from the disturbance at the main gate. A flood of airport security warnings blared over the loudspeaker in what I supposed was Hebrew and Arabic, then in English, advising of the apprehension of assailants and for everyone not to be alarmed. I didn't know if I was included in that.

"What are you doing here?" I asked, now that we were walking normally, though still with purpose. Nigel and I had a long history of hunting for the same artifacts for different employers, which made us competitive on our best days and frenemies the rest of the time. "For the record, I'm not in the mood to get handed off to your newest employer."

His lips quirked. "That would be entertaining. But I was in the area, merely called in to clean up the mess you were about to make. You should be more careful, Sara."

"Is that so?"

"Considering the trail of bodies you've left in your wake recently, yes," Nigel said. His gaze was cold as it raked over me. "Soo was a friend of mine."

"I didn't think you had those," I retorted, unreasonably stung. Annika Soo had died on my watch, but she'd walked into that danger on her own.

Nigel ignored my gibe. "You should know that Gamon has put out a bounty on your head to all his operatives—"

"*Her* operatives," I interrupted, which at least got the officious prick to shut up. Life was a balance. "Gamon is a her. That's why she always wears a mask. And so what if she wants me dead? She wouldn't be the first one."

"No, but *she* would be your biggest enemy to date. Her black market operations span the globe, her pockets are deep, and she's got agents everywhere. There's a reason she and Soo hated each other and it went beyond the war on magic." He glanced at me. "From all accounts, Gamon is willing to throw a lot of money into the search for you. Capture only, for now. Execution appears to be off the table, which doesn't bode well for your body parts. You should avoid public transportation until you two sort out your differences."

"I'll keep that in mind." Suddenly, all the fatigue of the past few weeks caught up with me. Even though I'd drunk none of the spiked vodka, bone-deep weariness made my legs too loose, my gait unsteady.

Nigel didn't seem to notice. "Good," he said, his voice clipped. He put his fingers to a spot behind his ear, and I realized he was carrying a wire.

"Um, who exactly phoned you in on this, again?"

Ignoring me, Nigel reached into his jacket as we entered a commuter plane terminal. "Your jet is waiting at gate fifty-three, up and to the right. I regret I won't be joining you on your trip to Paris. Your tickets say Belgium, but you will be rerouted in flight. When you are ready to leave France, call the number on the card, and your travel will be arranged."

He stopped then, looking at me fully for the first time. It was a critical, assessing look, and I didn't like it.

"You got a problem?" I snapped.

He lifted one perfectly arched brow. "Not at all. You're exhausted, and your reflexes are off. You'll need to be sharper in the coming weeks. Who were you sitting with in the bar?"

"You're the man with all the answers, you tell me."

"He appeared to melt into your arms, leaving behind only his clothing. I assume that was an illusion, but I don't know who was projecting it. You're not wearing electronics, and your Connected abilities aren't that good."

I stiffened, violated even though Nigel hadn't touched me. "You don't know that."

He waved his hand at me, drawing attention to the highly technical watch—as if I should have expected anything less from former MI6 with a Bond complex. "Electrical signature reader. Though I'm not Connected, I'm not without skills, Sara. Something for you to consider."

I smirked. "You sound like you're asking me out on a date."

His precisely winged brows lifted the tiniest fraction. "Something else for you to consider," he said.

Then he turned on his heel and left.

Chapter Three

Summer in the City of Lights was a far cry from spring. First off, it was hot.

Secondly, it was hot.

I disembarked from the private jet Nigel had arranged for me and descended to what looked to be an equally private airstrip. I squinted, trying to focus on the limo sitting on the tarmac, but it was virtually impossible in the heat rising up from the ground. Still, I made my way forward. I needed to get to Father Jerome and find out what was happening in the Connected community. I'd slept off and on for the four-hour flight and was feeling reasonably human, but I had more questions than ever before.

Namely, who exactly had spiked Simon's and my drinks in the bar—and why? I couldn't remember pissing off anyone specifically other than Gamon, and I wasn't sure how she'd found me so quickly. Mainly because nobody had known I was in Israel other than the Council.

If it'd been a normal situation and I'd been in the mood to deal with him, I would've simply asked Armaeus who they might have inadvertently tipped off. He was the Magician. Knowing things was sort of a pastime for him.

But every time I considered opening my mind to Armaeus, I recalled Simon's hints about the Magician's plans for me well before I'd known I was anything but a highly-paid artifact finder. He was taking the concept of messing with my mind to deadly levels. How much did I know about Armaeus, anyway? Clearly, not enough.

There was also the stupid ring. I clenched my bandaged hands, feeling the bite of the gold device. Armaeus hadn't trusted me not to disappear. Could there be something more to his concern than strategy? Or was Simon right, and I was merely an asset Armaeus didn't want to lose until the game played out a little longer?

I grimaced. There probably wasn't enough French wine in the world to make me feel better about any of this. But I would try.

I was about fifteen feet from the car when I registered that the limo driver hadn't yet exited the vehicle. Despite the heat, normally the driver was out of the car and standing. If he—or she—didn't want me to know who it was waiting for me...

Slowing my pace, I flexed my hands in their bandages. I wasn't really in the mood for a fistfight, but at least the pain would be blunted.

"Sara!"

I turned, gaping as a familiar young man fairly flew out of the largest outbuilding, his tuxedo shirt untucked, his hand smashing his chauffeur's cap to his shaggy dark hair as he raced across the superheated tarmac. "Come on—we've got to go!"

"Max?" I blinked, trying to make sense of what I was seeing, but the man didn't slow down. He cursed a blue streak in French and raced for the car, while I picked up my own pace. I reached the limo a few seconds after he did, allowing him to wrench open the back door with one hand and stuff his shirt into the waistband of his pants with the other.

"I can't believe we're so late." He practically shoved me into the sedan. "It's almost time."

"Time for what?" I asked as I slid across the back seat. Max jerked his own door open and tumbled inside, somehow managing to gun the vehicle before he was fully seated.

"Father Jerome is having a lunch prepared at the château. You'll love it—everyone's excited to meet you!"

I frowned, then jerked back in my seat as Max Bertrand turned the vehicle in a sharp arc, then roared away from the jet. A nephew of Armaeus a dozen generations removed, Max was one of the most interesting branches of the Bertrand family tree, even if he did revere Armaeus like the Magician was some sort of conquering warrior. I'd first met Max in Italy, where he'd been working as an on-call chauffeur for the family, and almost immediately sensed his Connected ability. From there, it was a short hop to get him hooked up with Father Jerome in Paris. The priest needed the help, and Max was meant for more than playing flunky to the Council.

Now, however, he was embracing the frantic-chauffeur role to the hilt. "What's the rush?" I asked.

"I've been late before. Father Jerome should expect it by now."

"Not late like this, you haven't," Max said, in his nearly flawless English. "You were supposed to land at Charles de Gaulle, remember? And then that got rerouted. Father Jerome got word of the new flight itinerary, and you should have seen his face. I told him I'd be there to greet you no matter where you landed." He lifted a hand to encompass the private airstrip we were barreling away from. "This place was the third redirection. Nice, huh? Big money out here."

I lifted my brows. "Third?" I hadn't realized the changes taking place. "It's owned by Annika Soo?"

"Haven't a clue." He shrugged, flashing me a grin in the rearview mirror. "But whoever it is, they're enough of a fan to go to these lengths to keep you safe. I guess you're getting pretty popular."

Once again I thought about pinging Armaeus, then discarded the idea. Instead, I focused on Max. It'd been two months since I'd seen him, and there was something…different about him. Different and good.

"How goes the work with Father Jerome?"

"Saved my life, Sara, you truly did," he said, flooring it around a turn. "Father Jerome, he takes one look at me and tells me I'm wasting my talents. He put me to work right away with the smallest Connecteds—I mean, they're little kids, right? And they've already gone through so much. Who am I to help them get over their fears? But the good Father, he says I must help in this way, so I do." He shifted his gaze again to meet mine. "You do good work, Sara, getting Father Jerome the money he needs to protect so many children. It matters."

"Eyes on the road," I said.

Max laughed but did as I asked, keeping up his stream of chatter. "And of course, being around the most vulnerable of the Connecteds, I could let my own skills show. Some I didn't know I had, some I'm still not sure what to do with. But I'm open to learning, and I grow stronger every day."

"Anything I should be aware of?" I teased him, buoyed by his good spirits. "You're not into mind reading or anything, right?"

"Ha! I wish. I would know what new terror Father Jerome is dreaming up for me." He shook his head. "What I do—it's far more subtle than that. I can sense the truth in someone. If someone is lying or being authentic, or what they perceive as authentic. I can also touch a thing and know where it came from, or the circumstances that brought it to me. That's all."

My eyes went wide. "Truth telling and psychometry? That's kind of impressive, Max. You didn't know you could do these things?"

"A good judge of character and a good guesser. It's easily explained away when you are not looking for a deeper answer, no?" His bright gaze met mine again. "And what of you? Father Jerome prays for you all the time, you should know. Says he's used up all his fear. He's so glad you've come."

Something in Max's voice caught me.

"Why?" I asked, hearing the sharpness in my own tone. "What's wrong?"

"Nothing's wrong." Max offered me a Gallic shrug. "He worries. And he has much on his plate." Max drew in a short breath. "The children. There are more every week, it seems. Too many."

"I know—" I grimaced, but Max shook his head.

"No, I mean legitimately, too many. They're getting shipped here from someone who deliberately is trying to overtax us, Father Jerome is certain of it. The children are too traumatized to speak, so we must dig to learn if they were targeted by dark practitioners or if they are simply cannon fodder launched by our enemies to distract us."

I blinked, taken aback by his harsh words.

"It's bad enough with the global immigration issues pulling everyone's resources," he continued grimly. "This is worse. These children may not be high-level Connecteds, but they are nonetheless terribly damaged. Far more than they should be, honestly. They are not strong enough to warrant the dark practitioner's attention and yet…they have been harmed and we don't know why. But of course we take them in because—how can we not?"

I heard the note of caution in his voice. "You think they were deliberately damaged to get accepted by Father Jerome? That they're some sort of plants?"

Max blew out a long breath. "I do not know what to think. Father Jerome doesn't hide his operation from the authorities. They know he's running a kind of orphanage loosely connected to the church. If the police know it, anyone can."

I frowned. Since I'd first learned of my friend's side mission to care for the most vulnerable of the Connected community, I'd funneled most of the money I made as an artifact hunter to his charity. I'd never questioned how Father Jerome ran his safe houses, but now… "If his operation is that open, then what's to stop the dark practitioners from ambushing one of your homes and taking the kids they want? The ones with the highest abilities?"

"Because—" Max hesitated. "That's sort of my third talent, I guess you would say. Assessment."

"Assessment...you mean of talents? You can tell that?"

He lifted one shoulder, dropped it. "I think so. Father Jerome thinks so, which is more important." Then his grin split his face again. "But we move any of the kids who we think has unusual talent. And we put out to the arcane black market that we've got secret bolt-holes for them. As a result, the dark practitioners focus on these unknown locations—places they'll never find—and not so much on the big houses, where most of the kids are. It's a win-win. Don't get me wrong, all the children have talent, but some..." He sighed. "Some of them are truly remarkable."

I nodded. "How does that work? The talent reading? I know Father Jerome had a battery of questions he'd ask the children."

Max nodded enthusiastically. "That's how he came to realize what I could do. He'd ask me to administer the tests, but there were so many kids—I had to sort of do a triage. Make sure we got the at-risk Connecteds out of harm's way before any slipped through. When Father Jerome realized the results were matching up with my shorthand sorting method, he got curious."

"Sounds like him." I glanced out the window. We were far outside of any city limits. Eventually, Max turned down a long private drive bordered on either side with thick forest. "Which house is this?"

"Les Anges," Max said, and I nodded, taking in the unyielding sweep of trees. It was well named, I decided. The trees reached up and over the lane, as if protecting the property beneath in angels' arms.

I'd long since lost track of the homes Jerome had purchased with my earnings—homes and staff to care for the Connected children. The kids weren't all orphans, of course. Parents existed, but they could no more stop the trafficking than the authorities could. As a result, they'd learned of Jerome and had sent their children to him. Or Jerome learned of a child with unique skills, a family gaining notoriety in the community. In those cases, he sought the children out himself. The result was that these gifted Connecteds entered a safe-harboring foster program that would last until the children turned eighteen. Then, at least, they'd have a chance. In the world of the dark practitioners, the focus was on youth, the more unsullied the better.

Which, more often than not, was the only silver lining in the vile underbelly of the arcane black market—that with so few pure children, the dark practitioners couldn't grow too strong, too fast. Not that it mattered. The idea of sacrificing any children to feed the slavish desires of the men and women who'd stop at nothing to augment their Connected abilities... It seemed impossible to believe. Yet it happened every day around me—was happening in far greater numbers than ever before, to hear Simon talk.

But it was Max talking now, and I blinked at him, forcing myself to focus. "—waiting for you," Max finished with a smile. "It's a little overwhelming if you're not used to it, but he really wanted you to meet them all."

I nodded as we pulled into another offshoot drive, this one quite clearly the lane to a grand home. The trees opened up to reveal a rich manicured lawn, and out of the valley sprang the quintessential French mini château—turrets and ramparts and even a water mill, churning at the river that ran alongside the property.

Max had barely stopped the car when a familiar figure appeared at the top of the stairs. I had to blink hard to stop the surge of tears behind my eyes.

"Father Jerome." I was out of the vehicle and up the stairs in a rush, then I buried myself in a long hug from the short, stout priest. "It's been too long."

"Two months and more," Father Jerome said, his perfect French accent a balm to nerves I hadn't realized were so frayed. "We are blessed you've arrived safely. The children have heard so much about you."

I turned and watched as the doors opened from several points along the house. Kids flooded out into the sunshine. They didn't look like they were being marched out for an audience, merely released for fresh air, but they converged on the main green in a tumble of humanity—some of them laughing and chattering, some of them quiet, walking in small groups of equally silent compatriots, and some of them moving alone, drifting in their own private world. There were dozens of them, and I goggled as they amassed on the front lawn.

"Max said you were getting too many to count," I said, taking in the worn faces, the gaunt cheekbones, the pale skin despite the bright and cheerful sun beaming down through the trees. "There has to be a hundred kids here."

Father Jerome nodded. "There is also the house in Toulouse, and another one outside Paris."

"And how many from these places did you pick out as specials?" I asked. "Max told me you had some children whose abilities far outshone the rest."

The look Jerome turned on me was bemused, then he transferred his gaze to Max as he bounded up the stairs to join us.

"I figured you should tell her," Max said, returning Jerome's surprised glance with a shrug.

Father Jerome sighed, then gestured to the children gathering in front of us. "All of these here are specials, as you call them," he said quietly.

I blinked at him. "They can't be," I said automatically. "There are too many."

He held up a hand, forestalling any further commentary. "But the fact remains. These are the children who've been identified with abilities or characteristics that would result in the arcane black market sale of their bodies, living or dead, in some cases for tens of thousands of dollars. They are visionaries, psychics, psychometrists like Max here, state changers, healers...and, in some cases, actual weapons, if aimed appropriately."

"But...how?" I stared around at the children and noticed many of them were looking back at me now, their eyes soulful and heavy with purpose even from a distance. "How did you find so many?"

"As I'm sure Max has told you—we didn't have to. Many have come looking for us. And before you ask—no. None bear the mark you sent me, of this Gamon. We have started receiving those children, but none of them are so talented as these."

My lips twisted. "I guess that makes sense. Gamon would have to give up too much power to bait us with a marked child. And she may or may not know we can undo her tracking device."

Jerome nodded. "The tattoo artist you spoke of. The Council Member. She has contacted me—well, your Magician has, on her behalf."

I bristled at his gentle words. "He's not *my* Magician."

"Ha! If you won't claim him, I will," said Max. "And Jerome's right. She said she'd send people to remove the tracking devices from the tattoos of the kids who have them, and she did. We haven't gotten a lot of marked Connecteds, though. And no high-functioning ones. Not that Jerome's let me near the marked kids."

"Too dangerous," Jerome said. "One of them could be as talented as you at reading abilities, and in communication with this Gamon as well. I cannot risk anyone knowing of your skills."

Max shook his head genially. "Father Jerome is taken in by my youthful smile," he said. "He doesn't realize I can defend myself."

"Not against everything," Jerome said firmly. Then he turned. "Come—you should meet some of the children."

He took me down into the throng of hyper-skilled Connecteds. Their energy swept over me in rolling tides the longer I was in their midst. Max was everywhere, introducing the children, goading the quiet ones into bright smiles and quick laughter, urging the more outgoing ones to share their stories. I'd heard many of those stories through Jerome already, but hearing them again from the children themselves tore a new set of holes in my heart.

"C'est bien, Giselle," Jerome murmured now. "She is here. She is safe."

I blinked as I looked down at the young girl Jerome was kneeling next to. But she wasn't looking at him. She was looking at me.

"Vous êtes ici," she said, and her eyes stopped me cold. They shone with a bright intensity I'd last seen in Las Vegas only a few weeks earlier, on an entirely different young woman's face. I seemed to have a knack for stressing out gifted girls. "You left this plane for darkness but you are back now," she said. "You can continue the fight."

Jerome smiled indulgently, and the child kept going. "And now you must become a fire that burns everything, defeating the usurper. Or all of us will die."

I flinched back, but the girl next to her turned and nodded at me too, her face set with tension. When she spoke, she used the same haunting cadence of the first child. "It's the only way," she said. "They'll strip away all that is left of us if you do not strike first. If your hand becomes a scythe that destroys the usurper, all will bow before you."

"Now stop that, Kaitlyn," Jerome began, but I lifted a hand even as Max reached out to me, his reassuring touch on my other hand holding me fast, grounding me.

"It's okay," I said and crouched down to meet the first little girl's eyes. "What usurper, sweetheart? What are you talking about?"

But the child simply stared at me, unblinking. I tried a different approach. "It's okay, it's okay," I murmured, until she blinked again, rapidly. "Have you seen—specifically—what it is that I must do?"

"Yes." And now the child did nod, with the solemnity only a little girl could muster. "You must take up your sword."

Chapter Four

It was another hour before Father Jerome, Max, and I left the château, only to repeat a similar scene at another house a few hours away. There the children were not the highest-skilled Connecteds—at least not anymore. But they were more traumatized to be sure. These were the children who had not escaped the demands of the dark practitioners unscathed. Some were missing limbs or were recovering from facial reconstruction surgery. Some were orphaned, their parents considered more important than the children for a particular ritual.

And some had been enslaved by Gamon.

"We followed your instructions," Jerome said as we walked down one hallway and peered through plateglass windows into hospital suites. "Even the local tattoo artists that we called in as reinforcements knew what was required once we gave them the name of Blue." He glanced at me. "That name opens a lot of doors."

"It should," I said. The incarnation of Death currently sitting on the Arcana Council was a shock blonde with a tattoo gun and a flare for painting hot rods. Known as Blue in the world of auto airbrushing, she ran a tattoo parlor in Vegas and had an international clientele of trainees. Trainees who apparently made house calls under the right circumstances. "She performed a similar job last week for maybe a hundred victims of Gamon. They can't be tracked now—and these kids you have here, hopefully they weren't tracked before you had their ink worked on."

"If they were, we're ready," Jerome said. "This house is not unknown. Our children have never been harmed once we've brought them in. Their value to the dark practitioners has already dropped by the time they reach us."

"Because they're tainted with awareness." I hesitated even as I said the word, a new idea occurring to me. "You know, maybe we should round up all the Connected children, both the ones who've been harmed and those that haven't yet, and let them mingle, so they know the evil waiting for them in the outside world. Once they know that, their magic might be altered enough to make them less appealing to the dark practitioners."

"Perhaps," Father Jerome agreed. "Though it would rob them of their childhood."

I grimaced. "Better that than their lives."

"As you say."

He directed us to an oak-paneled library that had been made over as a conference room, with a long central table and deep-cushioned chairs. Unlike the Arcana Council's meeting rooms, no electronics bristled from the corners of this chamber. Instead, a large map of Europe hung prominently along one wall, marked with pins in clusters. The white pins were the birthplaces of the Connected children; the black ones were known locations of dark practitioners. But another color had sprouted like wildflowers across the map.

I moved forward with a frown. "What's with the purple?"

"The highest skilled of the children are denoted by that color," Father Jerome said, and I could feel his gaze on me. "We thought we could identify hotspots of particular concern once we had enough markers." He chuckled wryly. "We didn't realize we would soon have far more data than beds. But you see the pattern." He waved at the map.

"Ley lines." I nodded. "The ancient arbiter of sacred grounds, tied to the earth's energy patterns. Makes sense." I turned to him. "But ley lines circle the globe, Jerome. That's like saying you're likely to find grass in a field."

"Our thoughts exactly. There is an uptick in the birth of highly skilled Connecteds at the intersection points, but most of the intersection points have been accounted for, at least in Europe. And there remain outliers."

"So it's a dead end."

"That line of inquiry, yes," he said. "We cannot predict where the next strong children will emerge. Of course, if we can't, our enemies can't as well." Without giving me a chance to comment on that, he moved to the map and picked up a ball of twine. "What we did notice, however, was perhaps more disturbing."

He began unraveling the twine from its bobbin, then hooked it on the tops of each cluster of dark pins, moving down and to the right, then up and to the left, back and forth. In no time, an image appeared in the center of the map, etched out in twine. I'd seen a deliberate incarnation of the image before, in Las Vegas.

Gamon had used it to mark a grisly diagram of body dumps throughout the city, but we didn't know why, precisely. There was no indication that Gamon was Jewish—but none that she wasn't either.

"Star of David," I said.

Jerome nodded. "The alpha and omega joined together. You'll note there's no population of practitioners in the center…that we're aware of."

My brows leapt. "But there's got to be something there." I moved closer, peering at the map. "Are we reading too much into this? Do we know anything about the distribution of the dark practitioners in Asia or the Americas? Africa?"

"They are active to be sure, but their concentration is not as large. The Old World, or what was known as such, seems to have held the highest concentration of practitioners for generations. And now this appears to be the center of those practitioners."

"What is that, Hungary?" I asked, leaning close. "The Ukraine, maybe. Okay, so—that's where Gamon is, you think? In the center of that star?" I frowned. "Why not Israel, if she's fixated on Hebrew symbology?"

I could feel Jerome's gaze on me. "I think perhaps there is a better question for you to ask yourself," he said quietly. When I turned to him, his hands were clasped in front of his stomach, and he looked worn—more tired than I had ever seen him.

"Jerome, what is it?" I took a few steps forward, but he waved me off.

"I'm not the one you should worry about," he said. "You're asking questions about Gamon, and in fact, they are good questions to ask. She has become the figurehead of evil—but"—he paused, lifting a hand—

"only the figurehead. You cut the head off a hydra, and it will grow a new head."

"That'll take time, though," I said. "In the meantime, this is one creature who deserves to be headless, even for the short term." I gestured to take in the grounds outside this room. "What if she's the usurper that little girl spoke of, the one I need to strike down?"

"What if she is?" Jerome threw my words back at me. "Help me understand why you should be the one to *wield* the blade, Sara, versus merely guiding this sword to the right hand." The priest's words were kind, but they struck to the heart of my own insecurity. "I've pleaded with you for months—years—to work more with the children. To not only provide for their safety, which you have done amply—but to help them recover. To bend your skills to their future, not simply their present. You have rebuffed me at every turn, and that is your right to do so."

When I would have spoken, he kept going. "Yet now, I find that not only have you taken up a call to arms in the fight to protect these children, you've gone further. You've been named the head of a Chinese death syndicate. You seek the blood of Gamon."

I stiffened. "Gamon is the reason why these children suffer."

"And you have pledged yourself already to their protection," Jerome said, his words as stern as I'd ever heard them. "The children talk of swords and death and retribution. Yet when I see you, I don't see swords and death. I see someone who finds the lost and shepherds them home. Why isn't *that* Sara enough in this war? How did you come to decide that the Sara you were is not the woman you can be and still serve the needs of the many?"

He pointed at the map. "There are many who would take up arms to fight this beast that wraps around our most vulnerable children. There are many swords to fill that army. Why must this blood be on you, when there is so much other work to be done?"

I took a step back, my mouth working, but in truth, I couldn't answer him. Not directly. "You don't think I can fight Gamon?"

Father Jerome's smile was the saddest thing I had ever seen. "I think most assuredly you *can* fight Gamon. I think you could fight her, and, in divine righteousness, you could strike her down. But this is a fight that does not end with Gamon. This is a fight that ends with the root of all that is fear and evil in this world. And that is a fight no one can win with only a sharp blade and a stout heart."

His words rang with a truth and a finality I couldn't disavow, but I still found myself shaking my head. "You don't know that, Father."

He stepped close to me. "I do not know," he said, taking my hands, the gesture so calm, so comforting that I inexplicably wanted to cry. "But I can hear, Sara. I can listen to what the children say about a warrior who is sworn unto death to save them. And I can hear them whispering about the pain and suffering this warrior will endure, the betrayals and loss. And I can think to myself—all these things, they do not have to fall to Sara Wilde. There are many roles in a war so big as this. There are many battles to fight."

He squeezed my hands. "Especially when you don't even know how to handle a sword."

I let out a choked laugh, but Jerome was right. Not half a year ago, I was secure in my position. I would make a mercenary's profit on a war fought by others, save the children in my path, and put the money toward the greater good. Rather than get caught up in the politics and perfidies of the opposing sides, I'd focus on the one thing I could do, and do well…finding and selling the artifacts to finance Jerome's work.

What had happened to that certainty?

A child entered the room then, her eyes bright and her manner shy, asking us to come to dinner. Another hour passed as the day drifted into night, Jerome making us laugh with stories of the children and their abilities, their improvements, and their hope for a better tomorrow. *You've done good work here,* his every anecdote seemed to say. And there was more good work to be done.

I couldn't deny that truth, especially when it was clustered around me three rows deep.

But there were other truths I couldn't deny either. When Father Jerome urged me to stay another few days in Paris, the tug to escape the city, to return to my own world, was visceral. His gaze was soft as he folded his arms around me.

"Think on it is all I ask, dear Sara. God has given you great gifts and the power to choose how to use them. It's not a decision to be made quickly." His smile was endlessly kind. "Even if you find yourself at the tip of a sword."

An hour after he left for one of the other houses, I let myself out the front door of the château…

And found Max waiting on the steps, his chauffeur's outfit looking freshly pressed.

"Was I that obvious?"

He shrugged. "Father Jerome said you wouldn't stay. He said you never did stay in someone else's house if you could avoid it. So he told me to get ready to take you somewhere else." He tapped the bill of his hat and grinned. "I'm at your service wherever you wish to travel in the greater European area."

I nodded, but inside something twisted. Jerome was right: I never stayed in someone else's house. But he of all people should know why. "Paris is fine. A hotel—someplace with a balcony. I want to see the stars." I smiled at his skeptical expression. "Or at least the lights of the city, if the smog is too great for stars."

"Smog, I can definitely find for you. And Father Jerome has many friends. There is a home I know for certain is unoccupied right now, a bit away from downtown but on the Seine. You will like it, I think."

I waited until Max got into the car to study him in profile. His manner was wound up—too wound up for the lateness of the hour. He knew what I was going to ask, but he let me work around to it. We talked of more nothing for a few minutes, then I leaned forward in my seat.

"So?" I asked, not missing the way he tensed. "What did you learn from me? I assume that's what you were doing when you held my hand as I talked to that girl."

"What, you don't like having your hand held?" he teased, glancing in the rearview mirror.

"Not by someone who practically sears it off with the brush of his magic, no." I gave him another moment, then continued. "You learned something. And you haven't come anywhere near me since you touched me. Was it really that bad?"

"Ah—no," he said, shaking his head ruefully. "Tell you the truth, I didn't know what to think. You have abilities beyond what I expected. Beyond any of the kids we have processed through here, even some of the ones who manifest as travelers and clairvoyants. And you can't do any of that. You don't wield actual magic." His gaze flicked to me. "Right?"

"Nope." I edged back in my seat, eyeing him. "That's why I use the cards."

"Spirit speaks to you, definitely," he said, almost as if he was talking to himself. "Through your intuition. That's certain. But the rest—your ability to travel, to jump dimensions, to command angels—to—"

"Whoa, what?" I sat up straight. "You can cross 'commanding angels' off your list. I'm pretty sure I'd know it if I had that skill."

"It's there." He shrugged. "The truth comes to me in words and images, sometimes both. That one was words. And there were swords—swords all around you. I know what that's about too."

"Jerome said the children were talking about the swords before I got here."

"They've been talking for days. All about the Houses in general, but Swords is the only one they'll name. Swords and you as its head. They don't seem to know the leaders of the other Houses—and we've asked. We figured you'd want to know."

"I would." I shrugged. "I will, eventually." I pinned him with a hard stare. "Father Jerome doesn't want me to lead the House of Swords."

"Father Jerome doesn't want you to be killed." Max gentled his words with a smile. "He is a big softie, for all his toughness. I get why he's nervous. But this…" Max shook his head. "I don't see you getting out of this one, Sara. Those swords were all around you. Not like the Eight of Swords either—they were out, flying past you. Like you had a battalion of actual swords at your disposal, and you knew how to guide them."

"Which would be impressive, if I could do something more than cut steak."

Max lapsed into silence, and I let him be. I suddenly wasn't sure I wanted to know what kind of skills he thought I had. Not if I wasn't going to use them. Not if I wasn't going to enter the war as the head of the House of Swords…whatever that meant.

I shifted in my seat, scowling as I watched the lights of Paris ease by. Eventually we turned closer to the river, but high enough past the city that we wound our way along large estates and manicured lawns, everything reeking of money and class.

"Father Jerome has friends here?"

"It's an amazing estate." Max turned into a drive, the gate opening almost before he glanced up to the camera. "We're expected."

"I guess so…" Still, it wasn't until we'd slid all the way around the perfectly curved drive that I realized my mistake in trusting Max Bertrand to take me anywhere.

The sight of the man waiting for us struck me like a visceral punch to the gut.

He owed a debt of thanks to his Egyptian mother and French father, the best of both their features comingling in his raven-black hair that now curled to his shoulders, his black-gold eyes, and the sharp, aristocratic cut of his jaw. His sensual lips were now tightened into a sneer, but the expression didn't detract from the raw perfection of his face. He wore his impeccably cut suit open, unbuttoned, and the fine material sat comfortably on his tall, rangy frame. He wasn't thick or heavy, but that grace was deceptive. I'd seen the muscles corded over his arms and torso, his legs, his—

Focus.

"You're killing me, Max," I muttered.

"Sorry," Max said sheepishly, not meeting my glare. "But the ties that bind, you know."

"Great." Still, I couldn't take my eyes off the figure standing at the bottom of the stairs to the elegant estate house, perfect and devastating in his burnished-bronze glory.

Armaeus Bertrand, the Magician.

Chapter Five

Armaeus didn't speak as Max parked the car. Out of a perverse sense of obstinacy I stayed in the limo until the younger Max came around to open my door. The younger Bertrand stood in awe of Armand on so many levels, he deserved to be a part of this handoff, to be addressed by his uncle, no matter how many great-greats there were between their generations.

I stepped out and immediately felt the intensity of the Magician's gaze on me, ice and fire. Ignoring Armaeus, I turned to Max. "You'll take care of Father Jerome? He looks tired."

"He's not so tired as that," Max said, his lips quirking up in a grin even as he seemed acutely aware of Armaeus shifting his gaze to him. "He puts on a show for you, to get you to do what he wants."

That made me feel somewhat better, but then Max stiffened, his eyes going wide as he raised up slightly on his toes.

I swung my gaze to Armaeus. "What are you doing?" I asked sharply.

The Magician had lifted his hand slightly—enough to make it clear he was the one holding up Max as if by the scruff of his neck. But the look he turned on his far-removed nephew wasn't angry, exactly. It was cold, calculating, his dark golden eyes now nearly black with intensity as he scowled at Max.

"Your abilities are not new. You've hidden this your whole life," he said, and his words contained a vocal projection that shivered through my bones. I grimaced. Max didn't have a lot of experience with Armaeus's auditory tricks. I did.

Max, for his part, looked frozen in shock. His words, when they came, were a babble of French.

Armaeus flicked his fingers, and Max stumbled back, regaining control of his body before he fell down. "Does Claire know?" the Magician asked, referring to Max's great-aunt, the matriarch of the Bertrand family who lived deep in the heart of France, knocking around an enormous mansion that had more bedrooms than a Hyatt. "She should."

"She doesn't," Max said, and to the boy's credit, he straightened under Armaeus's gaze, his shoulders going back. "She won't, not by me. I don't have time for anything but the children right now. And they keep coming, Armaeus. They keep coming, and if what I'm learning is true, that's not going to end anytime soon. They deserve someone to fight for them."

It was perhaps the most serious speech I'd ever heard Max make, and I kept utterly still as I watched them, afraid to interrupt the moment. Max had already done so much—committed so much—and pride swelled within me at how much more he could do. This was the reason to fight, I thought. People like Max, who dedicated themselves to those who needed a champion. This was the reason to lead.

Even if I couldn't handle a sword.

The two Bertrands stared at each other a long moment, then Armaeus turned back toward the house.

"As you will," he said, and strode up the stairs. "Miss Wilde."

Max looked poleaxed. I resisted the pull of Armaeus's command for a moment more as I gave Max the thumbs-up.

"You rock," I said. "Now leave before I beat the crap out of you for dragging me into his holiness's domain."

"Miss *Wilde*." Armaeus's pull was more insistent now, and as Max's faltering smile began to firm on his lips, I let myself be dragged up a step. Armaeus had not done this before, I realized with some surprise. Before, he'd certainly encouraged me to move where he wanted me to move, but never by using overt magical force. This was new.

I wasn't a fan of new.

Still, I climbed the stairs more quickly as Max started the car and eased the sedan forward, his night's delivery complete. Ahead of me, Armaeus paused to watch the vehicle move into the darkness.

"He's a good guy, you know," I said, speaking to the Magician's profile. "You should cut him a break."

"The likelihood of him dying a violent death has now increased exponentially with your interference in his life and your encouragement of his gifts," Armaeus said without inflection. "When he dies, and of course he will die, there is now an eighty-seven percent chance that his death will be directly attributable to the conversations you've had with him and the trajectory you've sent him on. I should think if anyone should cut the young man a break, it would be you."

He stalked through the open door.

I thought momentarily about turning around and trotting back down the stairs. Max wouldn't be far, or I could catch a cab—

Miss Wilde. As I waffled, Armaeus's words flowed through me, sensual and insistent. *Would you truly give up this opportunity? There's so much you want to know.*

My brows went up. So that was how he was going to play this?

Spinning the Magician's stupid ring on my finger, I climbed the last few steps and entered a palatial marbled foyer. I could see all the way down the long hallway to the veranda and Armaeus's imposing figure beyond. He was ready for a chat? I could chat.

By the time I reached the end of the corridor, I'd built up a full head of steam.

Armaeus stood at the edge of the stone veranda overlooking the tumble of forest down to the wide river. I stopped well short of him. I didn't trust him, and I didn't much like him right now. And due to a series of recent events, in which so many of my memories with him had been proven to be lies, I didn't exactly know how to base an opinion of him going forward.

"Okay, I'm here now. Let's chat," I said, and Armaeus turned. Once again, I steeled myself against his impossible beauty, as shocking in this moment as it was every time I looked at him.

For his part, the Magician's eyes glittered as our gazes connected, and I sensed the desire curl between us, more intense even than our shared fury.

"What is it you want of me, Miss Wilde?" he murmured, and his voice hinted at mysteries better left unexplored, treasures I'd do well to leave buried. It was magical hoodoo, a diversionary trick—but I'd be lying if I didn't say it was my favorite one. Armaeus might be a master of promises unkept, but they were always really, *really* good promises.

Unfortunately, I didn't have the patience for any of that tonight.

"I want the truth," I said, my annoyance ratcheting up again at his smirk.

"I find that's rarely the case of anyone, least of all mortals."

"You know, you've been immortal again for about thirty-seven seconds. And if you'll remember, I was the one who got you there."

His eyes turned a decidedly darker shade. "I don't think I'll be forgetting that anytime soon."

"Yeah, well, you know what I won't be forgetting? Simon, drunk off the poison *I* should have ingested in the Tel Aviv airport, telling me all about how you guys had the time of your lives trying to figure out what exact kind of freak I was."

His expression didn't change. "You're upset that we discussed you?"

"I'm *upset* that this whole time when I thought you were legitimately hiring me and paying me to find artifacts for you, you knew I was a walking time bomb of crazy. And rather than warn me so that, oh, I don't know, I could maybe watch out for myself, you simply observed me. Watched me like a bug. You put me in dangerous situations just to see what I would do."

He lifted a sardonic brow. "And paid you handsomely as well."

"Oh, don't give me that—what's payment to you when you can literally *create* money?" I spread my hands. "Don't get me wrong. I set a fair price, and by God, you paid it, but I didn't realize I was your science fair experiment. Every job you let me stumble around and fall and fail—and for what? So you could collect some new data about those wild, wacky mortals? Are you guys truly that bored?"

"You're hardly the *average* mortal, Miss Wilde." Now irritation sharpened his words, as I hoped it would. A cold Armaeus was a guarded one. But piss him off, and things got far more interesting. "That was clear before your family ties were uncovered—part of them, anyhow. Or has Willem told you who your mother was?"

His name drop of dear old Dad—current Hermit of the Arcana Council—was one too many stops along the crazy-train express. I hadn't even fully processed the fact that my father wasn't some drunken skirt chaser who'd stuck around Memphis only long enough to knock up my mom before skipping out on her again. No, he was sort of bodyguard of the universe, pledged since the Middle Ages to protect humanity from a magical being bent on our destruction. That still didn't clear him from missing all my soccer games, but it got him closer.

Either way, the woman who raised me wasn't even my mom. She was a paid caregiver in the Hermit's employ. Which pretty much meant my family tree should be clear-cut and turned into pressboard, but that was way beside the point right now.

"You can leave Dad out of it, and I'm not the one answering questions here. Why were you fixated on me? Why me, specifically? Because I know I'm not the strongest Connected out there. Not by a long shot. There are kids I met today who could run magical rings around me."

Armaeus was watching me intently, and I stared back at him until he shook his head.

"You're not the strongest Connected on earth right now, no," he said. "But from the first time I engaged you, your potential was clear."

"My potential. Right."

"There's a reason for dark practitioners craving the blood and bones of innocents, Miss Wilde. The Council is not so different. Many of the higher-level Connecteds available to us had already set their minds and hearts on a path from which they would not be dissuaded. Or they were too young, unable to make their own choices. You"—he spread his hands—"had every choice available to you, but no path."

"I *have* a path," I snapped. "One I was walking along quite happily without you."

"We do not have the luxury of ignoring our obligations anymore. The balance of magic had fallen hopelessly askew. With an Adept Connected also bent to the task of maintaining that balance—"

"A what Connected? Are you even listening to yourself?" I took a few steps forward to see him more clearly. As expected, he improved with proximity. Asshat.

"I'm not working with the Council as an all-you-can-freak buffet," I said. "You hired me for a job."

He shrugged, the movement aristocratically elegant. "And you're worth more than the job for which we hired you."

"Then why not simply tell me that? What's with the cloak and dagger?" I pounded my chest with my index finger. "This is me, Armaeus. Is there *anything* about me that suggests to you I couldn't be bought? My entire livelihood depends on me being willing to trade my time and skills for money. Why lie to me? Why make me think that—"

I broke off too late, but could see instantly that the damage had already been done. I'd strayed dangerously close to revealing the true reason for my sense of betrayal at Armaeus's cold treatment of me. Not that I could have died, not that I'd been injured in the course of working for the Council. That was to be expected for the amount I was being paid.

But Armaeus had become more than my employer. Much more, I'd thought. And that reality had made me incredibly weak when I most needed to be strong.

His next words confirmed my misstep. "So, is that your issue, then, Miss Wilde?" he asked. He'd somehow moved toward me, or my own traitorous feet had drifted me closer to him, the spider in the center of a glittering web. "You wish to know how I feel about you?"

"I couldn't give a crap how you feel about me anymore," I said, but my words were not as convincing as I wanted them to be. "I simply don't understand why you couldn't keep it all business. We had an arrangement. A good arrangement. I would have happily taken more money to push my abilities."

"You would have." Now Armaeus did move deliberately. As he stepped closer to me, the very air charged with electricity, and my breath seemed to grow thicker in my throat. I couldn't get enough oxygen, yet every one of my nerve endings was lit on fire with each foot he erased between us.

Then suddenly he was there in front of me, close enough to touch.

"Do you feel this current between us?" he murmured. He lifted his hand, and I flinched reflexively, causing his lips to curve into a cold, hard smile. He drifted his fingers along the side of my face.

Electricity sparked wherever he touched. My heart thundered, my hands went damp and clammy in their bandages, and my knees turned to milk. It was all I could do to stay upright, despite the anger building up inside me.

"This is exactly what I'm talking about!" I hissed, holding myself perfectly still. "None of this is necessary to accomplish your goals."

"Do you know so little about me, then, that you truly believe that?" Armaeus dipped his head so his eyes were nearly even with mine, and I couldn't break contact with their smoking depths. "My magic is born of the physical, Miss Wilde. The heat and electrical connections between two people is the most natural wellspring to fire it. And I needed it to be fired to understand you."

He leaned closer, so close that when he spoke, the whorls of his breath caressed my skin, teasing and tempting. My mouth opened of its own volition, and though I told myself it was merely to prepare to scream, I knew better.

I wanted Armaeus Bertrand. I wanted him with every fiber of my being. I'd somehow been exactly calibrated to match his frequency, so that when he was this close, everything within me hummed.

"You feel it," he murmured, and there was a roughness in his voice that skittered through me, flipping every switch to go. "That's what I needed, in order to build you up and tear you down and lay you open for my understanding. None of my research would have been possible without it."

"You could have simply asked," I said miserably, the desire racing through my veins impossible to ignore, the heat soaking through me as real as life itself. "You didn't have to trick me."

"If I'd asked, I never could have had this," he murmured.

Then he leaned the final few inches and brushed his lips against mine.

Chapter Six

There was no denying the hot, electrical surge that jolted through me, setting my nerve endings on fire. There was also no denying the anger that erupted on its heels.

"So you used me!" I shoved the Magician back with both hands, as much to create distance between us as to emphasize my point. "You used my attraction to you, whatever this thing is between us, as a means to get you information, to figure out how I could drag ever more complicated crap back to home base. First the artifacts, then people— For criminy's sake, I went to Atlantis for you!"

"You went to Atlantis for yourself," Armaeus corrected me. "I merely told you where to find the weapons you needed, and Death showed you the path."

"Yeah, well, did she know you were jacking me up on purpose? Were you guys all sitting around comparing notes?" I put my hands to my temples. "Sweet Christmas, Eshe. That pompous windbag crawled around inside my head, Armaeus. She—"

"Eshe and I do not discuss the progress of my work with mortals."

If he'd meant those words to reassure me, he was in for a shock. "Your *work with mortals.* Are you for real?" I stared at him, so unreasonably irate I could feel my split ends sizzle. "I…goddamnit, Armaeus. I thought—I mean, you said—"

I stuffed the words back into Pandora's Box as quickly as I could, but once again the Magician's entire body went tense, like a pointer closing in on a bird.

"I said what, Miss Wilde?"

I could feel the vocal projection shifting through me, but not even the magic of the Arcana Council could outweigh the survival instincts of a woman so totally scorned.

"You didn't say anything at all," I snapped, weighing my words with a healthy dose of self-disgust that was not remotely feigned. "I heard something in my head that I wanted to hear. But that's over—we've gotten that out of the way. From now on, though, you need something, you ask. Don't play games with me simply because it's a shortcut. It's not necessary." I rubbed my hands over my eyes, wincing as my flayed palms chafed against their bandages, but glad for the pain to steady myself. "Whether you need me to go to Atlantis again or astral travel or find stuff—whatever it is"—I passed a hand over my brow—"for the right price, I'll do it."

Armaeus watched me for a long moment before nodding. "Very well," he said, and crossed his arms over his chest. "Annika Soo has charged you with taking over the House of Swords."

"I know, I know—"

"Decline that invitation."

I pulled my hands away from my head. "Wait, what?"

"It's a simple enough request, Miss Wilde. It's not your place to become the head of the House of Swords. Decline it."

"Oh, geez—what *is* it with you people?" I demanded. "First, Father Jerome is on my case, then you? Him at least I can understand—he doesn't want me to get dead all that soon. But what do you care about the House of Swords?"

"It's a task that others are better suited to do. Moreover, it's beneath you. Your skills are such that you are made for greater things than an earthbound House."

I scowled at him. Something wasn't adding up here. "An earthbound House that you couldn't learn anything about until it practically fell into your lap thanks to me," I said. "But now you want me to step down?"

"You've not even begun to step up."

"Semantics. I would've thought you of all people would be into this side job. What better way for you to find out about this House that's eluded your grasp for lo, these past thousand years? And not only that one, but the others besides."

"A worthy consideration, but shortsighted. Now that the House of Swords has been definitely revealed to me and the Council, there are other agents who can be assigned to learn more about its inner workings and personnel." His glare bored into me. "And it is *not* a side job, as I suspect you well know. House leadership belongs in the hands of someone ruthless and unforgiving, and one willing to spend her every waking hour dedicated to action and self-protection."

"Maybe you missed the geisha brigade at the Bellagio when Gamon came to attack Soo," I said dryly. "Trust me, I've got self-protection covered."

He shook his head. "You're missing the key point of my objection. You're meant for more than House command, Miss Wilde."

"Yeah? So what color parachute have you picked out for me, then?" I waved off his confused expression. "Cut to the chase, Armaeus. You got that much work lined up that you're going to put me on retainer?"

Inexplicably, Armaeus's face lightened. "Retainer…" He pursed his lips.

Whoops, bad idea. "Never mind, it's not an option. What is it you need me to do?"

His lips flattened again. "It's not so much a matter of you doing something, it's you *being* something. You're an asset to the Council."

"And I'm mortal, and the Council isn't. So forgive me for wanting to ally myself with the home team a bit more."

"The Council is not arrayed against the Connecteds."

"You don't have a stellar track record of protecting them either. I've seen what the dark practitioners are doing to those kids, Armaeus. Adults too who're particularly gifted. If all that magic gets stamped out, you and your precious Council won't have anything left to balance, remember? So why shouldn't I get involved?"

"Perhaps because you could be operating at the position of puppet master, versus the doll dangling from a string."

I rolled my eyes. "Once again, you're not listening. I don't *want* to be a puppet master, Armaeus, I want to be down on the stage with everyone else. These people are *my* people. The Connecteds have a place in society that is determined by their own sense of what's right and wrong, even if that sense doesn't agree with what you think they should be doing. They deserve better than to be used as tools, whether by the dark practitioners or frightened organizations like SANCTUS trying to stamp out magic, or even by the Council. If they want to form an army, great—they can go to war. If most of them prefer to hide in the shadows, to protect themselves or their spouses and children, also great. There will always be those who are willing to fight."

"And since when are you one of those people?"

Since two wide-eyed Connected girls told me to pick up my sword and save the world. "What I do now or in the future is none of your concern, Armaeus. You can sit back and watch like the rest of the Council, and—"

"No!" Armaeus's outburst was so violent that the chairs on the stone veranda jumped, though he hadn't pounded a wall or stamped his feet. Still, the energy in the air turned crystalline, heat glazed by the intensity of his emotion. "*That* is where you are wrong, Miss Wilde. You've spent so long protesting your right to do whatever you want that you neglect to see what is right before you. The game has changed. *I* have changed. And I will no longer be satisfied with sitting by and observing, as you so succinctly put it. I have done that quite enough."

I'd snapped my mouth shut in surprise, but Armaeus didn't need any encouragement to continue. "Allow me to share with you what I saw in Hell, when I wasn't trying to keep you and your depraved twin soul from twisting events to your own despicable ends."

I winced. That was totally unfair, but now didn't seem the time to cry foul.

Armaeus barreled on. "The woman you saw in that plane was not a mirage or a memory, Miss Wilde. She was the woman I'd pledged my life to love and protect. And then the needs of the Council grew too great, and I did not return one fall as I had intended to. That year, the winter was particularly harsh. Though Mirabel had money and retainers, she could not outrun the sickness that ravaged the land. She came into contact with a stricken man at breakfast and was dead by dinner, as the saying goes. I was told weeks after her body was cold in the ground. Cold! Here I was, the Magician of the Arcana Council, able to move from state to state, plane to plane, and I could not protect the only woman I'd ever loved."

I really didn't want to hear this. I even more didn't want to see him as he spoke such words, their truth etched in every angle and plane of his face. But I couldn't look away. I'd known Armaeus had changed in Hell, but looking at him now, it was as if he was a different person entirely. Gone was the smug self-assurance, the mild-mannered certainty that he was righteously correct in all his actions. In its place was an almost feral outrage that defied anyone to stand in his way—including and especially, me.

"But she did not really die, it would seem," he continued scathingly. "Not in the manner she should have, the manner that would have taken her from this place and moved her to the next plane of existence, for her to live and love as she was intended to. No. Her spirit would not loose its hold on this earth, and for that she was consigned to the plane closest to our own, where mortals go to live out their regrets—their *regrets*,

Miss Wilde. That is what I found when I finally deigned to enter a plane I could have breached at any time in the last thousand years. A woman mired in the regret of a life she no longer held, all for the love of me."

I don't know where the words came from that welled out of me. I didn't summon them. I didn't want them. But that didn't stop them from boiling forth to spew at Armaeus in a scalding wash of pain.

"You're not the only one who suffered in Hell, Armaeus. You say that place was built for regrets? I regret ever setting foot in it, ever seeing what I was forced to see, forced to feel, forced to hope—"

Once again Armaeus's nearly preternatural awareness sharpened. His gaze raked over me so ferociously that I barely got my mental barriers set in time to avoid the blast of his attack as he reached out tentacles of ripping power, pounding into my skull.

"Get out—no!" I gasped, clasping my hands to my head. "You have no right—get out!"

"Make me, Miss Wilde." Though my mind was beset with a howling wind, I could still hear Armaeus's words slip silkily over the top of the storm, as insidious as the magic he blasted at me. *"That's twice you have wanted to betray something buried deep within you, so deep I cannot reach it. And I want to reach it. I want to know. You say you will do anything for money; then I will pay you. What is it you saw in Hell that gives you such pause? What is it that grips your entire energy with fury and despair whenever you rake over it, like a nail from the Holy Cross? I will pay you whatever you desire if you will tell me this—"*

"No," I seethed, wrenching back from him, though he made no move to restrain me. "Get your bony ass out of my mind—now!"

Without thinking, without even feeling, I pulled my hands away from my head and thrust them out, as if I was hurling a medicine ball out of my skull. The movement lit me on fire from my center up and out, and the world around me was suddenly too white—too bright—a fury of crackling energy blowing up between Armaeus and myself.

I yanked my hands back just as quickly, and the illusion shorted out, leaving nothing but singed air in its wake.

Singed air and a very feral-looking Armaeus. The Magician's touch was no longer on my mind, nowhere close to me, in fact. It was as if my brain now floated behind vaulted doors and bulletproof glass, and I stood taller for it, my shoulders lighter, my eyes clearer.

"What..." I said flatly, "was that?"

"That," Armaeus purred with a positively opulent interest that had never boded well for me, "was magic, Miss Wilde."

"Bullshit."

He took a step toward the side, as if he intended to circle me, the newest orangutan at the zoo. "Not the magic of illusion, or the psychic skill of a Connected able to astral travel or dimension hop. That was not a magic born of your mind. It was born of your heart, your sacral center. The magic of a Magician, some would say."

"So your magic returned back to you."

"I don't think so." Deep, fathomless speculation gleamed in his eyes. "Mortal sorcerers borrow magic from other entities—demons, the djinn, angels, there are a thousand sources they claim to channel. You pulled that burst of power from within yourself. Do you still think your role in the war on magic is one of bloodshed? To lead a syndicate known more for its executions and technoceutical drug deals than for the furthering of magic's place in the world?"

Back to this again. But at least this complaint I could handle. Especially without the Magician's infernal touch on me.

"This war you speak of is not the Council's war alone, Armaeus. It's a mortal war as well." My words sounded too loud, and I tried to modulate them, but I couldn't seem to control my voice. Or my hands and feet for that matter. I visibly trembled, and backed away from the Magician toward the house, only dimly aware that he paced toward me like a hungry leopard. "And as it turns out, I'm mortal. I'm also in a position to help. And I can help. I'm strong enough for that."

"There is no doubt that you are," Armaeus murmured, his eerie dark eyes glittering. "How are you feeling, Miss Wilde?"

"Fine." I took another few steps back, entering the house again. Its cool confines should have been soothing, but they were suddenly too close, too thick. As if the air was too tight against my skin, my skin too tight against my bones—

"Are you sure?" Armaeus's expression was entirely too aware. "The use of magic—especially when it is not merely channeled power—can have a significant effect on a person. One that is difficult to ignore."

"I'm solid." I turned, the front door of the house once more in my sight. I needed out of here, away from Armaeus, away from Paris. I needed time, space, breath. The heat that was pooling in my body, surging higher with each of Armaeus's words, might be an unfortunate aftereffect of whatever I'd pulled out of my brain…but it was simply an aftereffect, and one I could manage.

Really.

Armaeus had somehow gotten around me, and I stopped short as I realized he now stood at the front door. But to my surprise, he wasn't blocking me. Instead, he reached for the door and held it open, inviting me to pass.

"You remain, as ever, an enigma, Miss Wilde," he murmured as I finally moved past him. His words seemed to arrow straight into my core, and how I managed to keep walking was a bit of a trick, what with everything south of my navel threatening to dissolve into a puddle of need. "And I look forward to exploring your newfound abilities more deeply when next we meet."

I turned back to him. "Not going to happen," I said, and there was still the weird thing with my voice—too loud, too full. "At this point, I'd rather set myself on fire than let you touch me."

The Magician's smile, if anything, only deepened. "It would appear you're going to do both."

Chapter Seven

I'd texted Nikki Dawes the moment I hit US airspace, so I wasn't surprised she was waiting for me at the front doors of McCarran International Airport. Chauffeuring me around was one of the many ways Nikki earned her undisclosed monthly stipend from the Arcana Council, and she totally owned the position.

What did surprise me, however, was that she wasn't alone.

A white-haired Asian woman stood next to Nikki, and though they were clearly together, they couldn't have looked more different. Nikki had eschewed her normal chauffeur uniform for what could only be termed "bohemian chic." Her six-foot-four frame was draped in a poet-sleeved snow-white crocheted tunic that ended just above her jean shorts, and miles above the calf-high multi-fabric cowboy boots that adorned her size-thirteen feet. Her long auburn hair was stick straight today, topped with a man's fedora above oversized aviator sunglasses. Over Nikki's shoulder was slung a hobo bag that looked like she'd wrestled it off an actual hobo, and her wrists and fingers, ears and neck sported enough turquoise to open her own mall kiosk.

Beside her, the much older Asian woman held herself perfectly straight in her cream linen suit and elegant pumps. She'd focused on me the moment I'd entered the wide corridor that birthed the next generation of tourists into Sin City. Her eyes were a fathomless black, and her gaze only sharpened as I approached. She was petite—barely coming up to Nikki's bicep—and she appeared dressed for an international law conference, down to the expensive leather briefcase.

In contrast to the two of them, I probably looked like yesterday's lunch bag. Which would have been fine with me, since I couldn't remember the last time I'd eaten. My little face-off with the Magician had healed up my hands nicely but hadn't quite rid me of my need for food.

"Dollface!" When Nikki smiled, her entire face lit up like a neon WELCOME sign, and the icy fist I'd clamped around my guts the entire way to Vegas unkinked a notch. Then she was striding forward, engulfing me in her arms and turning me around.

"Nikki!" I managed. "I've only been gone a week."

"I've lived through a typical week with you. It's like a lifetime in other people's worlds." She swung me toward the woman in cream. "This is Madam Peng—Jiao to her besties. She showed up this morning at Eat and wouldn't leave, so we communed over shrimp and grits. She's one of Soo's people, which I guess are your people now."

Nikki's voice could have held a note of accusation in it, but didn't. I hadn't had much time to process the events of the past few days before Armaeus had offered Simon and me the rush job in Israel, and I hadn't debriefed her on Annika's unexpected legacy to me. I'd barely debriefed myself.

"You two talked?" I asked.

"Nikki was gracious enough to bring me up to speed on your travels," Jiao said. Her face was eerily unlined for someone with such bright white hair, and her eyes were coal black. But her smile was open and authentic, and I found myself warming to her for no reason. "Madam Soo would not have wanted you to journey so far without protection, however." Her gaze scanned the airport behind me. "Going forward, you'll need to accept additional security. Especially given the events of this past week. Your role with the organization is precious."

I hitched my messenger bag higher on my shoulder and considered her. "You called in Nigel Friedman, didn't you? He and I aren't the best of friends, you should know. But I appreciated his help."

Jiao bowed. "Mr. Friedman was the closest option for assistance," she said, though it felt like there was more to that story. Nigel, for his part, hadn't tried to reach out to me after putting me on Soo's plane, so maybe he *had* simply been in the area. But still…

"You call on him a lot?" I asked.

Jiao patted her bag. "There are many arrangements Madam Soo made during her tenure as head of the House of Swords. If you have time for a quiet conversation, there is much we should discuss." She unlatched the top of the bag, and I saw two thick folders of papers inside. Papers I had a sinking feeling I was supposed to read.

"Sure." I glanced at Nikki, but she'd pulled out her cell phone and was tapping furiously on it as she glanced at Jiao over her aviators.

"Jiao here said she's been in Vegas since Tuesday," Nikki said. "Lucky break that she found me when you were heading into town, yeah?"

I didn't miss the cautionary riffle in Nikki's words this time. Sadly, I was too tired to process it. "Right." I knuckled the grit out of my eyes, savoring the fact that my palms were no longer sliced up. The Magician could seriously chafe my chaps, but he beat Neosporin any day. "Look, my body is nowhere near on Vegas hours. If you guys can stomach another cup of coffee, I could use some—"

"Drop! Stay down!"

Nikki barked her words forcefully enough that her command intersected with my lizard brain. Without thinking, I collapsed to the floor like a sack of flour, just as something bright and white went skittering across the gleaming tile, smacking into the nearest trash can.

A knife? As chaos erupted around me I crab-scrabbled for the thing, making like a pill bug once I got it. Yep—long, thin, and made of Soo's signature white metal. Christ on a crutch, Jiao had thrown one of my own House's blades at me. I hadn't even had a job interview!

Four feet away from me, Jiao and Nikki were throwing punches at each other like a Boho MMA expo. Nikki might not know Krav Maga, but her days with the Chicago PD hadn't been so long ago that she didn't know how to defend herself. I moved to scramble upright, then remembered the second half of Nikki's command to stay down at the same moment a familiar voice barked from the front doors.

"Freeze! Police!"

What the…? My brain seized up as Las Vegas Metro Police Detective Brody Rooks strode forward, his worn loafers slapping against the tile in an angry but controlled cadence. Jiao bounced away from Nikki and allowed Brody to pull her around roughly without seeming to lose a fraction of her poise.

"My apologies, Miss Dawes. The test needed to be made," Jiao said as she nodded first at a bristling Nikki, then down at my own slack jaw and crouching body. "You are more prepared than we expected, Madam Wilde, and for that I am only grateful."

Nikki grabbed Jiao's bag from where Jiao had dropped it, her eyes remaining flat as Brody started barking.

"You have the right to remain silent," the detective said, signaling to two other uniformed cops to hustle up beside us. By now we'd drawn a small crowd. The apparent danger had passed, but my hopes for an egg sandwich seemed to be dwindling. Brody handed Jiao off to one of the uniforms, then turned to Nikki—scowling at her as she pawed through the contents of Jiao's bag. "Nikki, that's police evidence."

She pulled out the thick files and handed the bag over to him. "Then it's a good thing you're here to ensure chain of custody. Look inside for anything else you need, like maybe the baby Beretta in the front pocket."

I turned on her. "A *Beretta*? She was going to shoot me?"

Nikki scowled. "Honestly, I have no idea. These files looked legit, but I've never seen the woman, you hadn't prepped me, and something was twistier than a fish on a hook about her from the get-go." She stared after Jiao as the police officers escorted her to a waiting cop car. "Still, she totally pulled every punch after the first, as if she really was testing me out. Maybe she's one of Soo's people, maybe she isn't. Either way, she set us up. And that's not cool."

"Wait—Soo?" Brody asked. "Annika Soo? What the hell is going on here?"

"I've missed you, sugar lips." Nikki grinned at me, her good mood returning with suspicious speed. "That was fun, yeah? Not everyone gets attacked every time they get home."

"Isn't she..." My gaze tracked Jiao into the police car. She turned and stared back at me. "Isn't she on my side? Didn't you say she was on my side?"

"Car." Brody cut off Nikki's response. "Now."

The three of us exited the building and Brody's sedan was right out front, with his detective credentials guaranteeing he wouldn't get towed from the taxi lane. We slid into his beat-up sedan in positions that were becoming all too familiar: Brody in front, Nikki and I in back.

"You want to explain what the hell is going on, Nikki?" he rumbled the moment we buckled in.

"You know what I texted you," she said. "Nothing's changed. Woman shows up saying all the right things, looking the part, knowing shit she shouldn't know about Sara, but tighter than a tick on a dog."

I stared at her. "You did not just say that."

Nikki grinned, switching her attention to me. "Her credentials checked out—she's one of Soo's top officials, has worked with the syndicate for years. But something was weird, so I told Brody to shoot down here for backup without telling him about Jiao's background." She glanced back to Brody. "Good of you to get here so quickly. And that whole 'Freeze' thing—gives me shivers every time."

Brody's face didn't shift. "She had to know you'd contact me."

"I'm thinking so, yeah. Everything she did since the moment she ordered coffee was part of a script. Then she moved in public, testing me and Sara and you too, Brody—her attack on Sara went out over dispatch, and you know it was caught on screen somewhere. She was sending a message. I just don't know to whom."

"A message..." I scowled out the window. What kind of message was best sent via police scanners and amateur cell-phone videos? Surely nothing that important, but if not—why go through the motions? Annika Soo had a network of operatives and allies that spanned the globe. There were better ways to communicate with them—right?

Unless they weren't the intended recipients of the message.

My head started to pound as Nikki leaned back in her seat. She hadn't let go of the files, and I poked at them.

"So what are those, anyway?"

"From what I can tell, real estate holdings. *Your* real estate holdings, to be exact." Her gaze shifted forward. "Okay, sweet buns," she said, grinning as Brody rolled his eyes. "You wanna be useful while you're providing police escort, take us to..." She opened the top file. "Nine Fourteen Tallawanda Drive."

"Tallawanda?" His gaze met hers in the mirror. "That's industrial."

"Uh-huh. Well, if Jiao is who she says she is and not a very well-dressed assassin with piss-poor execution, it's a warehouse that's been deeded over to Sara's name."

"What? Already?" Time seemed to crowd in on me as Brody cursed in the front seat.

"Explain the whole thing at once, dammit," he bit out, his fingers white-knuckling on the steering wheel. "God save me from blasted female cops. Everything's a goddamn suspense novel."

Nikki dimpled at him. "Wasn't kidding about how much I've missed you. But here's the deal. I've picked up no fewer than five tails since Sara went to Israel."

Brody's groan was audible, but this time it was directed at me. "Israel? Really? Would it kill you to tell me when you're going out of the country?"

"Anyway, so this morning was the first time one of them approached me," Nikki continued. "I did my part dining out in the most visible restaurants I could, which I'll be billing the Council for, natch, but finally one of them bit. Knew something was a little hinky, but I didn't sniff a fake so much as, well, hinky."

"And she said she was with Soo," I cut in, sensing Brody's blood pressure starting to spike again.

"She did, and apparently Detective Dimples here will have his hands full if she's as plugged into Las Vegas brass as she said she was. Showed me her files—not her gun, mind you—and asked if you'd be in town. Apparently, Soo owns property in cities across the world, and lucky you, you get to manage them now."

"Which you're also about to explain." Brody's gaze slid to me, and I leaned back too. This part, at least, was easy. Or easier, anyway.

"My last job was for Soo," I said. "It turned into an audition for her role, which I didn't expect and wasn't planning on. But when she died, she asked me to take over for her—and, well…everyone assumed I said yes, and I didn't correct them."

Brody snorted, and I shrugged. "Hey, the woman had just died. I thought they'd…I don't know, forget."

Even as I said the words, they rang hollow in my ears. I couldn't unsee Soo's face as she'd stared at me, telling me to take control of the House of Swords. I couldn't deny the sense that I owed the woman—and her people—something more.

"Uh-huh," Brody broke into my thoughts. "And you've had no one else approach you since?"

"Some guys in the Tel Aviv airport, but they could've been anyone."

"Whoa, whoa, whoa." Now Nikki was scowling at me too. "You didn't tell me that."

"I'm telling you now. They didn't leave a calling card, and they didn't try that hard, frankly." I decided to avoid further mention of Nigel, or of the syringes filled with God knew what. That almost certainly was another black market kingpin on my case, with zero direct connection to Soo. No need to cross the streams of crazy. "I didn't think that much of it. There was no one in Paris, but I was more careful there, left with fake credentials."

"Thank heaven for small favors." Brody slowed the sedan. "This is the place."

We peered up at the building. "Warehouse, doesn't look abandoned," I said. "Can you figure out what's inside without a warrant?"

"Something to ask our new friend if she stays in lockup long enough," Nikki put in. "And, hey, it's in Sara's name, that should open its doors, right?"

She turned to me and I nodded. "Permission to search granted."

"Noted," Brody said. "What's next?"

There were three other properties in the listing, including another warehouse in an even sketchier part of town, which did look abandoned—and two houses.

We hit the road.

A half hour later, I squinted into the sunlight as we pulled up to the first residence. "This is the place?" I asked. "Seriously?"

It was a palatial estate up in the Summerlin district, a world away from the Strip—though you'd still be able to see all the beautiful lights at night from the rooftop deck. Nikki craned her head out the window, her gaze pinging from her printouts to the view.

"Curb appeal, total check. Pool, according to the sheets—can't see it from the street, but it includes waterfalls and multiple spas. There's indoor fireplaces, six bedrooms, seven bathrooms, media room—oversized walk-in showers." That stopped her, and when she looked up at me, her eyes were dilated. "We are going to have so much fun here."

"Nikki, this isn't really mine."

She flapped a hand at me. "Who's to say it isn't? According to Jiao, your name on the dotted line is about to bring you a world of crazy, not all of which is remotely close to good. Might as well float around in your pool for a while thinking about all that, right?"

"This can't be legit, though." The warehouses were one thing, but seeing an actual house at an actual address and imagining it as mine—that finally kicked my brain back online. "This is real live money and real live assets. And I didn't sign anything. It seems like I should have signed something."

"Oh, honey, it doesn't stop there." Nikki waved the file folder at me. "You're either going to be really popular or really unpopular in a very short period of time, once everyone figures out what all you own." She pounded the back of Brody's headrest. "Keep going, Jeeves, this next place is completely off the chain—head toward Lake Las Vegas."

Off the chain didn't begin to describe it. We reached the house in a little under an hour, a gated production off Northshore Road with an honest-to-Christmas gate attached to a high wall. Nikki gave Brody the code indicated on her paperwork and it worked like an Open Sesame.

Though other palatial homes were located on the lake proper, this one sat further back. Beyond the gate, Nikki recited a laundry list of amenities: the pool, the jacuzzi, the nine-bedroom estate house and half-dozen guest cottages. There was apparently a reflection garden, a series of ponds, and a fully equipped gym. The trees looked like they'd been shipped in aftermarket, far more than should have been sustainable in the desert, but between that and the fountains, they gave the place a more hidden feel, an oasis in the desert. The estate sat high on the ridge above Lake Las Vegas, and as we wound up the long drive, something else was immediately noticeable as well.

We weren't alone here.

"What exactly did this Jiao character tell you about the place?" Brody asked, his back going stiff as we passed two black-paneled vans parked off the drive, and a clutch of low-slung, high-rent vehicles. "Get those plates while you're at it."

"On it." Nikki's pen was already scribbling down numbers as Brody slowed, but no one halted our progress up the drive, and when we finally reached the terra-cotta roofed master house, all of us were staring.

The front courtyard was a watery wonderland, arched stone and patterned rock pairing with bubbling fountains that flowed into each other under a thick bower of yet more trees. It was also teeming with people—probably two dozen adults…all of whom looked decidedly familiar.

"Soo's people. The ones Gamon had taken," Nikki murmured, even as Brody nodded. "She stashed them here to recover."

"Oh…geez," I murmured. In that moment, the weight of what Soo had really gifted me sank in. She wasn't giving me money as she had in the past, not even the power to help the victims of the war on magic. She was giving me the war itself. The resources and power to truly make a difference.

And not only that. Here were people who could escape a terrible fate, if only I would lead. Here—and so many other places—were Connecteds who could turn to a brighter future, if only I would clear the way.

Here was a job that wouldn't end with a trinket safely locked in someone's vault…instead it was a job that might actually never end. If I took it. If I was strong enough.

I pushed those thoughts out of my mind for the moment. There were several attendants on the grounds as well, noticeable in their medical scrubs, but the place looked more like a Zen retreat than a recovery center.

Nikki eyed the personnel. "Does this mean I can't move in yet?"

I snorted. "Don't pick out your bedroom. There's still way too much we don't know."

Brody parked the car. "Gotta be someone in charge in this place. We'll start with that."

We emerged from the car, and even the heat somehow seemed less here, the foothills of the lake region and the intense fountains and trees combining to offer an idyll in the middle of the arid wasteland. I could see why Soo had picked the site, but what had she intended for it? So far as I knew, she'd never stayed anywhere in Las Vegas other than the Bellagio.

More to the point, why specifically had she given the house to me?

At the palatial entry to the house, two women stood, their hands folded over their stomachs. One of whom I recognized.

Madam Peng nodded to us, but my gaze rested on the second woman—a fierce Asian with an almost Vietnamese cast to her features, and the cold stone face of a warrior.

Brody hadn't gotten past Jiao, however, and the two of them locked stares.

"Now I'm starting to get pissed off," he muttered.

Chapter Eight

"You mind telling me why you are not at the precinct?" Brody's gruff greeting drew a gracious half smile from the older woman, while the second woman's gaze raked over me. Both females were pristine, while I still carried the heat and grime of Paris on my body. It'd been a long day. Come to think of it, it'd been a long week.

"A misunderstanding easily rectified, given your quick response and the grace of your office's commitment to the safety of an organization with such personal ties to the Consulate General of the People's Republic of China," Jiao said, her voice quiet and assured. "Should your travels ever take you to one of our consulates in the United States, please use my name."

Brody eyed her warily. "I made no response on your behalf, Ms. Peng."

Jiao waved her hand, revealing a cell phone that looked like it could blow up the moon. "You authorized several texts to speed my release. I regret the necessity, but Madam Wilde's life is in danger. When we realized that it was most likely that she would remain in Las Vegas, we had to work quickly to ensure the city's suitability. But though there is work still to be done, it will be a fitting base for the House of Swords."

This was all moving way too fast. I lifted my hands to protest, but the second woman stepped forward. "Please, we can talk inside," she said, her words clipped. "There is much to tell you and much for you to understand."

"This is General Som," Jiao said, her serene face etched with pride. "She is one of our strongest generals and came from her base in Cambodia to ensure our safety immediately after Madam Soo's death. She can explain much of your new role, Madam Wilde."

General Som didn't look like she'd relish that opportunity, but she nodded and turned on her heel, leading us into the house.

Brody held up a hand, frowning. "Cambodia?" he asked Jiao. "So your operation here isn't solely Chinese."

I'd suspected this, since I'd already encountered previous warriors for Soo who were decidedly Japanese, but I still focused on Jiao as she turned to him. "Not at all, Detective Rooks," she said. "Madam Soo built her House on steel and strength, wherever she could find it. You will find members of the House of Swords in every corner of the world. And that's exactly how Madam Soo preferred it."

She sailed through the door.

Reluctantly, I entered as well, still convinced that it bore nothing even close to resembling a place where I could live. Nikki clearly did not harbor the same reservations. She gave a considering "hmph" at every new room, muttering about needing a tape measure.

Brody, for his part, kept his hand at his waist, though this part of the big house was empty and silent, its high ceilings and enormous windows flooding the rooms with light.

We ended up in a drawing room that looked over a swooping canopy of trees, with more pools and pathways peeking through the breaks. "The home is situated on twenty-seven acres," General Som said. "It is equipped with state-of-the-art surveillance. You will know if you are being approached, even by air."

Jiao motioned for us to sit. Sealed water bottles in miniature ice buckets rested on trays beside each of the chairs, and while the palatial house was startling enough, the miniature ice buckets took me over the top. Jiao bowed to me, her expression serene.

"We regret not reacting sooner in Tel Aviv. It was difficult to track your actions, to know precisely when you left Hippos and where you were heading." She tilted her head. "Your companion—we are still unsure what happened to him, exactly. We did, of course, dispose of his clothing."

"His clothing," Brody said flatly, but I waved him off.

"Simon. He's fine." I leaned in, swiveling my gaze to both women. "Can you please explain what's happening here?"

"First, I must return these to you." Jiao moved to a small table in the center of the room, upon which sat an ornate box I'd seen before. I stiffened, and General Som's gaze also riveted on her. "I left that in my hotel safe at the Palazzo."

"And I stole it," Som interrupted, without hesitation. "It was not a safe location."

Jiao's smile was gentler. "Madam Soo long ago advised us that the pendants are meant to be worn at all times—ideally as a pair. We took the liberty to assist you in this regard."

She moved toward me and offered up the chain. The two jade pendants belonging to Annika Soo and her mother had been set into a necklace of intricate metal ropes, the discs linked by a series of silver chains, binding the two together.

"That's, um…very nice," I said.

Jiao nodded. "A local jeweler recommended to me by multiple sources." Nikki and I exchanged a look, but Jiao kept going. "While you are the head of the House of Swords, it is to your advantage to wear the pendants."

Not wanting to push the point, I bent forward as she settled the chain over my head. The silver rims fashioned to hold the disks kept the worst of their effect from my skin, but I could still feel the competing sensations of heat and cold arcing along my collarbone. I glanced to Som and gave the general a steady smile, and the woman seemed satisfied, finally.

"You are Soo's named successor," Som said, nodding once. "It is good you are here."

"Ah—thanks." I turned to Jiao. "Okay, that's done. Now what?"

"It is a complex question that you ask, yet we will start with what is simple." Jiao settled herself into a chair and folded her hands on her lap. She crossed her feet at the ankles, a movement so quietly elegant that even Nikki straightened.

"At Madam Soo's decree, you have been named head of the House of Swords. This is not merely a ceremonial role. You are expected to be a master of swordplay, as she was—" She held up a hand at my obvious shock. "She was aware you do not fight with the blade but with your gun. That will be rectified."

"Not anytime soon," I said. "That's a nonstarter. You need to know that."

"We are bringing in a master trainer to assess your abilities and provide you with the most likely path to perform your duties honorably," General Som said. With that proclamation, neither of them apparently considered my deficient fighting skills an issue.

Jiao continued blithely, "In addition, you will be the administrative head of the House."

I blinked. "Administration? Like paperwork?"

"You will have an entire staff at your disposal, of course." She nodded, but this still didn't sound anywhere close to being a good idea. My idea of bill collection usually involved a gun.

Jiao's soft voice drew me back. "The House of Swords is an organization that has existed in loose form for over five hundred years, most of that time based in Shanghai," she said. "That location no longer serves, however. The Waldorf Astoria Hotel sustained significant damage in an attack immediately after Madam Soo's death. The entire top floor was demolished."

"What?" Nikki barked as my own eyes widened. "Who bombed it?"

"They are calling the damage the result of faulty wiring, and the hotel is closing for renovations. Due to a longstanding arrangement between the Soo family and the building's owners, the repairs will be covered and expedited to ensure minimal loss from tourism. It is not a concern."

I forced my tone to stay steady, but seriously—a bomb? "Did any of her people die?"

"Not in that event, no." Jiao's attention flicked to me, and her smile deepened slightly. "Madam Soo anticipated the unrest her death might cause and long ago put in place instructions for the transfer of power. Even though she had not chosen a successor until you. Your existence will stay the internal chaos that often comes with such transitions, and allow us to guard against usurpers."

Usurpers. The word slithered through me, setting me on edge.

"She's not—married? No family?" I flapped my hand, suddenly feeling the weight of the pendants around my neck. "What would've happened if she hadn't hired me for that job?"

"She has no children, by choice. The leadership of the House of Swords is an honor that should be conferred, not inherited, in her opinion. There are several worthy generals in her hierarchy who anticipated receiving it." She nodded to General Som, whose face betrayed no emotion.

"Right," Nikki drawled, directing her question to General Som. "And how are they taking the news?"

"This is an honorable house. We will pledge ourselves to Madam Soo's preferred successor after the Test of Swords," General Som said matter-of-factly. "If Madam Wilde demonstrates her capacity to fight, we will follow her. If she does not, and we best her in battle, we will take up the challenge of leadership among ourselves. Either way, the House remains protected."

I considered that. "Or, you know, I could simply hand it off to one of you general people right at the start, or to all of you if that's better, and you could go ahead and fight it out," I said. "Because that's what you know how to do. Fight. With really sharp swords."

I'd expected General Som to jump on that idea. Instead, her expression darkened. "No. You must submit to the Test of Swords and meet the generals who challenge you in single combat. There is no other way. To reject the honor bestowed on you out of hand by Madam Soo would damage the House," she said. "It will not be tolerated."

Oh-kayyyy.

"You mean she *can't* say no to this?" Brody spoke, but both he and Nikki bristled, while I sat back in surprise. "She didn't ask Soo to give her that role."

"But she accepted it." Jiao's words were only about two percent question, but there was that two percent. I lifted a hand to my head, unsurprised there was a sheen of sweat on my brow. I hadn't really, technically accepted Soo's offer. But Jiao continued. "She accepted the pendants of the House of Swords."

Okay, that I definitely had done. "She was dying," I protested as Brody swung back to me, his gaze equal parts anger and anger. "She asked me to run her house. I didn't say yes, not exactly." I looked at Jiao, my words firmer. "But you're right, I did take the pendants"

"That was a *necklace*, for God's sake—" Brody continued, but Nikki's strident voice overtook him.

"What is the honorable exit clause in all this?" she asked, leaning forward until her elbows rested on her knees. "Because I've gotta tell you, Sara's not going to become Jackie Chan overnight, I don't care who you get in here to train her. So what does she have to do?"

I put aside my indignation, misplaced as it was, and focused on Jiao. She was looking at Nikki, but her words filled the room with their finality. "Madam Wilde must agree to do battle with the enemy of the House of Swords. The generals will attend that battle and step in when she falls."

"When she *falls*?" Nikki protested. "That doesn't seem reasonable."

Jiao inclined her head. "It is part of the Test of Swords. A very old tradition, and one that Madam Soo herself proudly maintained."

"Well, she could sword fight," Nikki groused. "So there's that."

I lifted my own hand to cut off Jiao's reply. "This fight—it has to be swords? It's stated that way, specifically?"

Jiao nodded, while General Som simply stared at me, silent and fierce. "Swords must be brought to bear," Jiao said.

"And nothing else? Like, a sword and say—an Uzi?"

Jiao frowned. "I do not know the specific wording. It is possible that something begun with a blade might be ended with a gun or a fist—"

"Or a bomb," Nikki put in dryly. "Or maybe an act of God."

Jiao folded her hands. "We will do the research."

Something about this still seemed off, but I couldn't quite put my finger on it. "What else, then? Let's say I hold on to Annika's commission. Who else is after me?"

Jiao's expression didn't change, but her gaze held mine. "The position is fraught with danger."

"Okay, so everyone." I grimaced. "And who's helping me?"

To my surprise, General Som spoke. "Ordinarily, the generals would be committed to your protection," she said. "But first they must confirm your right to assume the role."

Like that was going to happen. "Uh-huh. And that leaves…?"

"Your guards and staff." Jiao spoke up. Which sounded good, until one considered that she'd chucked a knife at me not ten hours earlier. "We will stand watch over you wherever you are in the world. And, of course, your Ace will serve as your personal bodyguard."

"Hold the phones." Nikki perked up, swinging her gaze to me. "You get a personal bodyguard? Is he hot?"

"Who's Ace?" I asked.

Jiao shook her head. "It is not a who but a what. The House structure has changed several times over the centuries, it's true. However, one practice that has stood the test of time for all the Houses is the concept of Aces: Unconnected mercenaries who can cycle through any or all of the Houses without betraying them to the general public, with the specific purpose of fighting for the highest bidder. The House of Swords has its current Ace, but you may draw from any of the Houses should your needs demand."

"Her needs definitely demand," Nikki said.

I was intrigued too, though for what I suspected was a very different reason. "So, where is he—or she? Here in Las Vegas?"

"The Ace assigned to the House of Swords was known only to Madam Soo. They aren't a personal bodyguard, they're a mercenary for hire, tapped only when needed—but one who is entrusted with the House secrets. We have not been able to contact the Ace of Swords directly since her passing, though we have reached out. There was no response. After that, we chose from the list of Madam Soo's more conventional hires."

"Right," I said. "And Nigel Friedman was on that second list, I take it. The conventional run-of-the-mill mercenary killers."

"He was the closest to Israel at the time as well." Jiao inclined her head. "I'm afraid I have no way to contact the Aces directly. We put out a request to a private server and offer up the details of the assignment. Whatever Ace is closest and can do the job, responds."

"Holy Mother in Chains," Nikki breathed. "It's Mercenary Tinder."

I grimaced, considering my options. My House Ace hadn't responded when called, which wasn't a good sign. But I at least could contact these people if and when I needed them.

"Okay," I breathed out. "So what's next? You clearly knew you wouldn't be stuck long in the precinct house, Jiao."

"Which is an entirely different conversation," Brody blustered.

"One I look forward to having, Detective Rooks." Jiao's words were ever so slightly inflected, and I watched with raised brows as Brody colored. I wasn't sure which of them would win in a throw down, but it would be a hell of a fight to watch. Then she turned to me. "But you are correct. We were prepared for your return, whenever you chose to leave Paris."

"Girl, you can't keep going to Paris and leaving me behind." Nikki pushed out her lip. "Maybe I can become one of these Aces people. I bet they get to go to Paris."

"And, as General Som has indicated, we have arranged for a trainer to assess your abilities with the blade," Jiao continued smoothly. "If you are fit and able, we could do it now. His assessment will go a long way toward helping you determine your best course of action."

"Fine," I said. I was exhausted and jet-lagged, but if I had to pick up an actual honest-to-God sword and fight someone in the future—I should get this over with. "It's not going to get any better from here, so he might as well see me at my worst."

After some argument, Nikki and Brody remained with the general in the sitting room, and Jiao walked with me deeper into the house. "Madam Soo custom-built the sword-practicing facility in the base of all her houses," she said. "It was a particular passion of hers."

Of course it was. "How long did you work with her?"

"I knew Madam Soo her entire life," she said. "I was her grandmother's cousin, though I retired from service when Madam Soo's mother died. When Madam Soo came to reclaim her rightful place, she asked me to return." Jiao straightened, her eyes flaring brightly. "I did so with honor."

"I'm very sorry for your loss, then," I said, but the fierce expression that had taken hold of Jiao's face fled just as quickly as it had arrived. Nevertheless...something about it tripped my trigger, and not in a good way.

Jiao accepted my condolences with a small nod. "That we all might die as honorably as she did would be the greatest grace of all."

Before I could argue the logic of that, she stopped at a large dark-paneled door.

"Master Kunh Lee will assess your abilities today," Jiao said. "You will learn much of what you are capable of within these walls."

"Great." As I turned, Jiao reached out and grabbed my arm.

"Madam Soo was a woman quick to decision and slow to regret. She would not have regretted choosing you, no matter what you learn here. Do all that you must, but know that she chose with her heart." Jiao shook her head. "I cannot say whether or not she chose wisely. Only you will be able to determine that. But know I will support your decision, whatever you do."

"Ah, thanks," I said, but Jiao was already turning away.

I watched her pace back down the long hallway in her sensible pumps, and still couldn't put my finger on what troubled me about her. If she was Annika's great-aunt, shouldn't she care more that the next head of the House of Swords was someone, oh, I don't know, capable of picking up a sword? Shouldn't she be wanting the position for herself, instead of doing all she could to ensure I landed the role? If that was even what she was doing?

I shook my head, squaring my shoulders as I pushed through the door to the workout room. Consoling myself as I entered the enormous space, complete with a rubberized floor and an honest-to-God water fountain flowing down one of the walls, I considered: how bad could it be?

There are certain questions one should never pose to the universe.

The guru hired by the House of Swords was an Asian Chuck Norris with way more confidence. A thin, wiry man of about five feet five, Kunh Lee wore a gi the way I wore yoga pants and a tank top. With a gesture and a grunt, he instructed I change into similar footless pajamas.

Then we fought.

The first battle was with fists, a flurry of movement I quickly recognized as a trick to tire me more than defeat me. It worked, however, though at least I felt at home with this style of battle. Kunh's face remained fiercely focused as we grappled. He never gave me any quarter, though I channeled every street-fighting technique I'd ever tried into fighting back—if only to prove to myself that Soo had not chosen completely foolishly.

When he stood back, I was so surprised, I fell to my knees, my lungs bellowing and my heart jackhammering out of control.

My respite was short-lived, however. Rods came next, and I was less successful here. I wasn't used to hammering on someone with a thin baseball bat, though I could see this too was an assessment of how I might handle the sword. I was beaten to a pulp by the time this second battle finished. As Kunh handed me a sword, I grimaced.

"This isn't going to end well," I muttered. He merely stood back and bowed to me.

He struck in one motion. First he was standing still, then he was flying, the very embodiment of the sword poured into human form. I could barely bring my own sword up to block him, and block was all I did—over and over again, but more and more weakly. He chopped at my arms, my legs, and though the sword was blunted, I could imagine the singing blade slicing my skin all the way through to the bone. This was my future, I realized. The strength of my hands gave way to uncertainty as our weapons changed again and I grew weaker, until finally there was nothing left but steel and blood. My blood, specifically. Mine and the House of Swords.

I couldn't even say specifically when my test ended. One moment, I was flailing away, and the next, I was lying on the floor doing my best interpretation of a semi-squashed bug, my arms quivering like antennae right before death.

Kunh stood above me, scowling down. "You are resourceful but untrained," he pronounced. "You are not in shape. You are strong but not disciplined. You are no warrior."

"Thanks for the update," I groaned, debating on whether it was possible for me to sleep where I lay for the next five years or so.

But Kunh wasn't finished. "You are weak of belief but not of spirit," he said, squatting beside me. "You are rash in your decisions but slow in abandoning a stance once you are committed. You would die rather than break, but so too would you also bend rather than die. You are not a warrior, but a messenger of spirit. And that spirit is strong."

That sounded slightly better, so I managed an appreciative grunt. But my head was still ringing from the colossal clock cleaning I'd received, so I didn't quite understand Kunh's next words.

"What you need, Sara Wilde, isn't a bigger spirit, nor a better-trained body, though the latter would certainly help you," he pronounced solemnly. "What you need is a sword that will show you the way. The Honjo Masamune."

Chapter Nine

It took another few hours before I was in any shape to leave the Soo compound, and when I did, I was buried in a phalanx of overprotection. Apparently, while I was getting beat up by Kunh, Nikki and Brody had been given a laundry list of Soo's enemies by General Som.

There were…a lot of enemies.

To head back into the city, Jiao and General Som took a lead car, while Nikki, Brody, and I piled into his sedan. Behind us, another sleek roadster pulled out, driven by what looked like your average Asian thug tourist couple, out on the town.

Nikki's pile of paperwork had grown in the interim, but her large hands clasped the thick folders without moving, her gaze on me. "Explain to me why we're heading back into the city," she asked, "if you're now Public Enemy Number One."

"I won't be for long," I said gloomily, staring out the window at the afternoon heat radiating off the desert plain. "And it's not like we're going to party. I just want to sleep. In my own bed."

"That would be a hotel bed. The kind of bed that has seen thousands of bodies in its short life. You know that, right?" Nikki said dryly. "There were nine bedrooms in that complex, and one of them with its own private dipping pool. A pool. Meant for dipping. And we're going back to the Strip."

"Anything of Soo's, I don't own, Nikki," I said wearily. "I won't own it. So one hotel is pretty much like another to me." I had more or less recovered from the beating I'd taken, but I was by no means in top form and I was still starving. "I'm pretty sure Jiao posted the results of my assessment to the House of Swords Facebook page. She and Kunh seemed less than hopeful that I was suitable Swords material."

"Unless you can find this magical sword of doom."

I creased my lips into a weary smile, but it was Brody's voice that made me open my left eye a sliver. "About that," he said heavily. "The trainer guy said the sword that'd help you out was the Honjo Masamune? He used that name specifically?"

"Yeah. I kind of got the impression he figured out what I do for a living and simply wanted me to track the thing down for the House."

"You haven't been approached by anyone else to find it?"

The question was odd enough that I opened my right eye as well and dragged myself higher on the seat. "I'll check my planner, but no. I think I'd remember something called a Honjo." I palpated a lump on my collarbone, helpfully located under the colder of the two jade pendants. "Why?"

Brody shifted in his seat, his gaze not leaving the road in front of him. "We interviewed all the people attacked at the Rarity show a few months ago, including

Soo. Asked them why they were here, what they were in the market for, you name it. Trying to figure out if they'd been targeted for what they wanted or what they already had. Soo listed a series of artifacts she wanted to buy. I don't have the list anymore, but I'd swear that sword was on it."

Before I could ask, he continued. "We didn't go any deeper than that. We got her list of artifacts, we checked that they were legit or reasonably legit, and we were out. On to the next billionaire buyer. But if Soo listed that sword, she must have thought she could find it at the Rarity, or she at least wasn't worried about anyone finding out about her interest in the thing."

"That sounds more like Soo," I conceded. "She had a pattern of letting her plans out to see what would shake out in advance of her actions. I never understood if it was strategic or stupid."

The others let the obvious hang in the air. Soo was dead. That argued for stupid. And yet…

"So—what was the trainer guy like?" Nikki asked too casually. "They wouldn't let me get close to that home gym they had set up, and I couldn't see anything." She tapped her head. "Not even here."

Nikki had the Connected ability to see through another's eyes. The closer her relationship with a person, the stronger her ability. If she'd been locked from my mind *and* Kunh's, it made me wonder exactly how that fighting room had been constructed. But the answer to Nikki's question was easy enough.

"About what you'd expect." I shrugged, then winced. Even shrugging hurt. "Mixed martial arts, which I handled better than I think he expected, rods, which I didn't handle badly, and swords at the end. That part went pretty quickly, but it was the worst."

"No marks on you, though, no blood." Nikki cracked a smile. "Couldn't have been too bad."

"There will be bruises later—I didn't have skin exposed, and all the blades were blunted. He could have beaten me to death with one of those things, but he wasn't going to flay me." I cocked a glance at her. "You've used swords?"

"Never once," she admitted. "Doesn't mean I couldn't learn."

"Ha, yeah," I said. "I can't tell if I should get that sword and really go after this—whatever 'this' is, or get it simply to fail honorably for the betterment of the House." I sighed. "I can't decide."

The words were solid—normal sounding. But once again they hung in the air at odd angles, awkward and unwanted. Because in some ways I'd already made the decision, and the conviction growing within me wasn't something I was used to, or something I particularly enjoyed. Nikki didn't seem to notice, and Brody straightened, distracted by whatever he was squinting at beyond his dashboard.

"What's this about?" he said, scowling as he slowed to angle into the Palazzo's parking section. "What the hell are they doing getting out?"

I peered forward as well. Sure enough, Jiao and General Som were exiting the car in front of the Palazzo as if they were arriving for a weekend getaway.

"I'm so not dealing with a sleepover, I don't care how worried they are for me," I said. "Make them go away, Brody."

"Who's the old dude with them?"

That made Nikki snap to attention as well. We both made the same realization.

"The owner of Grimm's Antiques," Nikki said, not bothering to hide the amusement in her voice. "I totally knew that's who designed that necklace. That's the Devil, love chop," she said, glancing at Brody. "Playing dress up."

"Why is he here?" I asked.

Brody snorted. "Must be a slow day in CrazyTown."

Brody pulled to a stop as a valet driver trotted down the stairs, and General Som and Jiao turned to us. To their credit, they did a good job scanning the area, as if trying to pick out snipers behind the plate glass hotel windows that surrounded us on all sides.

The Devil, however, paid no attention to anyone but the three of us as we exited Brody's sedan and Brody ignored the hopeful-looking valet. His smile wide, Aleksander Kreios bowed obsequiously in the nervous manner of the sixty-something dealer he embodied—thinning hair slicked back with too much gel, smooth fingers with a jeweler's manicure, the smell of expensive tobacco hitting us at a distance of three feet.

His eyes, however, were not disguised, and I resolutely didn't roll mine as his gaze landed on me. The Devil of the Arcana Council had taken on this mortal illusion for a reason, and I was more than willing to let it play out.

"Ah!" he said as we reached their small group. "Miss Sara Wilde. I'd thought it was you when Madam Peng asked me to reset the lovely jade disks. You have found them satisfactory?"

"It's a very pretty setting," I said, this time losing the battle with the eye roll. "Hopefully, it will remain strong through many wearers."

Kreios frowned slightly in his guise of Mr. Grimm. "Yes, yes, you are worried because you are not well equipped. But come! I have made us a reservation inside at a quiet table. We can talk, and I will tell you all I've found."

"What you've...found," Brody said skeptically, and Jiao turned to him.

"Mr. Grimm suggested when he delivered the necklace that he could help locate any piece we might need. Upon speaking with Kunh Lee, I placed a call." She turned to Kreios. "I did not expect you to find it as quickly as that, however."

"And I shall tell you all about it—inside," Kreios said.

The "quiet table" was located in the Palazzo Casino's VIP room, and quiet was relative in a chamber given over to high-end slot machines and games of chance. The whirr and clatter of roulette balls and the fluttering snap of cards was strangely soothing as Kreios ushered us all into the roped-off section where our table sat. I didn't need to ask how he'd gotten preferred treatment. What the Devil wanted, he usually got. Still, I contented myself with scoring a seat that gave me a prime view of the VIP room.

A half-dozen slot machines winked and glittered at the periphery, and at least a dozen baize-covered tables had drawn more high rollers than I would have expected. Then again—it was nearing nightfall in Vegas. That was when all the gamblers came out of the woodwork. Sort of like cockroaches and bed bugs.

"You are comfortable? Good, we are comfortable," Kreios wheedled, and he smiled with his yellow teeth at the black-clad server who'd appeared to take our order. "Champagne all around, if you would."

Beside me, Brody shifted. "We're celebrating something?"

"We certainly are," Kreios said, turning back to the table. "Madam Peng asked me to research the Honjo Masamune, which it has been my pleasure to do. But first you must understand that there is much to the Masamune blade that is sheer speculation. It is said to have been crafted near the end of the Kamakura period, perhaps around thirteen thirty Common Era, in the Soshu tradition. That tradition resulted in a unique line of crystals embedded in the blades, considered to be representative of a constellation of the night sky."

He paused with a self-important smirk. "Forgive an old man his indulgences, but the crystals are the important part of this history. There are some who believe Masamune was a gifted sorcerer as well as swordsmith, and the crystals in his blade were channels for higher forces."

Brody looked at Jiao curiously. "You know all this already, I assume?"

"It's good information for us to hear anew, and important for all to understand," Jiao replied, her smile devolving into a simper. Once again, my brows drifted up of their own accord. Was she flirting with Brody? The guy had to be twenty years younger than her.

Brody smiled back, and my own alarm ratcheted up. Was he flirting back?

Nikki didn't seem to be fazed by the byplay. She focused on Kreios in his Grimm suit. "How did the sword perform in battle?"

"Well enough—but the greatest story attributed to it has nothing to do with true battle. It is said that a student of the Masamune tradition wished to pit his own sword against Masamune. This would ordinarily be impossible, as the two were born roughly two hundred years apart. Masamune would have been long dead at the point the challenge was made. Nevertheless, the old master appeared, sword in hand, and the two proceeded to thrust their swords into a fast-flowing stream. The student Muramasa's sword cut everything in its path—leaves, fish, frogs—while the master's sword cut nothing except leaves that had fallen from the trees, already dead. Muramasa declared himself the winner, but the story goes that the true winner was Masamune. His sword did not harm the innocent, which made it a benevolent blade."

"Or a really dull one," Nikki said dryly.

"The sword was borne by shoguns and samurai throughout history, until after World War II," Kreios continued, warming to his tale. "It was lost in nineteen forty-six. Some rumors say it was given to a man named Sergeant Coldy Bimore, never to be seen again—some that it was another American soldier who took the sword for his own private treasury of memorabilia. But no matter which part of the story you believe, all signs point to the sword being in America."

"Well, that narrows it down some," I said, and Kreios glanced at me, his gaze filled with pure, indulgent humor. I shrugged and looked past him at the blinking arcade games. One of them was a five-card-draw-style slot machine, constantly running, so the cards blinking up on the screen would show three cards, then four, then five. I watched the spinning combinations distractedly, lulled by the blinking lights.

"That Madam Soo came to the Gold Show in part to locate the sword is telling," Kreios said. "There was no record of weaponry like the Honjo Masamune being at the exposition. That said, she was regrettably rushed from the Rarity without completing any transactions, to our knowledge, and she did not return."

He pulled out a card from his breast pocket with a flourish and laid it down on the table. "These are the names of the American vendors at the Rarity, and their specialties," he said with triumph.

Brody leaned forward and grunted. "None of those people are weapons guys."

Jiao leaned in too, their heads close enough to touch. I met Kreios's eyes over them, and judging by his amused glint, he noticed the energy between Brody and Jiao too.

Jiao's voice held more inflection than I'd heard in it before. "Their focus varies distinctly. European, South American, we can discount those. There are three with Asian ties. We start there."

"Well, all of them have outlets in LA, Chicago, and New York City—still, doesn't narrow it down much." Brody countered.

Kreios smirked. "That's smoke and mirrors in the main. Half the people in the show operate out of their homes, with their finest artifacts hidden in their basement, palatial though those basements may be. You find the home address, you find the sword, I suspect."

I flicked a glance again to the slot machines as the Devil sat back with obvious self-satisfaction. Nikki, Brody, General Som, and Jiao started arguing rapidly, debating the pros and cons of contacting the possible sword owners. I couldn't focus on anything but the glittering digital cards.

They'd...shifted.

I straightened carefully in my seat as I squinted at the machines. Before, there'd been a mix of hearts, clubs, diamonds, spades as the cards flashed up. Sometimes there'd been a straight, but more often, the cards had been a mess. But the last few rounds, they'd been flashing up spades with more regularity—and not just any spades.

Seven. Five. Ten. Knight. All spades. And then a random Five of Clubs.

Five. Knight. Ten. Nine. All spades. And another Five, this time of Hearts.

Three. Ten. Seven—

"Too many swords," I muttered, and Nikki looked up at me, her gaze going to where mine was focused. She scowled, but not at the machine.

"Where'd, ah, Grimm go?" she asked. "He was just here."

I blinked and then turned out toward the VIP section again, but the Devil was nowhere to be seen. General Som and Jiao looked up, their expressions puckering, and Brody reached for his gun—

Right about when the bullets started flying.

Chapter Ten

The screaming followed hard on the heels of the gunshots. To my shock, Jiao fell immediately, General Som right behind her, both of them collapsing into the cushioned seats. Security guards came running toward the VIP suite, but Brody had already yanked me hard out of the booth and shoved me toward the EXIT sign to the back of the room.

"Get out *now*. Nikki will follow," he growled. "Go!"

I flung myself to the floor as his cop voice roared out above me.

"LVMPD! Get down, down! Police!" he yelled, and Nikki was right next to him, body-blocking General Som's and Jiao's still forms in the banquette. Three assailants took up position behind the game machines. Most of the gamblers had dropped to the ground along with the dealers. I crawled between the tables as another peal of bullets rang out. Additional gunshots came from farther out in the lobby, and I reached the door in another fifteen seconds, leaning on it hard and bursting into a long hallway.

Another EXIT sign blinked urgently at the far end. Drawing my own gun, I headed for it. Everything had happened so quickly, I was on autopilot and running hard. This didn't feel right, though. It felt too rushed, too stupid. Where had the Devil gone? Surely the Council hadn't set me up. That made no sense. And General Som and Jiao? They were bleeding out—they couldn't have been behind this, right?

Right?

I pulled up at the door and hesitated, trying to work through my options. The door was hot to the touch. Not firestorm-on-the-other-side hot, but warm enough to know it was getting the full blast of sun most of the time. The sun had set not long before, so that would mean a western exposure.

I racked my mind, trying to remember the layout of the Palazzo and the surrounding access streets. Not a lot of parking, but trucks hit this place day and night, so there'd be an opening in the back—probably a large swath of open ground to get across, and—

My thoughts were fractured a second later as the original EXIT door burst open. To my surprise, it wasn't Nikki racing toward me but General Som, her arms pumping, her face set even as blood poured down her arm.

"Madam Wilde!" she yelled.

I didn't have time to puzzle out her motives. If she'd gotten past Nikki with Nikki's blessing, great, but if she'd somehow gunned her way through—

I shoved my way through the main exit door and out onto a concrete loading dock, a makeshift stage with one set of stairs leading down. Bypassing the stairs, I raced forward and hurtled off the six-foot-high dock. There was no one in the area, and the door banged open behind me.

"Madam Wilde, wait!" General Som shouted, the stridency of her voice at definite odds with her Asian accent.

I wasn't waiting, though. I had my phone, and I had my gun. Brody wanted me out of the action fast, which meant that in his mind, there'd be no reason to keep shooting if I was out of the picture. Which meant not only had I been the target, but I was also a menace to anyone around me.

Nothing like being the new kid at school who'd somehow pissed off the Mafia.

I picked up speed as I wheeled around the corner, taking the first alley that led out of the loading area. I realized my mistake immediately.

An enormous truck blocked the entrance, three men in front of it. None of them held a gun out, but instead they wielded scimitars the size of Detroit. These had to be more of Soo's generals. They were dressed in black Kevlar suits with Darth Vader-style helmets obscuring their faces. They didn't move, and I whipped around to head back inside.

No dice. Another five men now blocked that entry, and General Som was nowhere to be seen. The back-up guards rocked it less old school, too: they had guns. Big guns. And those guns were trained on me.

One of the generals burst forth in a furious round of Chinese, and turned back to him, holding up my gun. I could try to shoot my way out of this, but that seemed premature. No one had tried to kill me yet. If I could just stay alive long enough to get Nikki and Brody out here, I'd be set.

And for that matter, where was the Council? I was on their home turf, and not only had the Devil disappeared when the going had gotten interesting, but no one had swung out of the sky to smite my enemies. These people looked like they could use a good smiting too.

The man switched to English, apparently tired of being ignored. "You will fight as you were meant to fight," he cried out gruffly. "You will not make the House of Swords a laughing stock of our enemies. You will accept the order of Madam Soo and take up the sword, or you will die."

"I'm a little busy right now for all that." I turned slowly, scanning the walls for options. They were tall and windowless, useless for free-climbing. The men in front of the delivery truck were still doing their best immovable-object impression, and the line of men behind me advanced.

"Seriously, stop," I said. Surprisingly, the men stopped moving, though their guns stayed leveled on me. Not helpful, but I also still wasn't dead, and I willed my heart to stop trying to batter its way out of my rib cage as I assessed my options. I couldn't credibly fight these people. I was too damaged from Kunh Lee. I couldn't shoot them either. Minus the injured General Som, who apparently hadn't made it past the EXIT door, these were the mighty generals of the House of Swords. They wanted to fight me, not kill me outright, and I appreciated the distinction.

But where the *hell* was Brody?

One of the generals stepped forward and, more quickly than anyone I'd ever seen before, drew out a sword and flicked it toward me across the pavement. A moment later, the spinning sword arced to a stop at my feet, its journey swift and absolute. I kept one eye on it while staying focused on the thrower.

"You know I can't fight you honorably right now," I said, my voice echoing off the walls of this man-made box canyon. "And certainly not with that piece of crap."

He stiffened. "The Kamakura blade is a revered sword handed down for centuries. It will serve you well."

"Not as well as my gun."

"You must fight as the head of the House of Swords, or that head will be cut off," snarled the man. "We will settle this question once and—"

He didn't get the chance to finish.

Without warning, gunfire pelted down from the rooftop. Bursts of fire lit up the ground at my feet, sparking off the sword and the asphalt. More bullets rained down on us, and I crouched, scrambling toward the nearest wall—knowing that I'd never make it.

Whoever was on the roof, they couldn't be more of the Swords warriors. There was no honor in shooting fish in a barrel. And there was no chance of me taking up the generals' challenge now, that much was certain.

The generals themselves also started running as my body erupted in a fury of pain—my back, my shoulder. Had I been shot? Judging from the blood blossoming across my shirt, yes. Fire jolted through me, and I swung up my gun, my mind blanking as instinct took over.

I heard shouts but couldn't run as I unloaded my clip. Bullets whizzed by my shoulder and leg, another of them hitting its mark. I toppled heavily to the ground.

Pain swept over me in waves, and my eyesight jerked erratically, expanding and contracting to take in far too much for me to process, and then narrowing down to a pinpoint of focus that was all white-hot and icy-cold energy.

White-hot and icy-cold energy that centered in two crystal points on my collarbone. Soo's pendants fired to life as more shots pierced my skin, and power flexed within me, too much to contain within my body. Even as it flared, I feared it was too little, too late—there was another blast of gunfire, and pain radiated through me, in too many places to count.

I squinted through a haze of blood and sweat—then blinked, confused. The men closest to me in their heavy armor weren't running *away* from me in the face of the gunfire pouring down. Instead, they raced toward me, their screams defiant, their swords raised high. Swords, not guns, though they had guns holstered on their bodies, the weapons unfired, untouched. What were they *doing*? Why weren't they protecting themselves?

From my position on the ground, I could see their churning steps, their bulging muscles—their sudden, abrupt shudders as a new round of bullets crashed into them. But still they came upon me, as if killing me was more important than shielding themselves from getting shot by their own enemies. And yes, they might have been wearing body armor, but there was too much blood on the ground for it all to be mine. The asphalt seemed to be bathed in red, and still the bullets rained down.

Then the first man fell over me, bracing his fists on the ground to create a makeshift cage. A second knelt at my side. A third crashed heavily over my legs. We were being made into an impromptu funeral cairn, and all I could do was watch it happen. There was no way out of this blocked-off alley, no way to get to safety. But as I stared, the men's faceless masks jerked and jerked again as a new barrage of ammunition peppered into them, their bodies absorbing the bullets that were intended for me.

The energy crested in my body, emanating from Soo's pendants. Someone was screaming, but I could only dimly hear it as I lifted a hand to the first man who'd reached me. I curled my fingers around his shoulder. His helmet fell away with another sudden lurch, and I found myself staring into the eyes of a stranger.

A stranger who was dying to save me. To protect the unproven leader of the House of Swords.

"No," I whispered, and those eyes found mine.

These men—these generals—had intended for me to fight them for the right to lead. They had doubted me, hated the idea of me, to the point of lying in wait to ambush me the first day I surfaced wearing the amulet of their former leader. They had no doubt seen my reaction at the airport or been informed of my failures in Soo's house. They'd most certainly been informed of my disdain for fighting with a blade. And so they'd forced that fight upon me.

But in the absence of that fight, in the wake of an attack on me, this leader they did not know, could not respect...they'd laid down their lives for me instead.

"No," I said again as I locked gazes with the man looming over me. Sweat poured down his face, and he flinched back as I moved my hand to touch his temple. An emotion I couldn't name swelled in my chest, thick and heavy, the same kind of panic and desperation I'd felt in the Magician's mansion not two days ago churning again. But there was no anger here. There was only despair.

This was the first man to have reached me, the first to have laid down his body to save me when his own death would have been the only result.

"You will not die," I said again. "Not you, not here."

My hand firmed on the man's cheek and he looked at me with confusion—confusion from someone who'd not thought twice about defying bullets with his body. I could smell something burning, and my fingers grew hot—too hot, my whole body suffused with a new agony now as my blood seemed set on fire and my gaze remained locked with the stranger's, his dark eyes staring out at me from a weathered face twisted and broken from long years of battle. He'd probably been the first to seek to deny my place, but he also was the first to help me retain it, for all that it was useless, for all that there was nothing left around me but death and destruction.

But this man wouldn't die.

"No," I whispered a final time, and the heat left me, heat and sight, and the general's own eyes grew wide with a different kind of panic as, finally, silence settled over the alley and I dropped into darkness at last.

Chapter Eleven

Death seemed like it should be a lot more comfortable. And quieter.

Machines chirped and whirred around me, a symphony of bleating alarms, while the voices of men whispered in hushed tones. Those men were beyond the door, I realized, beyond the window, but the sounds of their earnest concern were still as evident to me as if they were murmuring in my ear.

One of the words was "miracle," which made me happy, since miracles were always a good thing. And then I heard the phrase "brain damage," and I got less happy.

I took stock of my perforated body. I had bandages on my shoulder and both arms, but my torso seemed fairly un-mummified. My head was swaddled in cloth and my legs felt like two lumps—no sensation at all below my hips.

The reaction of my heart monitor to that little realization had the men looking up outside of the ICU, but before they could burst in, I funneled a burst of desperate WTF downward and was rewarded with both legs jerking simultaneously—the blast of pain so great that I passed out again.

The next time I awoke, it was nighttime. I'd been moved to a room that allowed visitors, apparently, or Nikki had found a way in. She sat slumped in a chair several sizes too small for her body, her red hair locked down in a ponytail, her outfit a sedated version of SWAT—camo pants, combat boots, black tank top and work shirt. No glitter in sight.

Unaccountably, seeing her so unadorned was worse than the pain gnawing at me through the haze of whatever drugs were hooked up to my drip, and tears sparked behind my eyes.

I blinked and whispered her name.

Nikki's eyes popped open immediately, and she sat forward with so much force, I cringed back, though she was still five feet away from me.

"Dollface," she blurted, her voice sounding like she'd just come off a three-bottle bender. "How are you and where've you been?"

"What?" I blinked at her, lifting my hand slightly despite the wave of nausea. "I've been here, haven't I?"

"Not exactly." Nikki rubbed what looked to be tears out of her own eyes. "You've been out for four days. Came to briefly to hear the docs tell it, then coma city. I thought...I mean I hoped you were with Armaeus. But..." She scowled at my bandages. "You aren't better. Then again, you also aren't dead. So it was tough to figure."

"Armaeus..." I inched myself higher on the pillow, my brain starting to fire again. Nikki had a point. "He didn't send flowers, I guess."

"Uh, no. None of the Council has been by, other than Death, which didn't make me all that happy, I gotta tell you. Nothing like getting a house call from someone who trucks in mortal souls."

I smiled, then instantly sobered. Mainly because smiling hurt. "She say anything?"

"Only wanted to let you know she's been to the house in Paris, inspected the work there. The Gamon slaves have had their ink altered enough that they can't be tracked. They can go home when they're ready. She was glad you let her know they were there. Oh, and Father Jerome sends his love and prayers and his wish that you'd get your head out of your ass and be more careful."

I lifted my brows.

Brows didn't hurt.

"I may have taken some liberties with the translation." Nikki managed a grin, but her eyes remained clouded. "You scared me girl. What a cluster that whole scene in the parking lot was."

"Yeah..." I groaned, shifting position slightly. "What happened to General Som?"

"Found her right outside the door, but she's fine. Apparently, she'd known about the general throw down, not the impromptu firing squad. She's pretty shook up, though she's trying not to show it. Four fatalities, multiple gunshot wounds, should have been five." Her gaze slid to mine. "Or six, really. You lost a shit ton of blood and cracked your head when you fell. Two broken bones in your legs, one in your shoulder."

"My legs." I frowned down at the end of the bed, where I was happy to see my feet. "They're broken?"

"They were. That's why—" Nikki blew out a breath. "You broke out of traction the first night, snapped pins.

By the time they got to you, you'd passed out again, but the X-rays showed healed bone. The muscle and skin were still torn all to hell, but the bones were solid. And your pain was off the charts, so they pumped you full of morphine."

I stared at her, too shocked to speak for a moment. How had all that happened without me realizing it? And why was I still alive? I swallowed, then managed another question. "How could they tell I was in pain if I was out of it?"

"Heart rate. Seizures. Brain waves. You name it, you were radiating agony. Apparently, it hurt the hospital staff to stand too close to you. Which, again, kind of negated the whole likelihood that Armaeus was on the job."

"Death have anything to say about that?"

"Honestly? She seemed happy he wasn't here. But then she's kind of a twisted sister, you ask me. She said she'll be ready for your next tat when you are. Then she left, leaving a trail of staring docs and nurses behind her. Whatever she's got, there's no shortage of people who want it."

"They should be careful what they wish for." I lifted my left arm experimentally. "What else did you say I broke?"

"Nothing, anymore."

"Any...more." My body might have recovered, but my brain was clearly still shredded. I couldn't fathom healing so quickly without Armaeus's help—but there was no way he'd been here. Surely he wouldn't have left me in so much pain.

Right?

Then again...where was he? He'd never left me this broken for this long. Not once in all the time I'd worked for him. What had happened? What game was he playing?

And, more importantly, when would it stop?

"Yep," Nikki continued, oblivious to my growing hysteria. "You're pretty much un-Humpty-Dumptied. And your muscles are healing, obviously way ahead of schedule, but you ripped out your feeding tube three different times, once despite the fact you were restrained. So they stopped pumping food into you." She eyed me. "Hungry?"

I hadn't thought about it before she mentioned it, then my stomach growled, and I realized how…empty everything was. Hollowed out. "I must be freaking out the entire floor."

"We got you moved after the first day. That's why I'm not thinking the Council is completely hands off here. The doc on staff here is Dr. Sells, but she's acting like she's never seen you before—and doing such a damned good job of it, I don't know if she's doing it on purpose or simply trying to screw with me."

"Got it. Well, if she's here, then Armaeus knows my condition." Betrayal swamped me, but I forced the next words out if only to convince myself. "Apparently I wasn't that bad."

Nikki's snort was cut short when the door opened. A familiar face stood at the door despite the late hour—Dr. Margaret Sells, probably the only Las Vegas physician who made house calls to the Arcana Council.

Now she eyed me with patent shock. "You're awake."

There were so many possible snide comebacks, I was rendered temporarily mute.

Fortunately, Nikki suffered no such limitations. "You take a special class to figure that out, or does that kind of medical brilliance come naturally to you?"

Dr. Sells sent her a withering glare. "Visiting hours are clearly posted, Miss Dawes."

"Yeah, fortunately your staff thought better of trying to manhandle me off the floor. Special wing, special rules, sweet cakes. No one was willing to ring you up to confirm."

"Why am I still hospitalized?" I asked bluntly as Sells's gaze returned to me. "Did the Council drop me from their insurance plan?"

She moved over to check the monitors, as obvious an evasion as humanly possible without her running out of the room. "I've been providing them with extensive updates."

"Right. What you're saying is, they know, they've simply left me here to work things out on my own."

She finally looked back at me. "That's correct."

Sweet Christmas. I'd been cut off. Well and truly cut off. The shock was almost worse than the pain coursing through me despite the morphine drip.

Almost.

"They tell you why they put me in time out?" I asked, my tone as bleak as an executioner's blade.

Sells apparently didn't share my dismay at being cut off from the Council. "Do you actually want their help?" she shot back, her gaze challenging.

I squinted at her. "You're kidding me, right?"

"I'm not," she said. "From all accounts, you've managed to bring yourself back from death's door with no outside intervention. That's nothing short of miraculous for the average human, or even the above average Connected. Believe me, I've seen my share of gifted souls."

"Well, don't get too excited. I had help." I looked down at my chest. "Wait. Where're Soo's pendants?"

She frowned, stepping toward me. With a gentle touch, she lifted the collar of my gown away from my neck—but there was nothing there. Not even a scar to mark where Soo's necklace had lain.

"You had nothing on you when you came in except your clothes, which were pretty badly singed and bloodied. We gave those to the police for evidence."

I winced, imagining Brody getting a load of that laundry, but Sells continued. "Which is why I say your recovery appears to be completely self-generated, and as such, it's something you should be proud of. Celebrating, even."

Reaching over with my swaddled right hand, I tapped the tube feeding into my left arm. "There's a lot of morphine going into me right now, yeah?"

She pursed her lips, then nodded. "There is."

"Well, I still feel like road-rash flambé. Ergo, healing clearly hasn't been a bundle of fun. Ergo, yeah, all things being equal, I could use a little outside help."

Sells chirped something supportive, then spent a few minutes more going over my recovery points—skipping neatly over the one thing that worried me most. As she wrapped up her assessment of my no longer broken bones, torn muscles, deep bruising, and blood loss, I fixed her with as steely a glare as I could, given that my head was wrapped in fluffy white gauze.

"What about my brain?" I asked.

She quirked a look at me, playing Doctor Stupid. "I'm sorry?"

Her careful tonality made my stomach tighten into a thick knot. "My brain. I overheard doctors talking about possible brain damage. What's. That. About?"

"Your preliminary scans have been…anomalous," she said, again with the hesitation that ratcheted my worry yet tighter. "There's almost too much activity, and in quadrants of the brain not consistent for where your injuries are greatest."

"So my eggs have been scrambled is what you're saying." I stared at her, unable to force my gaze away. "Nothing's working right."

"That's not what I'm saying at all," she replied, too calm, too cool in the face of my clammy-skinned fear. "Your abdominal organ functions were not affected by the attack—nothing shot, barely a scratch—yet that section of the brain has been lit up since you arrived." She peered at me intently, clearly fascinated by the medical mysteries I presented. I couldn't drum up the same enthusiasm. "It's as if your sacral core needs attention, despite the fact that it has no injuries."

I frowned, then flopped my own bandaged hand in the general direction of my sacral core. Nothing happened. Nothing, at this point, was good.

"The areas of the brain associated with extrasensory cognition have also been engaged to almost alarming amounts, and your metabolism has become increasingly erratic." Sells said. Then her eyes widened. "Let me get some food in you before you pass out again. You removed—"

"I've heard." I blew out a pensive breath even as she pulled out her cell phone and tapped on it quickly. "Straight up, Dr. Sells. What happened to me? If the Council didn't heal me, how am I still here?"

She dropped the phone back into her pocket, and for the first time since she'd entered the room, her smile seemed natural...even a little dazed.

"We don't know, Sara," she said quietly. "You should've been dead. Without Council intervention, you would have ordinarily been dead before you even reached the hospital. There was significant cauterization at the bullet wound sites, blood vessels sealed off, muscles held in stasis. But there's nothing to account for such a large heat event at the crime scene. It's as if something burned through you and out of you, then was gone."

Fire. Agonizing internal fire. I did remember that, vaguely.

Dr. Sells shook her head. "As much as I don't care for this word, you are something of a miracle."

The door swung open, and she turned to the orderly who came in with a tray laden with dishes.

Nikki took the tray from the man and set it onto my bed stand, then reached for the silverware. "And now you're going to be a miracle who eats," she said sternly. "To make sure we can get you out of this bed as quickly as possible."

"What—" I managed as I sat higher on the bed. "What happened to the rest of the men? The ones who survived?"

Sells grimaced. "They were treated and released after they were stabilized, apparently under the care of the LVMPD and Detective Brody Rooks."

Nikki let out a sharp bark of laughter that was at odds with her haggard face. "Care, right. The men on the roof—hell, could have been women, I don't know—they got away clean," she said. "We figured there were three of them, no more. As soon as the sirens hit and there was nothing but a lump of bodies in the center of the alley, they apparently split. The attack was clean enough and professional enough that Homeland Security totally discounts homegrown terror. It was a hit, you were the target, the rest was collateral damage. No fatalities in the casino. Guns were shooting blanks."

"Blanks!" My eyes popped wide with that, and I looked up from my Jell-O. "But Jiao and General Som were hit?"

Nikki shook her head. "Jiao was clean, and General Som didn't get shot until she exited the casino. Even that was barely a skimmer. She's fine."

"But..." I'd seen them—their bodies slack, blood blossoming.

Had the Devil somehow...but no. It couldn't be.

"Yep. Blanks," Nikki said. "I had no idea either, until General Som dashed out and Brody started cursing a blue streak and hightailing it for the exit. Jiao was losing her mind at the gunmen, screaming in Chinese, so I followed Brody. By the time we cleared the second exit door, the snipers on the rooftop pinned us back, then unloaded on you."

Nikki's stark face spoke volumes about her reaction to the scene in the alley. "The generals didn't fare too well, all in all. Brody's got them under hospital arrest. Just to be on the safe side."

I grimaced as I reached for my second grilled cheese sandwich. "I'd forgotten about the other generals," I said, then spoke around a mouthful of gooey bread. "General Som able to explain their motives?"

"Jiao put the word out that the search for the Honjo sword would be commencing immediately," Nikki said. "Some of the generals were apparently already in town, like General Som was, put two and two together that if the new head of the household needed a magical sword, chances were good she wasn't awesome in a sword fight. They acted without sanction, according to Som, but…" she lifted one shoulder. "Who knows what kind of crazy is really going on there. The whole thing is dicey, you ask me."

"The men who fell with you in the center of the alley, they wore body armor," Dr. Sells put in, her glare intensifying until I reached for more food. "But it wasn't enough to withstand semiautomatic gunfire. Not that much of it. The snipers unloaded military-grade artillery into them. That you were relatively undamaged beneath them was another miracle." She smiled wearily. "There I go with that word again. I'm losing my edge."

"Yeah, well, a lot of that going around." I once again visualized the moment that I realized the men had been running toward me—toward me, not away. My instinctive reaction had been to run—only I couldn't run, not with my broken bones and so much blood loss. And then one had fallen on top of me, protecting me.

And then another.

Nikki's voice interrupted my reverie. "There's no word on who the external snipers were," she said, her voice a little forced. I wondered how much of the scene I'd just relived in my mind that she could also see. Sometimes, a Connected's gifts were as much of a burden as a blessing. "The remaining generals are unapologetic about their challenge but are uniform in their disavowal of knowledge of who their attackers were. Which makes sense, since they were the ones being shot at."

As she spoke, another figure moved into the doorway of the room. At first glance, I thought he was Chinese, but his height and bulk seemed more imposing—possibly Mongolian or even Russian. He was dressed in loose clothes with one arm in a sling, and he looked…familiar.

He spoke, startling Dr. Sells, but I couldn't understand the language, and the words seemed almost like an incantation or a prayer, despite the harsh tones. As if he didn't expect me to respond. I stared at him and shook my head, and he took another step closer.

"Sir—" Dr. Sells began, but I stiffened as he moved into my line of sight. And pressed back against the cushions of my bed when he half fell to one knee. Nikki was already up and at the man's shoulder, whether to help him or to crack him in the temple, I wasn't sure, but he stared at me with the same intensity he had the last time I'd seen him, his body bucking as a fresh wave of gunfire had strafed across his back.

"I am General Ma-Singh of the House of Swords," he rasped in heavily inflected English. "From now until I die, I will serve you as the lawful head of our House."

Chapter Twelve

I opened my mouth, then shut it again before I could gather my wits to speak. "You saved my life," I started, but my voice cracked, and his stare grew more intense.

"Up we go, big guy," Nikki said, dropping a hand beneath the general's elbow. "You know you outweigh me by like fifty pounds, and I don't think that fifty pounds is fluffy bunny weight. Cut a girl a break."

That broke Ma-Singh's stare, and he grunted in surprise as Nikki locked an arm around his waist and hauled him upright. She stayed that way as he leaned on her, and staggered a bit beneath his weight. Only then did I realize that all the color had gone out of his face.

"How bad is he?" I asked, turning to Dr. Sells.

"Should have been dead, no question," she said, eyeing the man appreciatively. "He's Connected, but low level—basically enough to help him fight, not much more. So what happened was even more unexpected. His body displayed the same anomaly you had, but more of it."

At my curious look, she pointed at the general's bandages. "Wounds cauterized from the inside out. Bullets pushed through—nothing left in the body, injuries clean and sterile. He's got a recovery in front of him, but he *will* recover, no question. He's in better shape than he has any right to be, given the givens. And he credits you with that, you should know. I didn't even know he spoke English until that little declaration, but he's said as much in Mongolian to anyone who will listen, once we got him a translator."

I frowned. "The Council?"

"They say they had nothing to do with his recovery. And again, his results are similar in nature to what you experienced, though yours was in stages. When you arrived, your bullets were gone, but the cauterization hadn't really taken hold. That happened later that night, after we set your legs."

I winced, remembering that pain. Sells nodded, and Nikki moved to steer Ma-Singh out of the room, but he stopped, turning back. He made a slight move with his right arm and grimaced, looking to Nikki and pointing.

"You are so lucky you don't know English," Nikki said, but she gamely reached into his right trouser pocket as he watched her, his brow knit with concentration. She pulled out a packet and checked it, then her smile split her face. "Here you go, big guy," she said, turning him back toward me. "We'd wondered where that went."

The Mongol warrior limped my way again, his face set with pain but his manner resolute. He shifted his hands, and the paper fell away, leaving Soo's necklace in his hands. "Broken—fixed," he said, showing me the clasp. It had been reinforced to the size of a bicycle lock.

"Ah, thank you." I didn't remember him pulling the necklace from my neck but then again—there was a lot I didn't remember about the Palazzo parking lot fight. I bowed forward to allow Ma-Singh to slip the silver strands over my neck. The new clasp clicked into place with a heavy thud, and the general straightened, clearly pleased. This time he did let Nikki lead him out the door, leaning on her a little more heavily than I suspected was necessary as she prattled to him in English.

"You're going to need additional healing," Sells said quietly after they'd gone. "What you've done is remarkable, but it isn't enough."

"I didn't plan on going it alone." I hadn't planned on living through the gunfire, truth be told, but Sells seemed to understand my meaning.

"Armaeus Bertrand is a complicated person," she said. "I've been on the Council's payroll for nearly twenty years, and he has altered more in the last few years than in all the years combined before, and in the last two months more dramatically still. I can attribute that to you, of course, but there's more to it than that. Something's changed fundamentally in him this time."

"I'll keep it in mind," I said. Right now, all that seemed to have changed was that he'd decided I was yesterday's news. Which was fine. I wasn't a big fan of him either of late. He'd hung me out to dry so many times, my soul was starting to bleach out.

I leaned against the pillows, unreasonably tired as Sells signaled for the orderly to take away my hospital fare. "How much longer am I in here?"

Her smile was intent. "I think in more ways than I usually intend the phrase, that is entirely up to you."

She nodded at my startled blink. "Good night, Sara. I look forward to tracking your continuing progress."

I was out before she left the room, unconsciousness lapping at my heels for only a second before it dragged me under and sat on me.

I drifted in a place where there was no pain, the sensation so welcome and familiar that I nearly groaned with relief. I could move my arms, my legs. My fingers stretched wide, and I fluttered my hand, reveling in each set of muscles firing in response to a thought. I drew in a deep breath, and it filled me up, redolent and pure. The entire world smelled of cinnamon and spices and—

Awareness struck me less than a breath before I connected with the rock-solid planes of Armaeus's chest.

"You!" I jerked back, but he moved with me, rolling over on top of my body, surrounding me with his warmth, his solidity. The Magician of the Arcana Council channeled a very particular kind of magic, based in profound sexual energy. As a result, he wasn't always big on subtlety, but when he did finally show up to party, he was very, *very* good at what he did. Right now, it appeared that he was ready to heal me. I struggled for another second, then abandoned myself to the jaw-dropping relief the touch of his body brought to every inch of mine.

Armaeus, for his part, didn't push—nor did he smirk. His dark golden eyes stared down at me impassively as he poured his energy into me, the quirk of his lips the only betrayal of his amusement as I moaned again, arching my body beneath his.

"Took you long enough," I groaned, reveling in the sensation of burned blood vessels opening up and reaching out again, muscles knitting and swollen dermis shedding its pain and inflammation. "Wanna tell me why?"

"You pushed me away quite effectively," he said, or at least I thought he said that. It was a little difficult to hear over my garbled sighs. Then he paused, apparently reconsidering his words. "At first," he amended. "I knew the moment you fell, was there to assist, but your reaction was—singular. You pushed out, and I remained out." I could sense his shrug, even in my dream state. "After that, it became more interesting to watch than to intervene."

"More interesting to..." I frowned, my brain slowly catching up to my ears, processing both his words and their underlying meaning. "You mean you simply *watched* me try to heal myself. I was in pain lying in a hospital room, and you decided it was more interesting to hang out and watch me instead of doing anything about it?"

"You hadn't asked for my help, hadn't opened your mind to me," he said, and we rolled again. I didn't know if we were in water, in the ether, or in his bed, and I didn't much care. "I could push through your defenses, yes. But in your state, I considered that unwise."

"My state." My lips twisted around the words. "Since when are you worried about my state?"

"Since you could do damage to me, intentionally or otherwise," Armaeus said succinctly. "Or, far worse, damage to yourself without realizing it." He pulled me up until my face was level with his and stared at me, his expression inscrutable. "Your abilities have intensified, Miss Wilde. You should not have been able to heal yourself as well as you did. By my calculations, you should still be in a self-induced coma."

I frowned. "For how long?"

"Approximately seven months."

"What?"

"I would not have allowed that to continue, of course. Your work with the Council is too important, and your position with the House has been thrown yet more fully into question, albeit for unexpected reasons. You will need to resolve that question before you can make decisions about your role clearly and without prejudice."

"Back to what's important here. You could have come in—at any time—even if I didn't want you to?"

"I just did."

I considered that, and Armaeus's eyes glittered. "There are many things I could attempt over your protestations, Miss Wilde. That has always been the case. And now, you are weak. If I pushed, you would push back. But if I wanted to, I could overrun you."

I realized I'd gone completely tense. "Then why aren't you pushing more?"

"Because in the end, I will not have to," he murmured. Somehow, his mouth had moved near mine, and I could almost taste the pressure of his lips. "In the end, you'll welcome me back to you—to your body and your mind. You will see the power I can guide you to, and you will want to drink in that power. And watching you have that realization will be infinitely sweeter than anything I would gain from forcing your hand...or from forcing my hand upon you."

As if to punctuate his words, Armaeus lifted long fingers to trace a pattern down the side of my neck, out to the shoulder that had been punctured by the first bullet. At the gossamer touch of his hand, healing warmth rolled out over my skin, sinking into nerve and sinew, knitting together bone, rushing oxygen into newly formed capillaries. Cells filled with light and life and magic, and I couldn't speak from the wonder of it.

The Magician drew his hand down my arm, and additional injuries responded, the pain drifting away instantly, as if on a puff of smoke. He stroked my fingers back to life and massaged the jagged scars along my thighs, erasing the evidence of the wide pin holes and stapled skin with long, mesmerizing brushes. All along, he murmured words I couldn't understand and that I didn't truly want to hear. I didn't want to think of Armaeus invoking arcane lore to heal me. It was more fulfilling to believe it was by his touch alone, by his will alone that I could become stronger, more whole.

"I can't believe you waited four whole days to do this," I groaned, and his laugh was low and challenging.

"There are repercussions to every decision you make, Miss Wilde. If you decide to learn on your own, you have the satisfaction of a self-determined path. But it is a path filled with pain and fraught with doubt and indecision. If you choose to open yourself to me—to anyone in the Council, you give up the power to direct your instruction as you see fit. But there are compensations for the release of that control."

"Compensations," I whispered, too lulled by his words to police my own reactions. I curled my fingers into his as they drifted down to my hands again, and pulled him close. Obligingly, he bent toward my face, and the touch of his lips against mine was a benediction. Something yearning and fierce opened up within me, responding to that light touch with a need too strong, too primal to be called back—

And on its heels rushed the whirlwind of loss, the endless wrenching pain that had consumed me, body and soul.

"Stop." I pulled myself back bodily, but Armaeus pursued me, and instantly I realized the trap he had baited for me so surely and so well. To allow his healing touch to take hold was to give him more access to my mind, and where I gave an inch, he invariably took a mile, pushing against cracks in my armor I didn't know I had.

Betrayal roared through me, quick and hot, and I was blinded by a sheer white wave. I screamed, and it screamed with me, and nothing else could matter—nothing else would matter as long as its tyranny held forth.

Ordinarily, once begun I couldn't untangle myself from Armaeus's hold. But by the time I finished thrusting myself away from him, I was fully awake—awake and alone.

Perhaps more importantly, I was in the Devil's penthouse office, about five feet away from his richly inlaid desk.

At night.

In a hospital bed.

A hospital bed. This seemed a critical detail as I scrambled out of the unit, my hands going for my clothes, my hair—I was dressed in lightweight scrubs. I was at least reasonably clean.

And I had no idea how I'd gotten here.

"Sara Wilde. Always a pleasure." The dulcet tones of Aleksander Kreios's luxurious voice drifted through the room, immediately prior to the appearance of the Devil himself. I stood, turning quickly, and staggered with dizziness.

"How long have I been here?" I barked. My voice sounded stronger. I felt stronger too, despite the head rush. "What happened to me—how long has it been?"

"Since you were in the hospital room with the charming Dr. Sells, screaming in Sumerian? Well, that's been about two days, I should think."

I blinked at him. "Sumerian?"

He nodded. "Of course, that could have been the result of the technoceutical Dr. Sells had pumped into you."

"Oh, I..." His words hit me with a thud. "Wait a minute. What?"

Kreios leaned against his desk, considering me. He was effecting his usual appearance once again, a tall, lean beach bum billionaire. His sun-warmed hair curled over his shoulders, and today he wore a linen shirt, untucked, over ragged-hem khakis. His feet were bare, his perfectly pedicured toes as tan as if he'd spent the entire summer on the beaches of his native Greece.

"Dr. Sells, it appears, took Armaeus's lack of interest in you as an opportunity to explore your abilities as well. Without his tacit instruction not to interfere with your recovery, she put two different combinations into your system. The first, I was able to remove in time. The second, I'm afraid I was not so lucky. That might have been administered via food. Your reaction was quite impressive once it set in."

"She *drugged* me?" I stared at him. "I thought that was Armaeus..."

Kreios's indolent smile widened as the blush spread over my face. "Armaeus was, in fact, there. You didn't imagine that—and in fact, the technoceutical effect lowered your mental defenses sufficiently that he assumed you'd reached out to him. And don't act so surprised about Dr. Sells's actions. Your abilities place you in a rarified league, one normally occupied by superstars and world-class athletes. Those who cannot be you will seek to use you to further their own aims. Not unlike Armaeus, though I would say he does so not out of personal gain but for the betterment of magic in the world. If that distinction is meaningful to you."

I couldn't process Armaeus's motives right now. "And Sells? Is she aware you're on to her?"

"An excellent question, and no, as it happens. We do not seek to limit the progress of medical science merely to ensure it doesn't inadvertently hurt one of our own." He smiled at my reaction to his words. "And, yes, make no mistake. You are on the path of becoming one of us, Sara Wilde. As much as you refuse to believe it."

For all his reputation, the Devil never lied. In fact, he delighted in inflicting the discomforts of truth. So as much as I didn't want to accept his words, I believed them. I believed him.

"I'll keep that in mind. What happened to Armaeus?"

"Nothing at all. He said he recognized the infiltration of the drug in your system the moment he got too close, and released his hold on you."

I narrowed my eyes at him. "He lied to you, then. I pushed him away, and he wasn't ready for it. I won that round."

"If you insist in making it a competition between you and Armaeus, I insist on taking a ringside seat." Kreios smiled. "But in this case, I wouldn't split the hair. Something he saw stopped him, or something you did stopped him, but in either case, he stopped. You returned to a coma-like state, much to Miss Dawes's distress, and we arranged to have you moved to this location forthwith. Miss Dawes has been gracious enough to relocate to my domain for the duration, and has stepped out to gather some actual food for you, since it became clear you would be waking within the next hour or so."

"Uh-huh. Became clear how?"

"Because I decreed it to be so."

"Right. Just like you decreed me to imagine Jiao and General Som covered in blood so I'd run out into the ambush the generals and God only knew whoever else had arranged for me?"

"Exactly like that," he said.

I'd guessed the Devil's trickery the moment Nikki had told me that Jiao and Som hadn't actually been shot in the Palazzo VIP suite. Illusions weren't lies to Kreios. They were games, and woe be to the idiot who didn't stop to question them.

Idiots like myself, as it turned out.

Kreios gestured to a nearby chair. "But I think Miss Dawes shall find herself delayed just long enough that we can have this next conversation quite completely. And quite completely alone."

Chapter Thirteen

Kreios moved away from the counter and approached me. His expression had changed to one less amused and more concerned. "You begin to worry me, Sara Wilde. I find I do not like being worried."

That…I wasn't expecting.

Suddenly tired, I sank into the plush chair, appropriating the small cushion on it as my personal stress toy. "And you're worried, why?"

"Because you're no longer behaving in any way that the Council can predict, and while I thrive on that reality, you must be aware that Armaeus does not. The volatility of your reactions has him wondering ever more what took place in Hell. And who else besides you might know about it."

I looked sharply at him. "Do you?"

"I know what he knows, which is everything you have spoken aloud, whether to yourself or to Nikki." He waved away my protest. "You forget that what you tell others is spoken into the wind, and the wind has its way of reaching me."

"Then Armaeus knows it too."

"Of course. But he also knows there is much that you have not shared with Nikki—or anyone on this earth. Much that can only be determined by returning to Hell."

"But he's immortal now. He can't go there."

He nodded. "Which presents him a perplexing dilemma, with only one solution—he must pull the information out of you, piece by harrowing piece. As you can imagine, I suspect that experience will not be particularly enjoyable for you."

I scowled. The event Armaeus wanted to know more about was no walk in the park for me either, though I suspected he wouldn't react to it the same way I did. Then again, it hadn't been his heart that'd been crushed.

Kreios watched me with almost a predatory fervor as I worked through that particularly unpleasant memory. "Your mind has held fast against me, but the expressions on your face..." He drew in an unsteady breath. "It's been some time since a mortal has been able to hold so much out of reach. So close that with a touch it should unravel. Yet it remains locked tight against me." His smile turned feral. "I can see why Armaeus remains intrigued."

"But you can't get in." I stated this as fact, but I was still relieved when Kreios shook his head.

"The Magician was right about something else: you've grown stronger for your time in Hell. It would seem the profound grief you experienced was worth it."

"I'm not grieving," I snapped, not missing the flare of interest in Kreios's eyes. "I'm pissed. Get your emotions right. And Armaeus is stronger too, isn't he?"

"He's—different is a better way to put it," Kreios said. "Not stronger, exactly, but more willing to use his strength as needs demand, and more willing to agree that the need is great more often than not."

"You mean he's getting involved with mortal magic." I thought about Armaeus at the Paris mansion, his thinly veiled goading of me until I'd thrust him back with a surge of ability I hadn't known I had. "It's not actually me he's interested in, it's the Houses."

Kreios shrugged. "It's mostly about you, admittedly. You fascinate and defy him. It's a dangerous combination. But to answer your question more directly, yes. He's getting involved with mortal magic. He would like very much to discover the remaining three Houses beyond Swords, and to explore the House of Swords more deeply."

I grimaced. Of course, Armaeus wouldn't want to emotionally invest in me. Not the way he once did, before our respective trips to Hell. That might have been too much to hope…and to bear.

"He is concerned that the dragon Llyr is stirring," Kreios continued, his gaze dropping to the pillow I clenched. "He wishes to ensure it's the Council's hand that's dipping into the pools of magic scattered throughout the world, not our enemy's."

"But Armaeus doesn't care about the mortals, does he?" This also wasn't a question, for all that I wanted Kreios to deny it. "He cares about the magic, the balance of it. But not about the practitioners."

Kreios lifted his brows, genuinely confused. "There will always be more practitioners."

"See? See? No!" Anger blossomed anew, quick and fierce. I flung the pillow at Kreios so quickly, it took him all of the one point seven seconds required to lift his own hand and stop the cushion a breath shy of his face, with a force that ripped through the air, far more potent than required. I mean, come on. The thing was a pillow.

Only it wasn't a pillow anymore.

Suspended in the air between us, the cushion had morphed into a writhing cat-o'-nine-tails, its leather strands spiked with sizzling barbs and coiling with power, ready to score across Kreios's face.

The Devil remained still, but his expression was arrested with pleasure as he surveyed the dangerous weapon. "I had no idea your tastes ran so eclectic, Sara Wilde," he purred. "Perhaps when you are finished enraging the Magician, you should come see me."

"Stop it," I said, and the projectile dropped to the ground, once again a harmless cushion. I stared at it, then up to Kreios again, the beginnings of fear gnawing at my stomach.

"Who did that?" I asked. "The whole leather thing. Was that you? Because I wasn't doing it. Not intentionally anyway."

"It was you." The Devil's expression had turned positively rapt. "I expected a pillow and had no interest in getting hit with one. Getting smacked in the face with a set of barbed lashes would have been even less appealing, I assure you. Though far more invigorating." He watched me as I sank back in my chair. "You seem...unduly concerned."

I grimaced. "I don't know what's happening to me, Kreios, and I want to know. Before I met you people—for a long time *after* I met you people, I was an artifact hunter. I'm good at being that. Successful. Now everything is changing, and it's changing too fast."

"Too fast for whom? I assure you, I'm enjoying the transformation."

"But what am I transforming into?" I drew my feet up, hunching over my knees. "I'm now supposedly responsible for the entire House of Swords. What was Soo thinking?"

"You don't consider yourself a worthy leader?"

"I can't even pick up a sword without cutting myself. So that would be no. No, Kreios, I don't consider myself ideally suited to manage an entire organization dedicated to the damned things. And I've got my own generals allied against me—well, most of them anyway—and if I were them, I'd ally against me too. Annika was out of her mind to choose me."

"You recovered her amulet for her, restoring the source of ancient power to the House. Some would say that's a sufficient test of your abilities."

"That was a job—and not an especially hard one. Weird, but not hard. It's not like anyone was attacking me when I grabbed the thing, other than Soo's own mom. And I outweighed her." I shook my head. "No. Annika wasn't thinking right."

"And then there's the healing you performed on her general at the Palazzo."

"For which I'm still pissed off at *you*, thank you." I glared at him. "Besides, there were a lot of people there that I *didn't* heal."

"Which is exactly the point. You do not have a sense for the dramatic, Sara Wilde, and it's something that you'll need to cultivate should you wish to truly lead. You were attacked on all sides and went down. The men who had previously opposed you could not by honor let you be killed by an outsider. It would violate their code."

"Lucky for me." I winced, recalling the thuds of the generals' bodies as they'd toppled over me. "They were dead men before they even reached me."

"Not all of them." Kreios lifted a hand, and a figure appeared before us, an illusion, of course, but a powerful one. General Ma-Singh stood with his cane and his sling, staring resolutely into nothing at all. But unlike the man who had hobbled up to me in the hospital, he was dressed in the same armor I'd seen him in outside the Palazzo—black and fitted, booted and belted. Only the helmet was missing. His eyes still carried the intense fervency they had when he'd taken bullets for me, staring me in the face.

"You held his gaze while the rage built within you, the healing fire. You thrust that fire toward him when it was your own body that needed repair. You kept his life burning within him, and he knows it. That is a powerful ally within your own House."

I sensed the truth of what he was saying, and Soo's pendants stirred at my neck as if to underscore that truth. The faint echo of fire deep within me stirred too. Kreios was right. I did that. I at least did that one thing. And yet… "If I were truly strong, I would have saved the others too."

"The others didn't see you. They acted out of honor, to be sure, but they were committed to the form, not the person. By the chance of his position, Ma-Singh *saw* you. And to him, that connection proved lifesaving. It is not a stretch for him to say to others who might be skeptics that they have only to look into your eyes to become committed to your cause."

I stared at him. "He did not say that to anyone. Please tell me you're making that up."

Kreios smiled indolently. "He can be quite convincing if he wants to be."

"No, no, no." My head began to throb. "I need to find that stupid Honjo sword. It's the only way I'll be able to fake my way through the succession fight and then figure out what I really need to do."

"Then it would appear you're lucky to have me."

I should have been expecting the person whose voice rang out across the Devil's office, but I wasn't, and the sudden appearance of Eshe in the doorway of Kreios's office took me aback. Today the High Priestess apparently had a business meeting, because instead of her usual toga-and-sandals, all-Cleopatra-all-the-time attire, she'd wrapped herself in a red bandage dress that emphasized every one of her multithousand-year-old assets. The High Priestess of the Council was its oldest seated member—or had been, up until Michael the Archangel had returned to claim his role as Hierophant. I wondered if she minded being the kid sister.

Eshe strode into the room, her stiletto platform heels sinking into the lush pile carpet but not deeply enough to keep her from making a grand entrance. Her dark, olive-toned skin and perfectly sculpted cheekbones needed no makeup, and for once she wasn't wearing any, while her thick black hair had been swept up in a tight chignon. If anyone needed a cat-o'-nine-tails to round out her outfit, it was Eshe, but she already came accoutered with a large flat silver disk, about the size of her head. She lifted it now.

"My thanks to you and Simon for recovering the shield," she said, and what appeared to be a genuine smile creased her lips. "I'd thought it lost for eternity."

I wasn't used to Eshe being nice to me, and I narrowed my eyes. "What do you want?"

"To help you," she said. She reached the collection of chairs and couches in front of Kreios's desk and perched on the edge of an antique sofa, her gaze never leaving me. "You're stronger now. You've been with Armaeus."

"Well, not been-with, been-with," I said, too quickly, and the High Priestess's smile turned condescending, which made me feel weirdly relieved. "But yeah, we chatted."

"He's disappeared into that fortress of his, refusing to talk to anyone, buried in his lore and spells." She tapped the edge of her scrying platter with a long, silver-tipped fingernail. "That makes me nervous."

It made me nervous too, but not as nervous as Eshe confiding anything in me. "What's he doing?"

"I would tell you that if I could put eyes on him. I can't, not even this one." She gestured to the center of her forehead, home of the third eye. "I suspect he is puzzling over the mystery of what you experienced in Hell. But you know him well enough to penetrate his defenses, should you wish to do so. Should you need to do so."

I considered that. I had peered into Armaeus's mind—once. Briefly. But what I'd seen, I had misunderstood. I'd paid the penalty for getting too close to the Magician, wanting too much. Now everything that could lock up inside me did so with impressive speed, from my brain to my guts. I had no desire to pry Armaeus into the open right now. He could stay locked in his basement for the next ten years, and I'd be okay with that.

"It doesn't matter what I saw in Hell," I grumbled, working to loosen my death grip on yet another of Kreios's pillows. "That place was full of illusions."

She shrugged. "It appears Armaeus does not subscribe to the same beliefs. In the meantime, I understand you need to recover the Honjo Masamune. I thought I'd assist you in locating it." She laid the disk on the table, and as I stared, something shimmered across its surface. A chill rolled down my arms.

"Or, you know." I shrugged. "I could simply ask the cards. That's usually good enough."

"But your cards will help you more if you have a place to get started, no?" Though she was keeping up her side of the conversation, Eshe's focus was on the shield. "You know what I say is true."

Her voice had already slipped into the overproduced cacophony I'd gotten more used to each time I watched her trance out. I could feel the pull of it and tried to maintain my hold on this reality.

"I don't need to astral travel on this job," I said. "I need a rental car. The sword was taken by an American soldier. So it's probably here, in the States. Sitting in someone's attic."

"No." Eshe looked at me, her eyes now covered in a milk-white sheen. "See what there is to see, Sara," she said. And she pointed to the surface of the shield.

Atop it now spun a blade that had to be the Honjo Masamune, the sword of the samurai. It gleamed in a pool of bubbling mist, long and perfect, unsheathed. There were lines and shadows etched into the blade as well as the crystals Kreios had described—but something more too, something apparent only as Eshe muttered and swayed, her hands drifting over the shield. An inscription—unreadable to me—glinted in the mists there, the promise of magic untold.

Then again, if I was the one wielding that sword, it would need to bring hella magic.

Eshe spoke again, chanting the words of traveling, and it wasn't one voice but twenty, worming into my ears, my eyes, lifting me until my skin no longer seemed capable of containing me, my bones separating as I sank into the trance right along with her.

The shield between us began to smoke, and more figures moved across its surface, eddies of a long-ago war fought with guns instead of swords.

"The American who took the sword was not who he said he was, not sent for the purposes of the allies but for his own quest, his own surety," Eshe intoned, and I watched the images her oracle was serving up.

"Connected," she moaned.

On the shield, a young man dressed in an army uniform carried boxes of swords and placed them into his army jeep. He drove away from the home of a Japanese shogun until the jeep dissolved into the deeper mist.

I dissolved more too. Eshe breathed the phrase "ley lines," and the images dancing on the shield shifted. My perspective lengthened and widened, and I now drifted above a Google map of magical earth—an earth covered in a net of connecting dots. Those lights flared highest where multiple lines intersected. Eshe spoke the ancient words of travel, while the image of the sword spun above the map, then triangulated upon it, pointing first to the southwest, then up toward northern Great Britain, then east to Belarus. But it wasn't until it shot deeper into Asia that the map transformed, an entire quadrant lighting up.

"Go," Eshe whispered, and the call to flight filled me, impossible to ignore.

My mind detached from my body, and I soared free.

Chapter Fourteen

Untethered from gravity, I burst out of the Devil's penthouse into the glare of the Strip at night, ripping over the imposing, glittering monstrosities of the Council's homes. There was Scandal, the Devil's domain, immediately below me, and Simon's foolscap palace above the Bellagio hotel. The Emperor's gleaming black tower hovered menacingly over Paris, but my attention was immediately drawn to Prime Luxe, the Magician's domain.

Somewhere amid all that stone and glass, if the High Priestess were to be believed, Armaeus had walled himself in with his incantations and spells. Somewhere, he was plotting ways to crawl inside my head and make himself comfortable. As little as I wanted him actually in my head, the idea of him thinking about me, wanting anything to do with me, swirled and eddied in my consciousness, a dark and heady desire unwilling to die.

Focus.

I shifted my gaze beyond the soaring turrets of Prime Luxe as I shot across the night sky. With astral travel, my vision was not a singular experience, but the result of a fractured perspective orienting on the earth's surface, like the eyes of a thousand satellites all turning to the same point at once. And my focus was the discovery of the Honjo Masamune.

As I gazed down, however, it wasn't the curve of the mystical blade that pointed back to me, but swords of all descriptions, angling toward me at points across the Americas and on islands in the Pacific. I turned west, my gaze raking over the surface of land and sea, and the swords shifted their orientation too. These couldn't all be the location of the Honjo sword—they couldn't. That was a weapon of unmistakable mysticism, of power recognized through the centuries. These were…something else.

I dropped into the mists of the world, soaring along the coast of California, far to the north. There were swords here, a half dozen of them, and I scanned the rocky coastline for their location. I flinched only slightly as I entered the building from which the strongest images resonated—an enormous compound perched on a cliff overlooking the stormy Pacific. I sank through walls and floors until I reached the swords. They were held by four men and two women, fighting in exact precision, executing training moves as elegantly as any dance.

Though one of the benefits of astral travel was that I was rarely seen, something clearly tipped off the practitioners as I entered their training space. They turned as one, their eyes and faces alight, and shouted in fierce joy even as I whirled myself away, my last sight that of swords being thrust in the air in triumph.

I whisked free of the world's embrace again and raced over the ocean, seeing more glints of light in the water—ships? Islands? These were weaker, less concentrated, individual swords tracking my progress across the earth.

I heard Eshe's voice in my ear, guiding me.

"Concentrations of ley lines," she said, and the web of energy glittered, superseding the placement of swords for a moment, before the blades took precedence once more. The islands of Japan and the coast of China radiated with concentrated swords, and I couldn't ignore their call. I avoided Shanghai, dropping farther south as if I were pulled. Here again there was a bright flame of focus, and I slid closer to it, unable and unwilling to deny my curiosity. More swords. More members of this House that spread across the world in silent power. How many people had Annika led? How many had pledged themselves to her cause?

The Chinese city of Chongqing lay deep in the heart of the country, and the home I entered there was half temple, half mansion, enormous and full of industry. Everyone was moving, rushing, but it was the center of the building I was drawn to, where a shrine rested—a shrine in which a dozen men stood in white clothes, their heads bowed in prayer, though no statue, no altar stood before them.

Once again, my arrival did not go unnoticed, but these men were not fighting, and their eyes, as they were lifted to me, met mine with recognition as much as surprise. They didn't know me, but they knew *what* I was, if not why I was there. More alarmingly, they could see me, recognize me. And that shouldn't be possible.

I scanned the room around them and saw the swords, each resting in a position of honor against the wall. My heart caught in my throat as I willed myself away, but I'd seen what I needed to see. In the center of the collection of Chinese blades…stood a white one. One of these men served Annika Soo directly, or had been rewarded by her. I could not know which one it was; no man's face betrayed anything more than resolution and fierce pride as I lifted my spirit out of the walls and soared once more into the ether.

"Focus, Sara. These are not your people. They are but a gateway."

I frowned as Eshe's words cut across my mind, instinctively rejecting anything the haughty priestess said to me. And yet—she was right, if what I continued to tell myself held true. I wanted succession; I wanted order. I wanted Annika's rule—all that she had built—not to be destroyed by my ineptitude. Nothing more or less than that.

And yet…

Finally, the net of ley lines superseded the pull of swords, and I concentrated anew. There had been a reason for me to journey this far to the Asian continent, and the glow of my destination beamed mightily from a coast far to the south of Chongqing.

"See what there is to see," Eshe urged. I swept down, spiraling toward a location that was not ancient so much as redolent with history and mysticism and power. Past Laos and Thailand, down through the clouds, the humidity so thick it was as if it was raining in full sunlight.

The sun had long since risen over the ancient monument, but the place was far from abandoned. Hundreds of people milled around, their tourists' clothes startling against the ancient reverence of the enormous temple. The entire structure was over half a mile square, bordered on all sides by a wide moat, and its statues and architecture were a mix of centuries-old design and modern reconstruction.

But there was something in this temple that did not belong, that had not been put there by its long-dead builder.

There was something in the grasp of a god that called to me.

I stared at the Bakan Sanctuary, the tallest spire in a forest of spires that made up the Cambodian masterpiece of Angkor Wat. The spectral light that spilled out of the tall windows and doors of the sanctuary nearly blinded me—there was no doubt this was my location.

But even as I edged closer, I felt something pulling at me, drawing me away. I sensed a presence I could not ignore, grasping, straining toward me.

"Sara." Eshe's voice held a note of caution, but I didn't need her to tell me of the danger I was experiencing. I'd been seen by members of my own House, but this wasn't the surge of interest and fascination. This was dead certainty.

And I had felt this touch before.

Gamon.

She was trying to *follow* me.

I shot up, scattering my focus as the swords flickered and winked out, the beam of light from the Bakan Sanctuary dividing to flow to all the points on the grid where the ley lines intersected. Now there were a thousand lit-up locations for what I sought, and I could sense the frustration of the woman who could not see what I saw, know what I knew.

The robed and masked figure filled my mind's eye anyway. And her laugh sounded across the planes of awareness to me, power redolent as she pressed against my mental barriers.

She was Soo's mortal enemy—and now my mortal enemy too.

"You toy with a war you cannot win, should not fight," Gamon said—though she spoke words in every tongue, as if she wasn't sure which one I could hear most clearly. "You have no place in the House of Swords."

Irritation fired anew, but I didn't want to argue with her. I wanted only to see her dead.

The realization of that anger, that dread promise roared through me with an insistence I didn't expect, and I threw up my hands at the image, forcing it back. It winked out almost instantly, but the violence of my movement shoved me back as well, even as the world brightened to an unbearable white.

A wall of crackling energy rose up all around me, robbing me of sight, of breath, of sensation—

"Sara! Sweet Jesus, someone get a blanket!"

Nikki's strident voice rang loud enough next to my ears for me to flinch away. A blanket was wrapped around me, the sensation completely disorienting. I blinked my eyes open, and only then did I realize that something was on fire.

Me, as it happened.

My screams shorted out as Nikki threw me to the carpet, beating out the flames that scattered into mist as Kreios and Eshe stood over us. I rolled to my side in a fit of racking coughs, my lungs suddenly filled with smoke. The two Council members stared at me in wonder as I finally stopped wheezing, like I was that night's final carnival trick.

"Get off me," I rasped. Nikki fell away, pulling the blanket free. What was left of my scrubs hung from my shoulders and hips, the light material scorched in several places.

I scowled at Eshe from my position on the floor. "Really? You set me on fire?"

"You stopped speaking," Kreios said before Eshe could respond. "When you travel, you speak—you always have. If you do not speak, we cannot guide you. You stopped."

I considered that, pulling myself upright. "And the fire was necessary because?"

Nikki flicked ash out of my hair. "I go out for doughnuts, and this is what I walk into," she muttered. "The human torch."

"Your abilities cannot be contained within your body any longer." Eshe's eyes still had remnants of their milk-white sheen, her hold on her oracular powers evident. "You are at great risk the longer you remain on this path."

"Gee, thanks." I blew out a breath, and could taste the heat against my teeth, as if I'd been charred from the inside out. That'd happened before, but not from a simple trip across the world via mental expressway. "What went wrong here? When did I stop talking?"

"You relayed the sword's location at Angkor Wat." Kreios gestured, and an image flickered to life in the space beyond his desk, the same colossal temple I'd seen moments before. The sun had now fully risen over the temple, but everything else was the same—minus the light pouring out of the tallest spire. "It seems our American thief was better traveled than you expected."

"Cambodia's a long way from Kansas City." Nikki's wide eyes fixed on the temple. "That's where he stashed the Honjo?"

"I think so," I said, though my gaze sheered away from the Bakan Sanctuary. Too much had happened on my journey for me to fully process.

I looked at Eshe. "I could be seen, this time. By people attached to Soo's House. What's that about?"

"You're undisciplined, and you foolishly put yourself at risk," she said, not hiding her annoyance. "Your task was the sword, not the House. You're not a true member of the House of Swords."

Her vitriol took me back a step. "What, you're angry too? I didn't ask for Soo's little legacy to fall into my lap."

"But you are considering keeping it," she said coldly. "You speak of succession and choices, but there is a part of you that yearns for this role—yearns for it even though you have no idea what it entails, the sacrifices you will make, the damage you will cause."

I lifted my hands. "You wanna enlighten me?"

Her smile turned craftier. "That would be foolish of me, I should think. Far better that the Magician is so distracted, he's turned his focus inward and is no longer seeing all that he should see. As head of the Council, he too walks a dangerous path following you. Perhaps I shall let him keep following that path. Let him and you both make choices that will be your undoing." She shrugged. "Perhaps."

I scowled at her. "You've been hanging around Viktor too long."

"The Emperor is better suited to leading the Council at least in one respect," Eshe retorted. "He knows you for the mortal you are. Gifted, certainly." She flicked her hand at the shield. "Useful, without question. But you are only a mortal, Sara. You'll always be only a mortal. And mortals have a ceiling on what they can and will do." She curled her lip. "Otherwise, don't you think the Emperor would have remained one? He was one of the greatest sorcerers of his time."

"He was also buddies with Hitler. So I wouldn't be singing his praises all that loudly."

"Allying yourself with strength is the hallmark of any great leader." Eshe sniffed. "He chose the Council when it presented itself, as you see."

"And angels wept, I'm sure." I transferred my attention to Kreios. "I'm going to need a plane, some kind of reason to be in Angkor. What I have to do isn't on the typical tourist itinerary."

"I'm going with," Nikki said. She folded her arms as I turned to her. "You are *not* going to Cambodia on a solo jump, girl. You may have forgotten the fireworks from earlier this week, but I haven't. And if you don't let me go, you'll just be stuck with Jiao's goons on your ass, and I don't think you want that either."

"Can't Brody keep an eye on her?"

"Not that close of an eye. He's up to his ass in paperwork over the whole shitstorm at the Palazzo. But you really think you're not going to have a tail on you the moment you show your face outside these walls?"

"Fair point," I mumbled.

Nikki gave me a toothy grin. "So I'm going with you. To protect you from your own people as much as anyone else. Besides, you were in a hospital bed a mere hour ago and spontaneously combusted just now. Hell, I'm coming along to protect you from *you*."

"Your concern is appreciated, if misplaced." Kreios nodded, clearly enjoying the byplay between us. "A helicopter is even now on its way to the rooftop landing strip atop the Flamingo, and a jet is being redirected for your needs. I can have you in Siem Reap in approximately a day's flight. I'll arrange for papers and accommodations to be ready for you upon your arrival."

"Thanks." I poked at the singe spots on my scrubs.

He nodded at Eshe, though his gaze never left me. "Do not discount counsel even if it isn't what you wish to hear, Sara Wilde. Eshe is correct, Armaeus is correct. Your own intuition, should you allow it to speak, is correct. The course you have set for yourself with the House of Swords will not end well, unless you allow another to fight in your place."

"I got it, I got it," I muttered, my mind already jumping ahead to the task of finding a sword in one of the busiest tourist locations in the Pacific. "I'll be careful."

"You'll need to be more than that," Kreios said amiably. "If you do not relinquish leadership of the House of Swords, you will die."

Chapter Fifteen

Like Paris in the summertime, Cambodia is hot. And rainy. And especially rainy and hot.

Nikki, being no fool, had stuck to her camo pants and waterproof hiking boots, her upper body on display in a skintight black cami beneath a flowing, sheer white rain jacket. Her hair was in a ponytail beneath her black CPD ball cap, and I eyed her broad back as we tramped through the rain-slicked streets.

"Um, have you been working out?"

"Girl needs to stay in shape," she said, lifting one impressive shoulder as she surveyed the scene. "Although right now, girl could use a beer, stat."

It was nearing midnight in Siem Reap, but the busy Pub Street showed no sign of shutting down. The recent downpour served only to force people inside the tiny cafés and bars lining the streets, or to spread plastic bags on the outdoor seating now that the rain had eased off again. The heat stayed at a constant, steaming off the pavement. We pushed our way into one of the more promising-looking bars, a place selling stir-fried beef and an international assortment of beers. There were no tables open, but the couple who'd entered ahead of us spent a second too long gawking at Nikki. She pushed past them, scoring a prime space at the bar. I sidled up beside her as the bartender came by, and Nikki ordered for the two of us with a pointed finger and an attempt at pronouncing the local fare that was so poor, it rivaled mine.

"I like this place," she said, grinning at me. She leaned heavily against the bar and snaked her foot around a stool that had been vacated a hair's breadth before. The disgruntled "hey" of a disappointed stool-stalker was cut short as he followed the reinforced-toe boot up to the top of Nikki's ball cap. I turned to take in the clientele, sipping on my own beer after making sure I watched the bartender uncap it and slide it my way without any technoceutical additives. Not that I was too worried, though. This wasn't Tel Aviv airport, it was a hole in the wall in the jungle, and we'd traveled with an Arcana-level of stealth, courtesy of Simon. Tainted food would be the least of our worries.

The bar crowd was an eclectic mix of tourists despite the rainy season, a scatter of Americans, Chinese, Australians, and Europeans. All of them carried on loud conversations over TVs tuned to what looked like a continuous feed of soccer. "We got, what, twelve hours before Soo's goons figure out where we are?"

"Soo's goons or the goons of her enemies," I said. "It's not like we've gotten debriefed on who we should even be watching out for."

"I get the feeling Soo'd shut up most everyone who needed shutting a while back." Nikki shrugged. "There'll be people who move against the House now that she's gone, but her generals clearly felt comfortable going after you instead of heading off the barbarians at the gate. I suspect her infrastructure is pretty tight."

"Probably true." I didn't like it, though, the sense that I was missing key information about a new purchase—like a rescue dog who was about to have puppies in my living room. Then again, I was almost certain I wouldn't be keeping the dog, so on a need-to-know basis, I didn't actually need to know much more than how quickly I could get the Honjo Masamune and hand it off to the first general I could.

"Don't you get that squirrelly look on your face. That always leads to trouble," Nikki said, tilting her beer toward me. "What're you thinking?"

"Nothing. I just want to get this op nailed down." I turned back to the counter, clearing a space on the scarred wood surface. Then I reached into my jacket pocket and shook loose my Tarot deck, the way an addict of a different sort might break out a pack of cigarettes. I shuffled the deck quickly, then pulled three cards, wincing as lightening flashed in the window, the roll of thunder following behind.

I looked back at Nikki, who was also grimacing at the renewed pelting of rain and the influx of bodies into the bar, everyone smelling of damp sweat. "Really?" she muttered. "Thunderstorms? That's kinda gonna put a crimp in the sunrise ceremonies tomorrow."

"I think people show up for sunrise no matter what, in case the weather turns—which it's already done like six times since we've gotten here, so probably not a bad idea."

"Yeah, maybe." Her gaze dropped to the cards. "You gonna flip those over, or do I have to guess?"

"You know, I'm not used to having a shadow when I pull these things."

"Well, I'm the most stylish shadow you'll ever score, dollface. Get comfy with it."

I shook my head but couldn't help grinning as I turned over the cards. It was strange having Nikki along for the ride, but it was good too. In a world where I no longer knew who supported me and who didn't, she was a constant I hadn't realized how much I needed.

Which was why I didn't begrudge her when she whistled low. "Well, that looks like a big pile of suck."

"You're not kidding." Hunkered down in Cambodia in a thunderstorm, I hadn't expected the cards to be cheery, but this read was exceptionally miserable. The first card was the Tower, complete with its super fun representation of victims flinging themselves off an exploding building. "Could be an explosion, could be the thunderstorm." tapped the card. "Could be everything falling to pieces."

Nikki snorted. "Glad to know we're in the right place.

I moved on. "The Ten of Swords could be betrayal, could be having to look for something along the ground. Could be attack."

"Or gall bladder surgery," Nikki supplied helpfully. "Can never be too careful with your gall bladder."

"Fair enough. Outcome is the Five of Wands. Could be a fight, or the fifth exit, or—"

"You know it's a fight, hon. A fight where we're betrayed. My favorite kind."

"Clarifying." I pulled two more cards out of the deck, flipping them upright: Hierophant and Death.

Nikki took another pull on her beer. "I'm glad you're the card reader and I'm the muscle."

"This feels like a location clarifier," I said, dropping the Hierophant between the first two. "We're going to a religious site, and there are statues dedicated to Buddha in there. So the statues are where we should focus."

"And this American GI was, what, a Buddhist? Drawn to the elbow of Cambodia as his personal mecca?"

"Who knows. Angkor Wat started out Hindu focused, but it's been Buddhist since the mid-1500s. That's a few hundred years after the Honjo Masamune was created." I shook my head. "I don't know the connection. Maybe there isn't one, maybe the guy simply paid more attention to the ley line configurations. They all converge beneath the temple."

"Maybe. All that matters is you think the thing is here." She flapped her hand over the cards. "And that we have enough lead time to get the hell back to the plane before the rest of *that* happens. What's Death mean in context here?"

"Probably not actual death, since the Tower is with it."

"Thank heavens for small favors."

I shrugged. "Change, something that takes us completely by surprise. That's what we're looking at, I think. Something that changes everything."

Our food arrived, and conversation halted enough for us to sample the delicacies that Siem Reap's Pub Street had to offer. Throughout the meal, though, Nikki's gaze kept casually sweeping the crowd, and I didn't miss how her hand strayed to her waist every time the door to the small bar opened.

I grimaced and downed another sip of beer. I was used to entering dangerous situations, thrived on it, in fact. I was used to ending up places I sometimes needed to exit equally quickly. But it was a different sensation to be walking around with a target on my back. Some of that was because of the House of Swords, admittedly. But how much would change even if I gave up that commission? Could I go back to the shadows at this point, even if I wanted to?

I looked over at Nikki, whose gift of Sight extended only to what her clients saw—or believed they saw. An excellent skill to have in her former role of cop, but not as useful now, when I truly needed to divine the future.

"You ready?"

"About as much as you are," she cracked, but she pushed back from the bar, throwing down a few bills on the counter. "Pretty sure that'll guarantee us a seat when we come back," she said, and the confidence in her tone bolstered my flagging spirits.

We headed back to our hotel, ostensibly to sleep for the rest of the night. Instead, a half an hour later in the middle of another rainstorm, we padded down the backstairs. The car Kreios had secured for us was small and nondescript, and Nikki folded herself into it with a curse.

"He did this on purpose," she grumbled. "He's thinking about me in this roller skate right now, laughing his exceptionally fine ass off."

"It's twenty minutes, and take heart. If the cards hold true, we're probably not going to be driving back tonight."

"That's great, Sara." She rolled her eyes. "You just keep the troops smiling, and it'll all be okay."

The downpour made the travel slow going, even in the dead of night—because nothing was really dead in Siem Reap, ever. People traveled on foot, on bike and motorbike in addition to cars, as numb to the rain as if it were a passing cloud of gnats. We dumped the car about two blocks from the temple and trekked the rest of the way on foot, pausing at an overhang to peer across the moat to the temple proper.

"I guess no one would really notice if we showed up wet," Nikki observed, and I grimaced.

"Whatever is living in that moat, we do not want to have it crawling into us," I said. "The back access road to the temple will take too long too. Kreios tapped into local data, and it's a barricaded nightmare right now. So that means we go over the bridge to pray at the temple doors with everyone else. And we stay there. We're die-hard pilgrims come to watch the sunrise celebration, and I bet we won't even be the first in line."

We weren't. Tourists sat huddled under makeshift rain shelters, their spirits bright and cheery despite the sweeping rain. The beach of Angkor Wat's opening to the temple grounds extended for several hundred feet in both directions, and trees hung over the high wall. It wasn't too much of a stretch for two soaked Americans to wander over to the edge of the tree line, looking for shelter.

We sat there another half an hour, until yet more tourists arrived, these singing drunkenly as they careened back and forth across the bridge.

"That'll do for distraction," said Nikki, and I nodded.

"Remember, the walls might have razor wire. So look for the biggest trees you can find."

"I just spent three hundred dollars on a full body wax," she retorted. "Ain't nothing going to gash open these legs if I have anything to say about it."

She moved off, melting backward into the trees as I watched the beach for five minutes longer. By the time I reached her on the other side of the wall (thankfully there'd been no razor wire), Nikki had holstered her gun for easier movement.

We set out, reaching the main temple area with surprising speed. It was approaching three a.m., and the place glowed with a skeletal lighting system, not enough to worry about. Still, up on the actual steps to the Bakan Sanctuary, the lights were everywhere. Only one of us would probably be able to slip up there unseen, and it wasn't the one who topped six foot four without heels.

"I need you on the ground until I get back," I said. "If all hell breaks loose, get out."

"Aye, aye," Nikki said, squinting at the light show. "Figured they'd dim the lights more with the rain."

"I think this *is* the dim version."

Nikki hunkered into the lee of the steps as I pulled a pair of climbing gloves out of my pants and slicked them on. The rain had kicked up in force, and the thunder had taken to rolling in ten-second rumbles, interspersed with bright pops of lightning. I timed my surges to fall as the bright static from the lightning faded, and made it up the steep stairs half running, half climbing—and half lying flat on my stomach, gasping for breath. Even the description of "stairs" was a kindness. These steps were more like a rock wall at a gym, despite sporting more regular handholds. By the time I pulled myself up to the central tower's opening, my arms were wobbling from exertion, and I flattened to the stone surface as a lightning bolt split the night sky.

"I get it, I get it," I muttered, squinting into the tower's central chamber with the aid of the heavenly light show. There were several statues of Buddha within, and I hopped the short fence to enter the monument, carefully avoiding the piles of ornamental offerings in tribute to the silent forms.

Four Buddhas stood at each of the cardinal points of the room, along with one in the center, the Maitreya Buddha. I looked at the feet of the four exterior statues, nodding as I confirmed they were bolted to the floor. None of the signs of reconstruction touched the statues' feet.

"Where'd you put the sword, soldier boy," I muttered, thinking back to the cards. The Buddhas all had similar poses, but I'd pulled the Hierophant card at the bar, symbolic of all things religious, yes—but also something more. The central Buddha had his hand in the air, as if passing on a benediction. That exactly matched the Hierophant.

Still, there was simply no way the sword was buried beneath or inside these Buddhas. The pit these statues currently rested on had been excavated and filled back in, everything of value carefully removed. A sword would have been found if it'd been buried in that gravel at any time over the past seventy years. I moved more closely to the central statue, brushing past the others.

The outer Buddhas towered over me and serenely watched my progress. I focused again on the Maitreya. It was virtually impossible to see the line where the head had been reattached after the original statues had been literally defaced by vandals. Had the sword somehow been placed inside while the statues had been undergoing construction? It was impossible to know, and either way—I wouldn't have the tools to unearth the thing.

Scowling, I reached inside my shirt for the cards, even as another rush of lightning illuminated the temple room. The shadows jumped, and I jumped along with them, yanking the card free and flipping it upright.

The Ace of Swords.

Helpful to know I was on the right track, but I scowled at the card, looking for hidden clues. The sword was held aloft over a rocky mountain range, a crown and garland surmounting it. The hand floated in the air, and I looked from it to the hand above me, Buddha giving his benediction.

Lightning cracked again, and I looked up farther.

The dome of the Bakan Sanctuary had been gilded with several layers of silver, gold, and other precious metals through the years, too high and too awkward for vandals to easily reach, only recently uncovered through careful restoration. The ceiling was covered in bas-relief carvings that glistened through that precious covering, heaven represented through the original Hindu artwork of a throng of warriors paying honor to Vishnu. The warriors carried swords, arrows, and knives, and as I scanned the elegant artistry, another lightning strike cracked through the sky, hitting the top of the temple.

Electrical sparks showered down all around me, and the lights blinked out.

But not before I saw it.

Chapter Sixteen

A long, slender sword stuck out near the bottom of the ridged dome, adding an extra bump that didn't match the other four arcs. Its scabbard reached out a scant inch farther than the other ridges, gleaming with the same metallic sheen as the rest of the gilded dome. I would bet my teeth that scabbard was lined in lead too. That might not have been done purposefully, but it had served to hide the sword better than anything else could have all these long years. After all, the dome was lined with metal—what was one more shard of steel?

Muttering an apology as the rain pounded down from above, I pulled myself up the Maitreya Buddha until I stood balanced, one foot on his shoulder and the other on his head. An outburst far below me on the grounds of Angkor Wat galvanized me to action, and at the next clap of thunder, I leapt, grabbing the edge of the sword—

And I hung there in midair, my feet pumping.

"C'mon," I gritted out, inching my way up the sword. I had a grip born of strength and desperation, but I couldn't miraculously put on weight. The sword refused to budge no matter how much I jiggled it.

"Dollface, where—sweet Jesus what're you doing?" Nikki's voice boomed across the small space and I glared down at her. "They've got the whole cavalry coming up these stairs in another five minutes. There's some sort of electrical fire on the roof. Get down from there!"

"The sword!" I gasped. "Grab my feet."

Muttering a curse, Nikki holstered her gun and ran forward, but her long arms were still too short to reach me.

"The Buddha," I managed. By then I could hear the rush of men on the steep stairs behind me, guards or priests moving up for reasons I didn't want to consider—whether for a fire on the roof or because they'd seen trespassers inside the dome.

Within the next fifteen seconds, Nikki had hauled herself up to the broad head of the Buddha. "Sorry, big guy," she muttered as she stepped on the crown of his head, one foot wedged onto his shoulder. Then she scowled at me. "Girl, you better have a tight hold and padded elbows, because this is going to hurt like a bitch."

"Just go already—"

Nikki hurtled herself off the Buddha and crashed into me, the sword giving way with a crack that sounded far too loud. Then both of us were dropping through the air. I hit the floor of the sanctuary so hard, my head bounced. I groaned, seeing nothing but stars.

"Buck up, Buttercup. We gotta skinny."

It was too late, though. A trio of cloaked monks cleared the entrance of the dome, chattering in outraged Cambodian. As Nikki stood, they waved long rods that looked like they would hurt a lot, but the men hauling themselves up behind them had guns. Those would hurt more.

"Out! Out! No trespassing!" the monks shouted, first in English, then French. I scanned the floor wildly for anything broken other than my body, but my vision was still processing double. The Buddhas appeared fine, still benevolently holding court, but another crack of lightning sent more sparks flying.

"Sorry! Sorry, heard it was a hell of a view," Nikki said, her hands up, her gun mercifully hidden beneath her knotted jacket. "That storm is something, isn't it?"

Another roll of thunder made everyone wince, and I cradled the sword close to my body. No way would I be able to run out of the temple without anyone noticing me or it, but I couldn't swallow the thing. The Honjo Masamune blade shivered in my hands as if possessed of a holy fire, but it was every inch a real sword.

My mind flashed to the Ten of Swords just as another bolt of lightning struck halfway down the temple, setting off new fires. "I'm stuck!" I cried, and when I staggered to my feet, the scabbarded sword was wedged between my arm and my side as if I'd been poked through. "Get it out, get it out—"

Not giving anyone a chance to do what I was begging for, I ran straight through the monks and into the startled guards, pulling one of them with me as I hurtled over the edge of the stairs. We both tumbled down, the sword immediately flying free of my grip. I righted myself and lurched after the weapon, half falling down the next several steps until I reached the blade.

By now, more men were rushing both up the stairs and down, and with Nikki clattering down behind me hollering that I'd been killed, I grabbed for the sword. It slid away from me, bounced sideways off the monument, then tumbled downward toward the stone floor of the courtyard. Without any other choice—I jumped after it.

The imagery of the Tower streaked through my mind as I smacked hard against the rocky surface of the monument. I hated it when my cards were that accurate.

There was no way I'd reach the blade before it clattered to the stone-studded base of the temple grounds but, arms windmilling, I tried anyway, bouncing down the side of the wall, sliding along the rocky incline and shredding my jeans. The hoodie protected my elbows and shoulders from the worst of the assault, but by the time I hit the ground, I felt like I'd been hit by a truck. My gloves were ripped, and I peeled them off completely, tossing them aside. I staggered forward and reached the sword as another round of orange-robed men barreled toward me, then grabbed the thing bare-handed and slid it free of its scabbard.

The Honjo Masamune practically exploded in my hand, the same hot-cold energy of Soo's pendants arcing from it and through my body in a surge of crackling electricity. Without having to fake my scream of half fear, half exultation, I lurched upright and swung around, waving the blade like a madwoman.

The sword gleamed in the pelting rain. Another crack of lightning illuminated the sky, setting all of Angkor Wat ablaze for a heartbeat. When it passed, I stood back, startled, my hands still aloft.

The monks had all sunk to the ground, their heads to the cobblestones.

"Go with it!" Nikki yelled, sprinting toward me from the bottom of the stairs. The monks there had also dropped, while the guards stared at them, confused, but Nikki didn't give me time to think as we dashed for the arches that led away from the inner sanctuary. We'd made it across the wide space before the monks came to their senses, apparently realizing that the sword was leaving their domain. Veneration was one thing—vandalism was another.

A strafe of gunfire broke out. Nikki yelped, hustling me to the side as a jeep with piercing-bright halogen lights swept up the wide stairs and into the inner courtyard. The jeep swerved toward us, and I squinted through the rain, recognizing the square-cut jaw even if my brain was currently sloshing through my ears.

"Get in!" Nigel Friedman roared as he came up beside us. "You've got another thirty guards out there, not all of whom work for the temple. You'll be cut down the minute you step outside."

"Not till you tell me who—"

"Go!" Nikki, apparently not having my same trust issues, picked me up and hauled me into the open door of the jeep, locking me down when I would have lurched back out.

Nigel cut the wheel hard as another round of gunshots flooded through the open entryway of the inner courtyard. He drove around the back of the building and down a service alley, bouncing down another half-broken road into the wide stand of trees. I nearly fell out of the jeep twice before Nikki pulled me bodily into a harness, snapping it tight.

"We kill him after he gets us out of here," she bellowed, and I didn't miss Nigel's hard smile as he turned to us briefly, then bent back to the issue at hand.

Namely, getting the hell off Angkor Wat's man-made island.

The back access road was as choked with debris as I expected, but Nigel angled the jeep over the side of the embankment, half into the water, until he was able to race up the other side and into the forest beyond. Sirens screamed from all directions as he turned onto a road that ran along a straggling river.

He slammed on the brakes and jumped from the vehicle. "Come on. We have to ditch this."

I unclipped from the harness and rolled out, sword in hand. Nikki was right behind me.

"We'll take this car." Nigel pointed, and there was another one there, similar to the one Kreios had given us. The British operative looked apologetically at Nikki. "Sorry for the tight fit."

"Clown cars are my specialty." Without slowing down, she dove into the driver's side. "Get in. Sara, down in back."

Nigel claimed shotgun. I clambered into the back of the vehicle, too winded to argue, and curled into the fetal position around the sword. It was larger than I expected it to be, almost as long as my torso, and Nigel threw a towel back at me with a barked command.

"Wrap it up as best you can," he said, turning back toward me. "We can't afford to—"

His words were cut off as Nikki sliced the wheel, running us down a side street, then braking sharply. By the time both of us had whipped our heads her way, Nigel's face was in profile—pressed up against the barrel of Nikki's gun.

"Thought we'd maybe work out that question of who you were working for right about now," she said.

To his credit, Nigel didn't lose his cool. Then again, he was British. The look he sent Nikki was exasperated, though, and he jerked his head back, lifting his hands to show his goodwill.

"Watch him. He's as slippery as a snake," I said, huddling around the sword like it was my newborn.

"Spill it, sexy," Nikki growled. "It's been a really long night, and we can't sit around chatting. Who's paying your freight?"

He rolled his eyes, his gaze shifting back to me. "You never were all that fast on the uptake," he said. "I'm working for you."

I straightened in the back of the car, staring at him. "Jiao contacted you again."

"She did. Now, if you would be so good as to keep driving, Miss Dawes, I'll explain on the way. You have accommodations at the Angkor Sayana Hotel and Spa, as well as six other hotels in the area, and two in Phnom Penh. I suggest we avail ourselves of none of those locations. In the last twelve hours, all known operatives of Soo's rival organizations located within a five-hundred-mile radius of Cambodia have taken up position, and there are more on the way. You have a private jet hangared nearby, I assume?"

At my nod, Nikki put the car in gear and started forward again. "Where am I headed?" she asked, managing to drive with one hand and keep the gun pointed on Nigel with the other.

He didn't take it from her, though I'd seen the man move and knew what he was capable of. If Nikki took on the British operative in earnest, she'd have her hands full, and not in the way she usually preferred.

"Out of the city—toward Damdek," he said, then turned back to me. "It's true, you know. You'd already begun asking questions. You simply weren't asking the right person. I've been in Soo's employ for the past several months."

"Yeah, well, I seem to recall you being in Viktor Dal's employ too," I said stiffly. "You get around."

His smile was decidedly self-assured. "As do you. The money has been good of late, but Soo was a primary client. And now that allegiance transfers to you, as long as you're willing to pay for it."

My brains jelled enough in my head for me to finally get it. "You're not simply a mercenary on this job, you're one of those Aces. You're an Ace for the House of Swords."

"Guilty as charged." Nigel grinned. "And Cups on occasion, though I've not been called on by Pents or Wands."

"But you're not Connected."

He shrugged. "I don't need to cast a spell. I need to shoot a gun. As long as the Houses aren't allied against each other—which they're not—there's no conflict of interest. It makes for good money."

I sat back in my seat. "I needed good money," I said, unreasonably put out. "How come you never told me about it?"

"Because you have a disarming habit of stealing things out from under me. And I simply didn't have the time to deal with all the explanations." He glanced back. "Plus, you're beholden to the Council. Or you were."

Past tense? "What do you know about them?"

"About as much as you did when you first started working with them—it was Rio, right? You got squirrelly after that job." He smirked. "Then again, with that much cash flow, I would too. I've met some of them—the Devil, Aleksander Kreios. The High Priestess, Eshe."

"The Emperor, Viktor Dal," I said pointedly.

"A good operative never shares his sources. But the work was always fringe. I didn't land the recovery work they assigned you to. Arguably, I didn't have the skills either." He regarded me. "You should know, you were seen twice last night, a floating vision surrounded by swords. Once in California, once in mainland China. That's a new trick."

"Yeah, well, I had a lot on my mind."

"It caused quite a stir. You're wearing Soo's markers, but she never appeared like that. The House is mobilizing. They want to act."

"Yeah, well, good for them." I drew my hand along the covered Honjo Masamune, drawing comfort in the solidity of it, when nothing else in my world was solid. I sighed. "I still have a long way to go. Floating in the air isn't going to cut it when they expect me to duke it out in some kind of cage match against the generals."

"Not only the generals," Nigel said cheerfully. "Other claimants too. There's a rumor of one of Gamon's lieutenants who is preparing to declare war on whoever Soo's true successor is."

Usurper… the word slid through my mind, unwanted, but Nigel kept going.

"If you don't hand off your role before he strikes, it'll be taken from you," he said. "Probably along with your head."

"Watch it, pretty boy," Nikki said mildly from the front seat, and Nigel transferred his gaze to her for a moment. Nikki didn't turn toward him, but I could see her jaw was locked.

"My apologies. But it doesn't change the fact of what is out there."

"We'll deal with that when we get there." Nikki pulled onto a main highway, no one behind us for miles. "What's in Damdek?"

"I have another vehicle, and we go overland to Phnom Penh. Two private planes are hangared there."

She snorted. "Thanks, but we kind of have a lock on transportation these days."

He smiled. "Not for where I'm going to take you."

Chapter Seventeen

In less than ten hours, we'd transferred ourselves from rain-soaked Cambodia back to...rain-soaked France. But there was no faulting the accommodations.

"Mercault know you're here?" I asked as Nigel ushered us up the long staircase to the imposing front entry of the fifteenth-century château. I'd been to several households of the French kingpin, but not this one. Still, Mercault's stamp was all over the place, his coat of arms decorating everything from flags to finials.

"Not specifically," Nigel said. "I tried contacting him, but he's too busy trying to undermine Soo's operation in Namibia. Her people have struck diamonds, and the conflict-free tag she can hang on those gems has attracted a host of new investors. Mercault, understandably, is interested in taking a large piece of that pie. Fortunately, he and I have an arrangement in place about the use of his homes."

I grimaced, feeling another headache coming on. "Soo has diamond mines in Namibia," I said. "That's something I should know, probably."

"What you should know now is that you have done everything precisely right since she handed over her House to you," Nigel said. "You took steps to determine your eligibility as the head of the House. You ascertained your weaknesses, then you recovered a centuries-old sword that had been lost for decades—all for the glory of the House of Swords. And you appeared in a vision to your acolytes. Check, check, and check again."

I blinked, and my cheeks flushed at the unexpected praise. Nigel and I weren't friends—we weren't even usually on speaking terms. But his quiet validation pooled inside me, shoring up my flagging spirits.

"Well, thank you," I said. "But you should know, that last one wasn't intended."

We walked through the richly carpeted foyer, heading deeper into the château. The entire place was silent as a tomb—reassuringly so. With all the noise and movement of the past few days, the sense of being ensconced inside rock walls that had withstood the French Revolution was deeply comforting.

Nigel shook his head as he glanced back to me. "Intentional or not, it was done, and your House has taken note. You are arguably the strongest Connected currently heading one of the Houses, though the leaders of all the Houses typically work at the height of secrecy, so it's possible others have unproven talents."

"And it pays well, this work you do?" Nikki paused at an ornate inlaid table, upon which sat a gold and silver carafe that clearly didn't come from Walmart. She drifted her fingers above it, careful not to touch. "This guy's got more money sitting around in a house he doesn't live in than I've seen in my whole life."

Nigel turned a speculative glance on her. "It pays very well, but there's a reason for that."

"Stop—just stop," I said, holding up my hands. "No recruiting my best friend into a life of crime in front of me, it's bad form." Nikki's gaze snapped to mine. She blinked rapidly, then a sound from the far end of the corridor caught our attention. Nikki had her gun out and had stepped in front of me before I could blink, and Nigel's smile deepened.

"We should continue our conversation later," he said to her, and I watched Nikki blush.

Would she truly want to become an Ace? And if she did, who was I to stop her?

Nigel motioned us forward, distracting me. "In the meantime, as you've surmised, I've arranged for a small gathering," he said. "It's time that you understood exactly what you're getting into with your leadership of the House of Swords...and what you're up against."

He led us down the hallway, not bothering to ask Nikki to put her gun up. I left mine holstered for the moment. It was hard enough learning to walk with the Honjo Masamune sticking out in front of me at an angle, my left hand resting on its hilt so the sword didn't slide out of the scabbard and clatter to the floor. Not that that had happened to me already or anything. Because that would have been disrespectful.

During the few bits of downtime on our trip from Cambodia to France, Nigel had shown me a few cuts with the sword, though he was the first to admit that he was by no means a master of the weapon. Apparently, Aces could choose their own methods of killing people, and antique swords rarely fit the bill.

Now he stepped ahead of Nikki and held up a hand, cautioning us to stop as we approached what looked to be the entry to a library. Despite the fact it was high summer, I could hear a fire burning in the hearth, smell wood crackling.

He turned the etched brass doorknob and slowly opened the door.

"Nigel!" A woman's voice I didn't recognize rang out from the room. I tensed along with Nikki, but the speaker sounded friendly enough. "It's about time you showed up. We've got six contracts to go over."

"It soon might be seven." Nigel put his hands behind his back, the epitome of British civility. "I would like to introduce the new head of the House of Swords." He turned to me, and I glanced at Nikki, rolling my eyes.

"Shoulders straight, dollface," she whispered. "Own it."

I barely contained the snort as I moved into the room, Nikki right on my heels and stepping to the side. I could tell she'd kept her gun at the ready from the sudden tension of the other people in the room, but they betrayed no other reaction.

There were three of them, only one I knew by face, a Nigerian with coal-black eyes and a ready smile. He turned that smile on me now, hooking his thumbs in his belt. "Sara Wilde! I'd heard the rumors, but I did not want to believe them to be true. I have seen the way you fight." He shook his head. "You'd better have a lot of money. We Aces do not come cheap."

"I'm surprised you can get a job fighting anything but a bad cold, Mobo," I said, settling on the balls of my feet. The assassin was legendary in the arcane black market for using any tool or implement at hand as a deadly weapon. I'd once seen him take out an opponent with a handful of chess pieces, and I made it a policy not to get within four feet of him. Or to offer up a game of lawn darts.

His gaze dropped to the sword. "And the Honjo Masamune," he said, his laughing voice taking on a different note. "You wear it well."

"YouTube videos," I said. "Came with a makeup tutorial too."

The woman to Mobo's right cracked a smile, but her face otherwise was hard as granite. She was older than I would have expected for an Ace, maybe fifty if the gray of her hair was any indication, and her icy-blue eyes and sharp cheekbones screamed a Norwegian heritage.

"Alaina Dodd," she said, her European accent impossible for me to place more closely. "Why did Soo choose you?"

"I don't know," I said, and my words had the ring of honesty to them. "She could have done far better."

"She could have done far worse." The fourth Ace nodded as I shifted my gaze to him. He was smaller than Nigel, wiry, also older. His accent was French, which might have explained our location, and his eyes were hooded beneath his wrinkled brow and close-shaven hair. "I'm Luc Banon. The House of Swords is the most progressive, the most visible of the four Houses. Soo chose not merely a warrior but a Connected. Not the most skilled perhaps. Then again, perhaps you are. Rumors are running rampant in all the Houses about the change of succession. Rumors and fear as well. It is a dangerous combination."

"Thanks, I think." I inclined my head.

Luc's attention shifted to Nigel. "Why have you brought her here?"

"As Mobo believes, I suspect we'll have the opportunity for employment, and there is no secrecy about the identity of this House's leader." He nodded to Alaina. "Far better for you who work exclusively with Cups and Wands to be able to tell your employer that you've met the woman."

"Generous of you," Alaina said, her suspicion clear.

"I've worked with Sara well before the incidents that led her to this impasse." Nigel flicked a rueful smirk my way. "I owe her, and she has questions about the Houses. Some of which can be answered, some of which can't. It's up to you what to say to her."

I blinked, forcing myself not to stare at Nigel. Here were three people who knew more about the mythical structure of the Houses than anyone in the world, assembled in Mercault's living room. And I was being granted an interview?

More to the point...since when did Nigel owe me? I'd missed that, and it wasn't the kind of detail I would ordinarily forget.

"So we answer her questions, in return for what?" Alaina's question was sharp. "Information is power. There's no point in giving it up easily."

"I don't want to know about your Houses," I lied. Still, we could come around to that. "How exactly do I contact you, normally? Do I throw a pigeon out a window?"

"You've got Nigel," Mobo said gravely. "It is rare that more than one Ace is required for protection."

"Let's say I'm up against a full house, and I need four of a kind," I said. "Can I do it?"

"For enough money, you can do anything," the Frenchman said.

"Not if I can't find you."

His smile didn't reach his eyes. "We are very friendly, eh? You can find me through Nigel. You can find all of us through Nigel. And if Nigel, he is dead, then it is likely we will not want this job for which you are seeking to hire us."

"No one has hired all four Aces before." Mobo's deep voice flowed over the room, and the look in his eye was speculative. "Connecteds prefer to use their abilities over their muscle to solve their quarrels."

I shrugged. "Some quarrels take both. And you're not beholden to your Houses, right? You're true wild cards, and can flip to another House if the need requires?"

"If the need requires," Alaina said stiffly. "And if there was no damage to our own Houses."

"How would I know if my job wouldn't cause that kind of damage?"

Her smile was arctic. "You tell us the job. If we do not respond, it's one of the potential reasons."

I blew out a breath. This was the shiftiest group I'd run up against, and the arcane black market wasn't known for its high trust quotient.

"I have a question." Mobo leaned in, putting his hands on the chair he stood behind. "If you want to be forthcoming here, among friends." He stared at me. "What is your connection to the Arcana Council?"

Mobo's question held an unusual weight, but it was easy enough to answer. "I work for them on occasion, much like you do your Houses," I said, keeping my manner light. "As their needs require."

"You aren't their only finder."

"Of course I'm not." Even as I said the words, I wondered at them. I hadn't ever thought about the Council employing other Connecteds, not recently anyway. But who's to say that they didn't have a whole stable of finders in their contacts list? "You looking for a job?"

"A House leader so closely allied to the Council, that is a curious thing," Mobo said, and I saw where he was going with that. "It might not be so well accepted among the other leaders."

I shrugged. "My understanding is, all the Houses used to be allied with the Council. One big happy deck and all. They aren't now, but it doesn't mean they couldn't be."

"That is what you're going to try to do?" Alaina asked.

"I've had this job for about fifteen seconds." I lifted my right hand, my left still firmly on my sword as it rested at my hip. "But each House is free to choose where to throw its support, as I understand. Working with the Council is simply one of those options."

"So is working against it." Mobo again, and his words sent a frisson of concern through me. I wouldn't be surprised if the Houses allied against the Council. The whole, the half, or even individual members. I could see Viktor Dal dangling the bait to draw a House into conflict with Armaeus. Then again, the Emperor professed to have no knowledge of the Houses. Who was to be believed?

Still, I played it cool. "Where would the money be in that?"

Mobo's broad smile told me I'd hit the nail correctly.

"If it's cash you want, I can get you that," I said. "The Council has enough to spare."

"Mobo," Alaina said warningly, clearly anticipating a tirade, but Mobo ignored her.

"Ah, the Council," he said, still smiling…though his expression had turned harder. "Smug in their magic towers. There are those whose memories are long who would sooner rot than see themselves once more at the beck and call of such overlords."

Overlords? "Well, they can be a touch overbearing but…they have their moments," I said cautiously.

He fixed his gaze on me. "Some who would see *you* dead before you turned the Houses into the Council's private serving garrison again. That won't be tolerated, no matter who stands for you."

His anger was real and near the surface, and I wondered at it. "What did the Council do to your House, Mobo?" I asked.

If the question took him off guard, he didn't betray it, but his words were sharp. "They destroyed it long ago. The House of Wands was once the strongest of all the Houses, a far-flung family of businessmen and builders. Some of the most beautiful architecture in the world could be traced to their work and the work of their acolytes. Then they got too strong, and their power was snuffed out like a candle. The House itself was not destroyed, no. The Council is too careful for that. But the Wands' leaders were exposed and executed, its adherents chased underground. They stayed underground too."

Alaina sighed, her lips pursing. "The House of Cups experienced a similar fate when they got too strong."

Mobo's damning gaze burned through me. "Now it is the House of Swords that is showing its ambition. Built on the backs of the samurai tradition, but so much further flung than that, as you will see. As you've already seen. I would caution you to be wary. It is a dangerous thing for a House to get in bed with the Council."

I considered the Aces' words. All of them had concerns about the Council, none more eloquently stated than Mobo's. I was standing before a group of mortals who had information that the Council could not get at—resources and knowledge that could help protect the Connecteds I longed to keep safe. Resources and knowledge that could help me keep the House of Swords safe too. The Council would want to know more about the Houses, but what had it done to help those mortals in the past?

Nothing.

These were people who helped themselves. And who were beholden to no one.

These were future allies in the war on magic.

I didn't have time to consider the matter further. Because as Mobo drew breath to unleash another screed against the Council, the enormous windows of Mercault's beautiful French château…

Exploded.

Chapter Eighteen

"Deploy!" The command from Nigel was so incongruous that I jolted away from him even as the wreckage blew inward, throwing us all deeper into the room. Alaina now held her face together with one of her hands, blood spurting between her fingers as she staggered back from the wall. Around us, a half-dozen men in Kevlar suits poured in from inside the house, assault rifles at the ready.

They secured their position not a moment too soon.

A flare of gunfire burst through the now open walls of the château, and Nigel's men returned fire on a ring of assailants that came pounding out of the forest, shooting a combination of flamethrowers and machine gun blasts. We fled into the interior hallway, Nigel barking orders. Apparently, site security was his detail, and his face was mottled in fury.

"Go! Separate jeeps in the back, standing guard." He swept our group and cursed. "Luc!" he growled before heading back into what was left of the study.

Mobo stumbled into the hall. His arm swiped out to hold on to something, and found Nikki, who grunted beneath his weight as he pulled himself up…

Then he reached past her and assassinated Alaina.

Mobo's gun was steady and his aim sure as he shot the Nordic operative in the head, finishing what the blast had started. Then he pulled back his gun and held it to Nikki's temple, swinging her toward me.

"The three of us," he said tightly. "We are going to run out of here as if we're the best of friends. Luc is dead, but it'll take enough time for Nigel to work through that, and by then we'll be gone. Go."

Nikki bristled. "What the hell do you think—"

Mobo shot the gun immediately in front of Nikki's face, her scream unfeigned as residue blasted against her skin.

"I said go!" he snarled. I turned and fled down the corridor, my heart in my throat.

I was used to putting myself in danger; I sucked at putting my friends there. And my brain could not comprehend what the hell had just happened. Nigel had secured the château before we'd arrived—of course he had. His men were embedded both inside and out. They might not have been watching the forest, but the initial blast—the initial blast hadn't come from the forest. It'd come from inside, inside the very walls, it'd seemed.

Had Mobo arrived with the others, then planted the explosives to go off once everyone was in position? But if so, why?

I didn't have time to figure it out as we pounded down the corridor to a teed-off hallway that led into an enormous kitchen, then out the back of the château. Mobo loped along behind me, dragging a nearly blind Nikki with him. She managed as best she could, but her choking gasps were all that was needed to encourage me to run and run hard.

It took me a few seconds too long to realize the foolishness of that move. We clattered across the kitchen as the gunfire grew more boisterous outside, but I still timed my own steps with those of Mobo and Nikki, and realized they both were decidedly slowing. Mobo wasn't growling threats at Nikki, she wasn't gasping anymore, and I turned mid-stride to see him throw her against the island hard enough to crack a rib, his gun coming up to aim point-blank at her face.

I didn't have time to think. I definitely didn't have time to get my gun out for sure. Nudging the sword forward to loosen it in its scabbard, I turned fully around as I slid the Honjo Masamune out of its scabbard and flung the sword at Mobo. There was no precision in my throw, and there was definitely no style. The thing arced out over the kitchen as I screamed in fury and desperation, anything to distract Mobo and throw off his aim.

The sword slashed through the air and clattered harmlessly across the kitchen counter and against the far wall, but still close enough to Mobo that he jumped back. With an unearthly growl, Nikki piled into him, her head down and her shoulders hunched as if she were a bull intent on charging a toreador. She caught Mobo in the chest and lifted him off the ground, shoving him forward as I ran up. I pulled out my gun and shot him in the shoulder, unsure of whether to kill him or pump him for information.

I turned to Nikki, and that was my second mistake since everything had started exploding. Her face was a mass of blood, from where I didn't know, and my heart surged too hard in my chest as I gasped her name, even as she wheeled away, one hand roughly clearing her eyes. I strayed too close to Mobo, and he lashed out with one leg, tripping me hard onto the stone-tiled floor, I held on to my gun even as I bounced, but he'd scrambled upright, ignoring the shot to his shoulder that really wasn't pouring out anywhere near enough blood.

Of course he'd been wearing a vest.

I squeezed off two more shots, enough to send the Nigerian skittering back behind the island, and Nikki dropped to her hands and knees, uncharacteristically silent. Whether she was dead or injured or playing possum I didn't know, but Mobo's rich laugh reverberated off the acres of granite and stainless steel, distracting me.

"You shouldn't bring a sword to a gunfight," he chortled.

I winced, popping up over the countertop to confirm that the Honjo Masamune remained where I'd flung it, propped against the far wall of the kitchen. Too distant to reach, and my Jedi Force skills were sadly lacking at the moment. I didn't think it would spontaneously leap into my hand just because I willed it so.

That left the gun, but that was okay. I liked guns.

Mobo was on the move, evidently deciding that Nikki was down for the count. He headed toward the back of the kitchen, as if daring me to follow him.

"You would never have survived this visit," he gloated. "That Nigel didn't know it paints him as the fool. Alaina's Cups would not have let you live, not with your connection to the Council. The Pents are also no fools. They remain close enough to keep tabs, but lifetimes apart in position on mortal and immortal magic. They will never be servants to a greater power again."

"You think so highly of Alaina, why'd you kill her? Doesn't that go against some kind of code?" I inched along the counter as well, but Mobo seemed content to toy with me. I could hear him throwing down one pistol, doubtless pulling others free. And here I was with a gun and a sword I couldn't reach. Stupid.

"Because Aces really are wild cards," Mobo said. "And I've been dealt into an entirely different game. You think the Houses are no match for the Council, and you may be right. But there's a new player on the board now, and she will take no prisoners."

I grimaced. He could only mean Gamon. I crawled across an open space, and a bullet pinged at my left ankle, making me lurch to the side. Mobo's laughter rolled across the kitchen again. "She wants you alive, if I can manage it. The money's triple for that. But don't think it's for your conversation. She plans to harvest every last piece of you to build her army even stronger. And then, when she takes the Council apart, she will use their own precious pet against them."

My eyes flared wide. Mobo was right about one thing—I did have abilities. Abilities I might not know how to use, but they were there…dormant.

Dormant but within reach?

I focused on Soo's pendants against my collarbones, but had no idea how to direct them. And I couldn't go all fugue state and simply give myself over to the rage growing within me. Not with Nikki so close.

Nikki. I reached the edge of the counter where she lay sprawled, my heart pounding as I sought out her gaze. She stared at me out of a face coated with blood and smoke, but when our eyes met, she winked.

Her right hand appeared useless for the moment, her shoulder severely dislocated, but her left hand still clutched her Beretta. I hadn't even known she'd been carrying a second gun.

Relief surged through me, but I kept going, picking up my pace. "You ever wonder how much the Council would pay you not to slice and dice me?" I asked, playing to Mobo's avarice. "I can guarantee you it's more than Gamon would pay."

"Ah, but one betrayal is smart, two is bad for business," Mobo goaded back. "And Gamon's pockets are as deep as her reach is long. I will not betray her." He spoke the words a little too loudly, as if even the walls had ears, and I pulled myself into a crouch. I only had one shot at this. I needed to make it good.

"You have chosen the wrong ally after all, Mobo," I called out, deepening my voice by several octaves as I surged upward with an Academy Award-winning performance. I swirled my hands impressively in front of my chest as if I was massaging an air kickball, and Mobo halted the swing of his gun, his eyes riveted on me. "You have heard of the powers I have, and now you will—"

Two gunshots rang out simultaneously. It was as if Mobo's body had nowhere to go, a punching bag stuck between rival combatants. He fell backward and then thrust forward, his eyes still wide and startled even as twin bullet holes started gushing rivers of blood.

I turned to Nikki, crying out as she sagged forward.

"Scalp wounds always bleed like a bitch," she gasped, dropping her gun on the floor as she sagged to her knees…then rammed her shoulder against the edge of the counter. Her expletives rang out across the kitchen as her shoulder popped back into place.

"An excellent shot." Nigel stepped into the corridor behind Mobo's body, rolling him over. "I can't say I'm happy yours entered first, though. Mine was the better vantage point."

"Anything to shut up the great and powerful Oz here," Nikki cracked, her voice only a little thready. She winced as I pressed a towel to her face, wiping off the worst of the gore. "Was he really buying that?"

"He was buying something." Nigel's voice sounded a little strained, but I didn't have time for him yet.

"Are you hurt bad?" I asked her. "Can you walk?"

"Gut wound. Too close to the damn windows." Nikki winced as I pressed the towel against her side. Even Mercault's kitchen towels were luxury on steroids, and she scowled down at the blood staining the thick cloth. "You know that's never gonna come out. Might as well be mustard."

"Sara—"

"Hang on." I cut off whatever Nigel wanted to say, draping Nikki's arm over my head as I noticed a second patch of red. "Shit, Nikki, your leg?"

"That was all Mobo. Dickhead." She growled. "Missed hitting me full-on, though."

I grimaced, moving with her toward Nigel, who was looking at me like I'd grown two heads. "Luc? Is he dead too?"

"No. Mobo's bullet went wide, but Luc went down with a convincing thud, banking on the chaos to keep him out of the fray." He smiled wearily. "There's a reason why he's lived so long." Nigel seemed to shake himself into awareness and stepped forward, "Let me take her. I'm bigger than you are."

"Hey," groaned Nikki. "I'm sensitive."

But no sooner had Nigel settled her weight onto his shoulders than he turned to me. "Perhaps that might explain Mobo's surprise at your performance," he said quietly, nodding behind me.

Both Nikki and I turned, and while she said something, I couldn't hear it—couldn't process anything except what was right before us.

There, hovering above the kitchen counter, was the Honjo Masamune, twisting and spinning in place, exactly how I'd been guiding my imaginary kickball. It pointed at the space where Mobo had been standing, but as I breathed out a startled "Whoa," it flicked again toward me, the point of its mythical blade mesmerizing in its lethal beauty.

"I can kind of see how Mobo might have gotten distracted," Nikki said, her words barely audible. "Can you, uh, tell it to sit?"

"I have no idea." Swallowing, I took a step toward the blade and lifted my hand, exactly as if it were a wild creature I was somehow expected to tame. Before I embarrassed either of us, though, the blade suddenly clattered to the counter, inert.

"Good God," Nigel breathed. "When did it start doing that?"

"Pretty much right now." I hesitated, then picked up the blade, once more feeling the shock of its power in my grasp. The sword had championed me. And more importantly, it had kept Nikki alive, all without shedding a drop of blood.

Pretty good trick for a samurai sword.

I slid it into its scabbard at my hip, surprised at how natural the movement was. Maybe I could learn to wield the thing after all.

The courtyard was a mass of activity by the time we got outside. I folded Nikki into a Parisian version of a minivan that was about the size of a toaster, but she could almost lie straight. There were no emergency vehicles this far out, but the hospital in Amboise had a full surgical suite, according to Nigel. He sent three armed guards with Nikki and a car trailing behind. He watched the vehicle bounce off the lawn and onto the drive with a fierce scowl, and I liked him better for it.

Luc stood surveying the mess, then looked up as we approached. "Pretty clean job, it seems, for all of that," he said in his querulous French accent. "Didn't see Mobo turning so quickly, though. Alaina had her doubts." He spat. "Should have listened."

"And you should have kept me apprised of that." Nigel turned his sour glare on the bombed building. "Mercault isn't going to like it."

"He's got about six more châteaux in the valley. He'll survive." Luc lifted a hand and rubbed his chin, then transferred his gaze to me. "You've certainly made an impression."

"So Alaina was Cups, Mobo, Wands?" I asked, my mind split between the question and the image of Nikki's face, spread with blood and grime. "That leaves you what, Pentacles?"

"Or Coins, if you prefer to call a spade a…well." He shrugged. "Unlike Nigel and Mobo, I didn't split my allegiance between Houses. Gets messy when you do that. As you can see." He gestured to the mess. "Alaina was exclusively Cups, Mobo played in both Wands and Coins. Had to have, in order to plant those bombs, I'm thinking. They've been there awhile." His expression was bleak. "Mercault will have to spend more money securing anywhere that bastard went."

"Whoa, whoa, whoa..." What they were saying finally dawned on me, and I stared, rocked by the realization. "*Mercault* is the head of the House of Coins?"

Nigel and Luc stared at me, then Luc shot him a glance. "Not much gets by her, does it?"

Nigel lifted one shoulder. "It's a gift."

At that moment, a soldier trotted up, waving a familiar-looking cell phone. I swiped for my pocket out of habit, even as the man stopped in front of us. "It's been ringing constantly," he said with an apologetic smile as he handed it over.

"Thanks." I frowned as I scrolled through the calls, instantly worried about Nikki.

But it wasn't Nikki's name on the screen—it was Father Jerome's. Over and over again.

I clicked through to the voice mail, meeting Nigel's gaze.

Then started running.

Chapter Nineteen

We reached the outskirts of Paris in less than two hours, arriving at Jerome's secondary safe house well after the area had been cordoned off with police tape. I ducked under it, Nigel on my heels, ignoring the gendarmes as they tried to stop me first in French, then English.

"Sara! Sara—" I turned as a familiar voice called out, then Father Jerome was there, hastening forward with a dirt-stained face split by a wide, relieved smile. "You didn't have to come, I told you we are fine, I was simply worried—"

"Do you know anything more?" I stood back and surveyed him critically. As always, he wore the simple clothes of his position, black pants and black shirt with the white collar, no robe or cap to distinguish him further. He shook his head.

"There was simply the blast. The front windows were blown out, you see? We were away from the house by accident, actually. Wednesdays are usually quiet days, but the museum—" He held my hands, and his weren't the ones shaking. "No one was hurt, Sara. The children are safe."

"You'll have to move them."

"It's already done." Father Jerome looked up, noticing Nigel for the first time, his gaze pinging back and forth between us. "You've been hurt. You said there was a similar explosion, that your friend Nikki was injured. Others killed."

"Windows blown out there as well," Nigel said crisply. "If I may?" He gestured to the house, and I nodded, feeling slightly awkward at giving the man permission to do anything. He stopped briefly to show something to the police, who also nodded him on his way. No one had more fake identities than Nigel Friedman. Which made me wonder why he kept the name Nigel Friedman.

Father Jerome linked his arm in mine and steered me toward the gardens. "What is happening, Sara? What have you stumbled into?"

I forced my own breathing to steady. Father Jerome was unharmed; the children were safe. The bomb that had been set in this house hadn't been followed this time by a horde of Gamon's operatives—though it could have. Should have, really. The safe house didn't have a phalanx of guards around it. It didn't need to—it was supposed to be secure.

I tightened my jaw, the sudden image of a skull overrun by scouring beetles flashing in my mind. That was what Eshe's shield had shown me, what Gamon's operatives were capable of. That was the fight I was undertaking. Poorly, as it happened.

"How many of Gamon's children went through here, how long ago?" I asked, a new image of tattooed arms assaulting me. "Any one of them could have been the leak."

"Or a hundred other children in a hundred other places," Father Jerome said quietly. He lifted his hand to brush my cheek. "Your friend, she will be all right?"

"She will." I nodded too quickly. Nikki had been admitted for overnight observation, to her strident and outspoken dismay, and I'd spent most of the ride into Paris assuring her that Nigel wouldn't leave my side. She'd then asked to speak to him, and while I couldn't hear her side of the conversation, he seemed to be of a mind to agree with everything she said. "She got pretty banged up, worse than I thought, but—she'll be okay."

"And how banged up did *you* get, this time? How damaged will you be the next?" Jerome didn't continue with a tirade, contenting himself with patting my hand as we walked together beneath the trees. Then his words took a decidedly different turn. "The children have started to speak of you again. The gifted ones. They have a name for you."

I pulled away from him. "Is it a name you can repeat in public?"

"It's an interesting one," Jerome said. He released my right hand and it dropped to my side, my left still resting on my sword. Surprisingly, the gendarmes hadn't blinked when I'd come striding up with a thirteenth-century blade strapped to my body, but then again—this was France.

Jerome waited until my attention wandered back to him, smiling benevolently as I blushed. "You do not sleep enough for all the lives you live, Sara. You'll have to be more careful."

"I'm fine," I said, giving him my best healthy-and-happy grin. "Distracted is all. So—the children have given me a nickname?"

"Vigilance," he said, without preamble.

He kept speaking then, but the word blasted through me with a strength that shook me to my toes. In a single heartbeat, my mind exploded with a dozen different images—places I'd been, people I'd known—things I'd seen. I'd heard that name before, seen the image. A picture, high on the wall of a domed throne room, an image of a woman holding the scales in one hand and a sword in the other. So very similar to the Tarot depiction of Justice, but undeniably more forceful. Instead of being seated with a placid demeanor, the woman of Vigilance rushed forward, her sword outstretched, the scales as much a weapon as the sword...

The sword.

"Sara, what is it?" Jerome's voice broke in. "I didn't mean to alarm you. They meant it as a compliment—a compliment!" He was back to chafing my hands, and I blinked at him, trying to regain my balance.

"It's okay," I managed. "It's okay. I just—it took me by surprise. The name. I've heard it before, hunting items for the Council. It's some sort of older goddess, maybe a precursor to the Tarot, I don't know."

He pursed his lips, then turned to walk again, distracted by this new question. "I'm not familiar with a mythology that incorporates that imagery with that name, but as you say, there are any number of esoteric societies that sprang up during the Renaissance and even before. That one of them would have taken on the depictions..."

I let Father Jerome's words wash over me as I strode beside him, a thousand miles and several dimensions away. The denizens of Atlantis had reacted strongly to me when they'd seen me come storming out of the abandoned throne room, dagger and scales in my hands, my hair and eyes wild. They'd known me, recognized me, from a picture that had been painted thousands of years before Christ, etched into the stones of a lost civilization. Why were the children using that name to describe me now? Had they been given it by someone? Fed it by a scholar of the ancient city? Or were my gun and my perpetual state of darkness enough to bring the name to their minds organically? I grimaced. It could go either way.

Nigel stood on what was left of the front steps of the house when we circled back around. "Exactly the same configuration of device, remote detonation, not a timer. Someone knew to blow this second set at the same time the first set went off miles away."

My adrenaline jacked, and I turned to Jerome. "You're sure the other houses—"

"Not affected. I checked. We're having bomb teams come in to be sure. And there is nothing damaged here other than what you see." His lips turned down. "I suspect there is extensive damage to Mercault's château, however. What was its location again, specifically?"

He asked this last as my phone buzzed in my pocket, and I jerked it free from my hoodie, hoping for another of Nikki's rants. Instead, a different name flashed across the screen, and I smiled despite myself. One rant was as good as the next, I supposed. I hadn't planned on being out of town this long.

I swiped the phone on, then held it to my ear. "Sara," I said, bracing myself for Brody's explosion.

There was nothing on the line for a moment. Then a familiar rasping feminine voice filled up my whole world.

"I'm afraid Detective Rooks took an untoward step today, Sara Wilde, investigating a property you have no claim to."

I went stiff, only dimly aware that Nigel and Jerome kept walking. "Where is he?" I asked stupidly. "How do you have his phone?"

"It seems he's not the only friend of yours convalescing in a hospital," the voice continued. "You're becoming dangerous company to keep."

"If you hurt him…"

"The day you are a threat to me is a day I will relish," Gamon scoffed. "But it is not today. Stay out of a war you cannot hope to win. Give up your sword. Let others do the fighting while you lurk in the shadows. I have spared the foolish children you seem so intent on saving. Believe me, I've kept the ones I've found who are truly useful. And those you snatched from me before I could find them—life is long. I can afford to be patient. You cannot, however. Your every associate is at risk, from the lowest to the highest reaches, unless you let things flow to the fullness of their—"

I clicked off the phone. With every word, I was getting more convinced that Gamon was insane, but insane was tricky to manage, and I was full up on my allotment of crazy for the day. Hitting speed dial, I reconnected with Nikki, who picked up on the first ring.

"You're coming to get me," she said.

"You're still on a morphine drip."

"I'll take it to go. What's up, dollface? Hit me."

I filled her in on Brody, asking her to connect with anyone she could back home to find out what was happening to him—and to let the police know his phone had been swiped. Doubtless that meant Nikki would be contacting Dixie Quinn, Brody's current girlfriend, but she was the least of my problems. Nothing like being responsible for all your friends landing in the hospital to give you some perspective on what mattered.

I rang off to find Nigel and Jerome back to staring at me. "Gamon blew something else up," I said. "One of Soo's properties in Vegas. I get the feeling it might not be confined to there."

Nigel nodded, fishing his own phone out of his pocket. "I would've been advised if it was a widespread attack, but there may be more outlying events. We'll track it." With a curt nod, he moved off, leaving Jerome and me staring at each other again. With a start, I realized I hadn't asked about Max.

"No one was hurt?" I pressed him. "Not Max either?"

"Max?" Jerome looked at me with a bewildered smile. "Sara, I thought you knew. He went on vacation immediately after you left—to visit family, he said. I've been working him diligently for weeks, and before today, things had been going so well with the children. He has more than earned a respite. I don't expect him back for several more days." He reached for my hand and pulled me toward the back of the house. "He'll be fine, I suspect."

I let Jerome take me to a quiet courtyard, accepted his French wine and soothing talk, but I knew in my heart that Max wasn't relaxing somewhere with cousins in the south of France. He'd delivered me gift wrapped to Armaeus, and I'd fled within the half hour. But something had tipped Armaeus off to the changes going on inside me—both then and when he'd touched me in my dreams. And no one knew my abilities more clearly right now than Max Bertrand.

Which meant he could only be one place right now: spilling my every secret to Armaeus. Even those I didn't know I had.

I waited until Jerome was called away by the police before I settled back in my chair. Everything hurt on my body, most especially my heart. Nikki was in the hospital—Brody as well, if Gamon were to be believed. Everywhere I turned, someone was insisting I give up Soo's commission and relinquish control of the House of Swords.

But I also had an uptick in my Connected abilities that hadn't been on my radar screen before now. The burst of power that I'd thrust out to keep Armaeus away, that I'd used to keep myself and Ma-Singh alive, that I'd distracted Mobo with long enough for Nikki to plant a bullet in his skull. My odd connection with the Honjo sword—something else I hadn't been prepared for.

There was too much I didn't know, too much I needed to know. I needed to be able to combat the darkness that seemed to be rushing ever closer to me, threatening my friends, my people…

A darkness I had no idea how to fight.

And in the entire world, I had only one person I could truly turn to, one infernal teacher more than willing to teach me—if only I asked for his help.

I was asking for it now.

The barriers to my mind were thicker than I remembered them, knotted snarls of defiance that took longer than I expected to loosen. But when the first knot finally gave, he was there. The way he was always there, his assured arrogance palpable despite the distance between us.

"Miss Wilde," Armaeus said into my mind, his voice dripping with condescension. *"For what you truly want, I need you here. Here and ready to do all that I ask, exactly as I ask. Unless and until you tap the power you need to survive, you will not win this battle. Once or evermore."*

Chapter Twenty

It took another full day before Nikki's doctors consented for her to leave the hospital in Amboise, but I suspected that had more to do with the moony expression on the face of her head physician than any lingering complications of her injuries. She left with shopping bags full of French lingerie and a promise to return, sashaying out the front doors of the hospital in a jaw-dropping nurse costume that ended well north of her knees.

We kept the conversation light until we boarded the plane—this one sent by the Council, over Nigel's protestations. But at this point, I wasn't going to fool around with mortal protection schemes. The Council would get Nikki back to Vegas safely. What happened after that was a problem for a different day. And Nikki was taking full advantage of her pain medication, barely staying conscious until we strapped her into her seat.

We were cruising at twelve thousand feet when Nigel finally swung his chair to me. "You've avoided the question of your succession for too long. It will be waiting for you once we land."

"There's no real question," I said, absently drawing my finger over the hilt of the Honjo Masamune. "I'll go through the ceremony with whatever generals I need to convince, and one of them can fight over who wins. The houses, the money—I don't care about that." I pulled my hand away, resolutely ignoring the flare of heat along my fingertips. "The House needs someone who can run it—independently. And all the Houses need to feel secure. Not hiding in the shadows, afraid of the Council or Gamon or anyone else."

Nigel unbuckled his seat belt and stood. From her captain's chair, Nikki didn't lift a lash. I envied her medicated state.

"Come on, then," he said, extending a hand. "Your Council saw fit to give us an airplane wide enough to stage a rock concert. Let's see how we can orchestrate your sword fight with the generals so you don't do harm to yourself."

"Nigel, you don't need to practice with me." Still, I got up a little too quickly. I didn't want to embarrass myself in front of the generals, for all that I knew I would lose.

"Have you ever fought seriously with the blade?" he asked, shucking his jacket. His compact frame bristled with muscles.

Despite Nikki's drugged condition, I'd swear that she swiveled her seat slightly to get a better view.

"I try not to fight seriously, period." I pulled off my hoodie and slid the Honjo Masamune out of its scabbard. The sword glinted in the artificial light, so heartbreakingly beautiful, it made my soul ache. "What are you going to use?"

"I brought a practice sword." Nigel moved over to the side of the cabin and slid open a bin, unearthing a bundle of cloth. What he unwrapped was a sword surprisingly similar to mine in size and heft. "This is a Muramasa blade. It will cut you if I'm not careful. I get the impression that would not go over well with your employers, so I'll endeavor to be careful."

"Yeah, you'll endeavor not to be embarrassed, anyway." I held up the sword like a baseball bat, knowing it was wrong, but before Nigel could correct me, the sword dipped heavily in my grip, aligning itself to a more natural position.

Nigel lifted his brows. "Defend," he said and moved in toward me, slashing his blade in a vicious arc.

My arms moved with a jolt of energy I couldn't explain, thrusting up to meet his blade squarely so that his sword bounced back from mine. Nigel was taller than me, and stronger, but I met each of his attacks. Blocked every thrust. My arms and hands and core and legs moved in concert as if born to the art of sword fighting, and I shifted in perfect symmetry to combat the British operative, strike for strike.

At length, he directed me to attack, and I was more tentative. The blade never got close to nicking Nigel's skin or presenting him with a serious threat, even when he urged me to strike more actively. Time after time, I feinted away, artfully moving around him rather than cause him real danger.

"What are you doing?" he growled at length, and I held the blade up, pacing evenly to match his steps.

"Nigel, you're hysterical if you're thinking I'm doing any of this at all. The sword is not your enemy; therefore, I am not your enemy."

As soon as I spoke those words, I stopped, frozen in place. Nigel stopped as well. He straightened, and I followed his lead, lowering the Honjo Masamune. When he bowed, it was the most natural thing in the world for me to bow as well. We had come to an understanding, he and I. And an understanding of the sword I held.

"The honorable blade," he said, his eyes wide with surprise. Across the cabin, a now fully alert Nikki was leaning forward in her seat.

"Meaning what, exactly?" she barked. "It's a sword that won't cut anyone? Because news flash, that's not a super useful attribute when you're in the middle of a sword fight."

I held the blade out in front of me, and it gleamed in the soft cabin light, the dance of stones embedded in the base of the sword evoking the brilliance of the night sky. "It strikes down its enemy cleanly, or it doesn't kill at all," I said. "I read that somewhere. A samurai was attacked by a man wielding this blade. It cleaved his helmet in two—but didn't harm a hair on his head. The samurai eventually bested the guy who attacked him and took the sword. I thought that was weird at the time but didn't realize…" I shook my head. "I don't know how successful it was after that. I still can't believe its owners simply gave it away to some random American guy."

"Well, that's the story that was put out, certainly," Nigel said. He watched me as I moved the sword back and forth in the light. "But who's to know the truth? Perhaps the family who owned the sword wanted it kept far out of allied hands, while appearing to be following the path of the righteous. I wouldn't have thought to look for the blade in Angkor Wat, and I doubt many American servicemen were that familiar with the spot in the nineteen forties. It could have all been an elaborate ruse."

"I guess." I slid the sword back in its scabbard and rested my hand lightly on it. "Who among Soo's generals are Connected, do you know?"

"Haven't a clue," Nigel said. "They have a tendency to die before that becomes an issue." He laughed as my mouth turned down at the corners. "Relax. These men and women are not stupid. They will put forth as their champion the best of their number, and as we have proven here, you'll face that champion honorably. After that, the fate of the Honjo and the House will be in the hands of the best candidate. It is all you can do."

I nodded as the twin pendants of jade fired along my collarbone, one cold, one hot. I didn't know what Soo would think of any of this, but Soo wasn't here. She'd never told me of her plans for the House, or even that she'd led the House of Swords, until her dying breath. Had her reticence been purposeful?

I turned my gaze out the window, staring into the darkness beyond the airplane's wings. What truly had been Soo's thinking, to assign her House to me when there were so many better choices in her ranks? In doing so, she'd painted a target on my back—mine and those closest to me. Granted, she'd also stopped an immediate crisis among her generals, making them stop and assess her choice of their leader before discounting it out of hand, forcing them into the established protocol of succession. She had further denied Gamon a win of the highest order by not allowing her House to die with her.

So where was Soo now? Hopefully not roaming through Hell, with nothing but the shadows of her mother's bedchamber and my own lost spirit to guide her. Hopefully she was somewhere far beyond that desolate plane.

Hopefully.

We landed at McCarran International Airport before dawn, the lights of Sin City still shining despite the hour. I gazed at the bright towers of the Council, somehow feeling a million times older than I'd been when I'd left the city days earlier. My gaze roamed farther afield, toward Lake Las Vegas and the home Soo had built on its banks, safe within its surrounding trees and fountains, hidden from the harsh realities of the desert.

But there was no hiding for me anymore, I knew.

"You'll be safe?" Nigel asked, scowling as I helped Nikki into the back of a limo—one I would be driving for a change. The empty car had been waiting at the Jetway when we'd landed, and I'd felt strangely comforted by its presence.

"We'll be safe. We're getting Nikki some clothes—"

"And a shower. Trust me, this is a good thing," Nikki piped up, but I could hear the strain in her voice.

"Clothes and a shower. Then I'll be out to Soo's house. If you've got generals coming out your ears, cool them down. Try to figure out where else we've been hit, if we have, and where we might be hit next."

Nigel eyed me oddly, and I waved him off. "Go. And let me know if I should lie low. I could put off the Battle of the Bros for at least another decade, and happily."

He smiled, shaking his head. "You'll comport yourself honorably," he said. "You can count on the Honjo for that."

The Honjo was currently in the backseat with Nikki, keeping her as honorable as she was ever going to get. "Noted."

We watched him head off to wrangle with customs, but no one stopped us as we left the tarmac and headed into the city. "I always wondered what it'd feel like to sit alone in the backseat," Nikki said. "I'm not so much a fan."

I shifted my gaze to the rearview mirror. "Would it help if I wore a hat?"

She snorted. The trip to her condo was short, and as we turned into the development, I realized that in all the past several months of living in Vegas, I'd never once been here. Nikki had told me only briefly about her place—about a picture I should ask about, if I ever visited. But we hadn't had time. Nikki had been staying at the Palazzo, and I'd been traveling to Israel. But now, as I made tight turns down residential streets, it was almost surreal to imagine her living a life among these pink-and-white stucco tract houses, each more faceless than the last.

"Brody didn't say one of Soo's Vegas houses had been leveled, did he?" I asked out of the blue, stirring Nikki in the backseat.

She blinked at me beneath her Chicago PD ball cap, then shook her head. "Nah. It was the warehouse—the occupied one. Caused a bit of a stir, because apparently Soo was stockpiling guns there, always what you want to find out when you report up through Homeland Security. But he was mostly still pissed he hit the building thirty seconds before the bombs went off. Had he been a minute earlier, he'd have missed the blast site. A minute later, and he at least wouldn't have been knocked into the opposite wall."

I winced. "What does Dixie have to say?"

Nikki's laugh was wry. "She's about to fall apart with joy at having someone to fuss over. Brody better hope he stays injured on a regular basis, because that girl has found her calling."

I couldn't help but smile too as we made the final turn to her street, and I parked in front of the third house down and to the left. I stared at it. "You live in a duplex?"

"Hey, a little respect," Nikki protested. "We refer to it as a Gemini. Much classier that way."

"A twin." I got out of the car as Nikki unbent herself from the backseat, handing me the Honjo sword. "Yeah, I can see that."

The duplex—and it was a duplex—was small and nondescript, the exact opposite of anything that seemed appropriate for Nikki Dawes. But I kept my silence as she strode up the front walk, clearly still a little ginger as the stitches tugged in her thigh and hip. In deference to her injury, her heels were only three inches tall, but her freshly painted toes stuck out proudly from her gladiator sandals. French manicured, of course.

"In we go," Nikki said, and if she was self-conscious about opening her home to me, she didn't show it.

Inside, I swept the room with a quick gaze, again struck by the ordinariness of it all. The main living area was done over in IKEA and knockoff Pottery Barn, cool and neutral to combat the infernal heat outside. The carpet was springy beneath my feet, and the walls were painted a buttery taupe.

"You don't have a cat or anything I need to guard against, right?" I asked, and Nikki chortled, throwing her bag on the couch and checking the stack of mail on the end table.

"That would be negative. Dottie next door brings in my mail and makes sure my plants are watered. I don't have the heart to tell her they're plastic." She grinned at me and pointed to a picture of her with a septuagenarian wearing huge cat-eye sunglasses and grinning ear to ear. "She reminds me of my grandma who pretty much raised me, south side of Chicago. They both would do anything for a laugh."

Nikki entered the kitchen, and I followed helplessly behind, amazed at the number of photographs on her walls. Most of them were from Vegas—Nikki posing with burlesque dancers and sequin-covered singers, magicians, and fortune tellers, all of them looking happy to be alive. There were a few pictures from her childhood, her family apparently a big fan of the 90s plaid revolution and boot-cut jeans, but none of her parents. On the refrigerator was a picture of a woman with on-purpose blue hair, a grinning childhood Nikki beside her staring with wide eyes.

"Gram Betty," Nikki said, tapping the photo. "She dyed her hair that color the summer I moved in with her for good, my parents having long since given up on me."

"The summer you…" I squinted at the picture. "You look all of twelve."

She shrugged, an ocean full of water sliding under a bridge somewhere. "I was a trying child. But Gram Betty never minded. She called it the way it was, at a time when being different wasn't always a good place to be. And she protected me until her dying breath."

I swallowed past the lump in my throat. "How long ago was that?"

"Long time." Nikki's smile was far away. "The year I got married." She shook my head as I gaped at her. "I know, right? All that drama."

She turned and headed out of the kitchen again, her voice floating back to me as I stepped into the narrow hallway. "I need stuff for—what, a couple of days?"

"Maybe longer," I managed, trailing behind her. The longer I stayed in this home, the more I realized it actually did fit Nikki, or at least a part of her I'd never glimpsed before. More pictures lined the wall to her bedroom/office, and I blinked at the narrow bed and enormous desk, crammed with enough electronics to make Brody blush.

"You like keeping up with the news, I see."

She grinned at the collection of monitors and scanners, reaching over to turn one of the dials. "White noise. Keeps me company. I'll just be a jiff."

My gaze raked the desktop as she busied herself in her closet—which was actually the entire second bedroom. But what I wanted to see was in plain sight on the edge of her desk. A picture of a tall, proud Nikki, not a curve to her frame—dressed in a police officer's uniform. The face was more angular, the hair nowhere near fabulous, but the eyes were hers. The smile was hers.

And so were the three children with her, two of them grabbing her legs, and one, the smallest, hanging from her neck. She'd told me about this picture, told me to ask about it, but I couldn't think of anything but how beautiful and alive these small souls seemed to be, even in a fading picture.

"They're perfect, aren't they?" I didn't put the frame down as Nikki came up behind me, and it was her hand on my shoulder, comforting me, when it should have been the other way around. "Three beautiful babies that I'd do anything for. I told you, remember? To ask me about them."

She glanced at me and I nodded, not trusting myself to speak.

"Yeah," she said softly. "Eventually, I couldn't be what they needed me to be. So I became what I had to be for myself. When they're ready, if they're ever ready, they'll find me again. And I'll be waiting for them when they do."

She stopped and took the picture frame out of my trembling hands, her voice gentle with concern. "Aww, it's okay, sweetie," she murmured, turning me toward her. "It's okay."

I buried myself in her embrace and cried tears I didn't know I had in me.

Chapter Twenty-One

By the time we reached Soo's house in the brushy foothills of the Lake Las Vegas area, it was clear the cavalry had been summoned. A dozen rental SUVs lined the expansive parking deck, each bigger and burlier than the last.

"I'd make a joke about overcompensating, but it's too easy," Nikki drawled. She was back in her customary seat in the front of the vehicle. I sat beside her, my nerves too jacked for playing our usual roles. She apparently felt something of my nerves too. Rather than her usual eye-popping ensemble, Nikki's hair was once more tucked beneath her CPD ball cap, her uniform positively staid—a gray technical T-shirt and deep charcoal cargo pants, with reinforced gray Chucks beneath. She looked like she was ready to rumble.

"Nigel hopefully has filled them in. I don't want this to be a big deal," I said. My hand rested protectively on the sword across my lap. I'd switched out my hoodie and jeans for the thick tights I employed on night raids, and a technical T-shirt that allowed movement, also in black. So much easier to hide the blood that way. Otherwise, it was me, my sneakers, and the Honjo Masamune, against the arrayed ranks of Soo's best warriors.

I gave myself about even odds.

"You're going to be great," Nikki said, parking the vehicle. Instead of exiting immediately, though, she put her long, Miss Kitty-manicured fingers on the steering wheel and stared straight ahead at the mansion for a long moment before turning to me.

"And when you are great, and you find yourself wondering if you could ever do this thing, be this person, I want you to know this. You can. You may not have all the answers yet. You may not understand fully the ramifications of the job. You may be years away from being able to handle it well—but you can handle it. And no matter what you choose to do, whether it's running your sword down the center of Soo's generals or using it to draw a line in the sand between you and the Council, I'm here for you. I'll fight in front of you as long as you need me to, beside you as long as we can, and behind you until I can no longer stand."

My trembling hand reached out and closed over one of her great big ones, and I let it sit there for a few moments before I squeezed. Once more I couldn't speak, my throat too tight around the lump wedged in it.

"There. That about covers it." Nikki slapped the wheel, her eyes bright. Then she got out of the car.

It took me a moment longer to compose myself, but by the time my feet hit the sizzling-hot pavement of Soo's luxurious desert mansion, calm draped over me like a ceremonial cloak. I followed Nikki, fixing my gaze on her broad back until she reached the door. There she stood aside and opened it, grinning at me.

"Go get 'em, cowgirl," she whispered, and I managed a smile back.

My triumphal entry was marred by a workman exiting the building, followed by Jiao.

"Apologies, Madam Wilde," Jiao said, bowing to me. Her serene manner shifted slightly to a scowl at the worker. "He should have been completed hours ago."

"He..." I frowned at the man, then stiffened as he turned his capped head toward me. Beneath the crisp tan uniform with a patch of an HVAC business whose name I forgot even as I saw it, stood Simon the Fool, grinning like a twelve-year-old. I stared at him. "You had work here?"

"Checking the systems, ma'am. We had reports of damage to the coils in your main AC unit, and as hot as it gets out here, you don't want to mess with that. The company wanted to make sure we checked everything was safe before things got out of hand. They worry."

I blinked at him, hearing the layered message in his words. What was going on? "And what did you find?"

"Monitors were acting up, but we've got the right eyes in place now. You should stay cool for the duration."

He tipped his cap again and Jiao shooed him outside, leaving Nikki and me frowning after him.

"He bugged the place?" Nikki asked under her breath.

"Who knows what he did," I muttered. "But no hanging your bra on the camera unless you want to get called on it later. I have a feeling we're going to have a live studio audience for whatever is happening in here."

"Roger that." We moved inside the foyer and waited for Jiao.

Jiao returned seconds later, her heels clicking on the gleaming blue tile. "The generals are assembled in the fight center. I'll brief you as we go," she said.

Nikki and I fell into step behind her, and I mouthed *Fight center?* to Nikki, who gave me a broad wink.

The Honjo weighed heavily at my side, a welcome pressure against my hip, and I dropped my left hand to it, more for my own reassurance than because I was worried it would slip out of its scabbard. Technically, it wasn't a scabbard, but a *saya,* I'd learned from Google. I didn't need to know the language of the blade, but it made me smile anyway to recall the term.

"There were no casualties from the assault on the Tallawanda warehouse," Jiao said crisply, my attention returning to her. "It's our only semi-manned warehouse in the city, and that day it was free of employees. Detective Rooks's timing was—unfortunate. We don't know if anyone entering any of the unprotected locations would have tripped them, or if Gamon set them off on a predetermined schedule."

"Good that it wasn't worse."

Jiao glanced over her shoulder. "It's odd, though. Typically, for maximum effect, Gamon prefers an audience and collateral damage."

"Brody's still in the hospital?"

"Convalescing in private care," Jiao corrected.

Nikki's eyes rounded as she turned and matched my grin. I didn't want to imagine what Dixie Quinn's version of private care consisted of.

"We've settled the disputes with local authorities about the contents of the warehouse," Jiao said, continuing her briefing. "There had been no activity in or out of the building in over a year, as corroborated by their own surveillance cameras placed by the city when Soo purchased the building. So the weapons were legal, for all that they continue to be a concern. We'll be transporting them out of the city at the LVMPD request, or we may simply donate them. The decision is one of many to be made after today."

After whatever happened in the fight center, she meant. "What about other locations?"

"They've been swept with bomb squads, but there appear to be no other breaches." Jiao flashed me a serene smile. "You understand, we do not often advertise the location of Soo's holdings. So our exposure is limited."

"No other member homes have been struck? Warriors for the House of Swords?" So many people in this House. Families who depended on strong leadership and a steady sword.

Jiao's smile turned more speculative. "No. The only disruption to the network of Soo's personnel was the one you orchestrated earlier this week. It created more traffic in our communication channels than we've experienced in a year...and it's been a very busy year. So thank you for that."

I winced. "I didn't intend—"

"No." Jiao stopped and placed a hand on my arm. "I mean that in all sincerity. Thank you. The true call to arms for the House of Swords has been long in coming. For years it's been too heavily draped in ceremonial trappings, as the work of the samurai became at the end of its long run."

"I thought they were still going strong," Nikki said.

Jiao shook her head. "The ancient Chinese practice of warrior philosophers also died a slow death as the vaunted warrior life became the province of peasants and not those seeking the greater way. In every society on every continent, there has been the divide between warrior mystic and base killer."

"Now that I can understand," Nikki smiled wryly.

Jiao shifted her gaze to me. "Your appearance in the homes of two schools of practice, an ocean apart on the same night, went further than you can imagine to stir the spiritual energy of the House members. With energy flows fervency, and with fervency, we can mobilize if and how we need to." She bowed. "We are already in your debt."

She turned again and moved forward. Nikki bumped my elbow with hers and winked at me. The three of us arrived all too quickly at the familiar door deep inside Soo's fortress. Jiao's serene smile had returned to her face, but her eyes were alight with interest, her expression rapt.

"You will fight honorably, Sara Wilde," Jiao said, straightening my shirt like a pageant mother. "Of that I am certain."

She pushed the door wide and motioned Nikki to precede me. Her shoulders back, Nikki stepped into the room like she owned it, her body language shifting only slightly as she came into contact with the springy, rubberized floor. Watching her almost telegraph "bouncy house" aloud in her adjusted step resulted in my reluctant smile as I crossed the threshold as well.

But the men and women on the other side of the room were not smiling. My hand tightened on the Honjo, thumb at the ready to kick against the base of the hilt and free the blade.

There were nine generals, including Ma-Singh, standing tall in his black uniform. General Som stood near the back of the group. All the generals wore black, the sole nod to their ranks the stylized helmets placed carefully beside them. They all wore kendo swords similar to mine, and no apparent other blades. Their legs and arms were padded, but I hadn't had time to hit up Amazon for "modern samurai fashion." What I had would have to do.

The diversity of the House of Swords was readily apparent in the assembled generals. The two women were split—one looking strikingly like Alaina, though much taller, and then, of course, General Som. The men ranged from the Mongolian Ma-Singh to a crop-cut American or Western European, to three more men of decided Asian appearance. We stared at each other a long moment, then I stopped. I was nearly halfway across the room, but they had not moved.

Nigel was there, but his role in this exposition was clearly one of spectator. He nodded to me as my gaze swept over him and the people beside him. The room had become a gallery with men and women three rows deep—far more than I would have expected given the number of cars outside. These were not the injured souls of Soo's ranks either. These were silent and intense men and women, unspeaking, unsmiling.

So, okay. This fight was a big deal. I got it.

Jiao stepped forward, her soft voice cutting through the silence. "The generals have elected Ma-Singh to do battle against Sara Wilde, for the right to rule the House of Swords, to lead its warriors and defend against usurpers."

Ma-Singh? I flicked my gaze to the warrior even as he stared at me with fierce pride, and tried to remember how many days it had been since the shootout in the Vegas lot. Surely he couldn't be ready to lift a sword, I don't care how cauterized his wounds had been. The man had been Swiss cheese.

He apparently agreed.

"I relinquish my right to lead the House," Ma-Singh said. He widened his stance, his left hand on his own sword's hilt. "I serve Soo's true successor."

No one seemed surprised by this, but I found Nikki's gaze in the crowd, and she shrugged, clearly sharing my WTF for the smoke and mirrors.

Jiao bowed to Ma-Singh, then straightened. "In second succession, the generals have elected General Som to do battle against Sara Wilde, for the right to rule the House of Swords, to lead its warriors and defend against usurpers."

If I'd thought General Som and I could settle the dispute over a handshake and a game of Words with Friends, I was mistaken. She strode forward, the most samurai looking of everyone, despite her gender. Her face was set into fierce lines, her snarl heartfelt. Her black hair was now wrenched into a topknot at her crown, and as she took up her stance opposite me, I knew she would not go quietly into the night.

It suddenly occurred to me: I should have watched more YouTube videos.

Jiao said something, but I couldn't take my eyes off General Som. Her glare consumed my whole world. She didn't blink, but I had the curious sensation of her mind momentarily laid open to me, as if I reached inside her to the place of anger and ferocity and drew from it what I needed to know.

At Jiao's next musical command, I kicked my sword out another inch with my thumb, then reached for it, withdrawing it smoothly with my right hand. I brought the sword around at the same time General Som brought hers, but her motion didn't stop. She lifted her sword high and brought it down at me, aiming for my head—yet her gaze never seemed to leave mine. It was as if she'd sent me an instruction guide when I was six years old, and all these years later, I was reacting the way I'd been taught for decades.

In a sweeping arc of the Honjo Masamune, I countered General Som's blade. The abrupt, resounding clang echoed off the walls, but we didn't stop fighting, didn't stop moving. Instead, we danced. I met her thrust for thrust, never attacking, always defending—but I *could* defend, it seemed. Or, more precisely, the sword in my hands could. It seemed larger than life in my loose grasp, twisting and leading me so that all I truly needed to do was hold on.

This was what the fight instructor Kunh Lee had told me in this very room. That I wouldn't be a fighter, I'd be a messenger of spirit. And the Honjo Masamune was making a great noise.

Then my concentration slipped, and General Som's blade snapped into the breach, catching the flaring edge of my collar and nicking the skin of my neck before I could duck away in time.

What happened next I couldn't fully process. The slice was not a killing blow—General Som pulled back with the smoothness of long years of training. I, however, spun away and kept going, my feet bringing me back around in a movement that had me leaving the forgiving floor of the fight center and leaping up, whirling through the air in a *Crouching Tiger, Hidden Dragon* move for the ages, my left elbow out with my hand cocked, my sword arm arced high.

I fell on General Som fast enough that she was taken by surprise, and knocked her backward as my sword arced down. It didn't cut her—it could have, but it didn't. Instead, it passed harmlessly in front of her face as I was brought round yet again, following its arc, until once more I stood on the rubberized floor, my stance wide and both hands wrapped around the hilt of the Honjo Masamune, poised for a killing blow.

General Som stood, gaping at me, her blade down and to the side. For a second time, I could have killed her, or at least drawn blood. I didn't.

I was not a warrior here. I was a messenger.

"You have been judged by the Honjo Masamune," I said into the shocked silence. "You are a worthy leader for the House of Swords."

I tried to move a step, but it was General Som who shifted, stepping back and bowing to me, offering me her sword, though I clearly had my hands full.

"I relinquish my right to lead the House of Swords," she said, her voice ringing out. "I serve Soo's true successor."

Chapter Twenty-Two

Two more of Soo's generals stepped forward to do battle with me. They each started out with snarls and growls, but toward the end, it seemed like they were doing it more for the opportunity to fight the sword, not so much me. In each case, one defining attack of the Honjo Masamune stopped the fight, resulting in wide, knowing eyes and an assertion of following Soo's true successor. By the end of the session, I had several slash marks to my arms and torso and one impressive one along my thigh.

Importantly, none of Soo's generals had so much as a scratch on their bodies. Anywhere. I hadn't even managed to give one of them a hangnail.

Which was why their goodwill seemed problematic. Jiao stood in front of me now, her face serene, her manner beatific. Something was definitely not right.

"What am I missing here?" I asked between my teeth.

She looked over at Ma-Singh, who apparently, as first elected general, still carried weight with the group as their unofficial leader. His hand was cupped to his ear, apparently to trigger an earpiece I hadn't noticed before. He nodded to Jiao, then to me. "We have confirmation," he said, his voice slightly strangled. "The witnesses are talking."

Jiao pursed her lips, then spoke. "We have arranged for audio of the battles taken place here today to be transmitted to House members worldwide. You understand, we did not wish to allow video—"

"No." Ma-Singh kept talking, his words stronger now but no less stressed. "The witnesses received audio feed through their computers, yes. But there was visual feed as well—in the sky, on the walls. The ceilings." Ma-Singh waved his hand, turning his startled gaze to me.

I grimaced, my mind jumping immediately to Simon. The Council clearly hadn't had any concern that I would embarrass myself on international channels. "And—is that good?"

"It simply is," Jiao said, bowing slightly. "Those who would question you have been answered. You are worthy." She turned to Ma-Singh. "What is the count of external claimants to the House?"

"Before today, five different warriors attempted to attack our generals and claim the right to lead the House of Swords," he said. "Three challenged General Som alone."

The feral woman smiled, and I forced myself not to take a step back. General Som was one scary general.

"My size is their undoing," Som said. "My size and their arrogance. It makes a powerful combination, but only for me."

Jiao continued. "There are rumors of another warrior, though, one who will only fight Soo's true successor."

I lifted my brows. "Gee, I wonder where that phrase came from. And you mean Gamon?"

"A lieutenant of Gamon's, certainly." Jiao nodded. "One we have heard rumors of for years—ambushing our people, delivering them to Gamon's foul cells. We have never been able to discover the warrior's identity, though. Now we can."

"O...kay." I frowned. "Except I'm not the best swordsman here. Any one of the generals can fight with the Honjo Masamune and have far better results than I could."

It was Ma-Singh who responded, not Jiao. "The usurper would have gone unsatisfied if there was anyone less than Soo's named successor who wielded the sword for the final battle."

Usurper. I grimaced. I couldn't seem to get away from that word.

Ma-Singh continued. "Though we need to draw out the warrior, we could not send you into battle if you were not prepared. The ceremony of succession is not yet finished, but our pledge holds. We serve Soo's true successor. That is you."

"Yeah, well, after me, it's you," I said, staring at him. "I don't think I'll much care who you tag after that."

"Yo, Sara." Nikki was staring at her phone. I turned, and she lifted it to me. "Simon texted his congratulations. And, ah...an invitation."

"Nikki, I don't really have time—"

"No, I think you're going to want to take this one," she said, eyeing her phone and then me again. "You've been called to speak to the Council. As, um, the Head of the House of Swords."

Beside me, Ma-Singh and Jiao stiffened. "Madam Soo refused to be summoned like a dog," Jiao said mildly, but there was no questioning the steel underlying her words. "To go now is to set a dangerous precedent."

"Yeah, well," Nikki cut in before I could respond, "she's not the only one. The head of the House of Pents is already there, according to Simon. He looks forward to meeting you too."

I blinked, my gaze going first to Jiao, then to Nigel. Both of them registered patent shock. "Any precedent for that?" I asked casually.

"The Houses have not worked together in more than five hundred years," Ma-Singh said. There was no denying the undertone of reverence in his voice, his attitude shifting exactly that fast. "That you are already bringing two together…"

"Let's not get ahead of ourselves—"

It was too late, though. Jiao was already turning, issuing orders in crisp Chinese, then English for an armored escort, alerts to the House warriors, pleas to the generals to stay close and stay alert. Even General Som watched me with grim satisfaction, the closest I suspected she ever got to a smile.

Before I could protest, I was handed a change of clothing that looked like an exact replica of my usual jeans-and-hoodie combo, and ushered into a sumptuous bedroom to change. Minutes later, I was out of the house and into one of the House's armored SUVs, bouncing out of the compound. I sat with the Honjo resting on my lap, and Nikki watched me from opposite the large, open space.

"I never understood how people liked to ride backward in these things," she said, scanning the scenery as it flowed by in reverse. "I'd flat-out refuse if I was drunk."

I smiled, my face seeming unused to the expression after the bizarre events of the morning. Nikki had also changed, and was now dressed to impress in a jet-black sheath with silver-heeled platform pumps and enough jewelry to rival the High Priestess. I wondered who'd picked out her ensemble. My bet was on Nigel.

When we reached the Luxe's faux Egyptian kitsch palace, though, we weren't the first ones at the party. Monsieur Mercault's opulent white Rolls-Royce sat idling in the valet parking area as we pulled up. When Nikki popped the door of the SUV and stepped down, that seemed to be the cue for the Frenchman's vehicle as well.

I watched a driver exit the vehicle and hustle around to the side, and as I stepped into the Vegas heat, so did Mercault. The Frenchman was short, elegantly dressed in a suit that cost more than my monthly rent at the Palazzo, and smiling from ear to ear.

I'd done work for Mercault in the past, and we'd survived some sticky situations together. I was happier than I'd expected to see him again.

"You destroyed my château!" he exclaimed, striding toward me with his arms outstretched. "It was my mother's."

I winced. "I'm sure we can find a way to—"

"You misunderstand." He leaned forward and bussed both of my cheeks in the accepted European fashion, while I gritted my teeth and scrunched up my face in the accepted American fashion. "I have never liked my mother. I could not be more delighted."

He stood back, eyeing me with keen interest. "And now you have taken the place of Annika Soo. I can only hope that this will mean the House of Swords will stop stealing from me."

"Right after you shut down your smuggling operation in Namibia, I'm sure we'll take that under advisement," I said wryly.

"Mon Dieu!" His expression turned to one of shocked dismay, even as he held out an arm to escort me inside. "So young to be cynical. It is a sad day for both our Houses."

We entered the Luxor, and as usual, I had the disturbing moment of seeing the two realities converge—the gold glitz and outsized glamour of the Vegas casino that everyone could see, and the platinum-and-onyx sophistication of the Prime Luxe overlay, the Magician's domain that was visible only to Connected eyes…and to those Armaeus allowed to see it.

Mercault stood back, watching me. Sudden realization hit. "When did you tell them you were the head of the House of Coins?" I asked. "I would swear Armaeus didn't know."

"He didn't, until that ass Luc Banon allowed the right words to be spoken where the Magician could hear them. The House structure is one of the few bits of mortal magic the Council cannot break. But humans are the weak link, you see? They have been so over the centuries. That's how awareness of the Houses surface, and it takes some time for us to drift back into obscurity again." He shrugged, eyeing me keenly as I bypassed the Luxor elevator keypad for one that wasn't completely visible to the ordinary eye.

"I see it there—barely," he said, his voice bemused. "How many times I've been in that infernal Bellagio lobby and looked, but never once could I pinpoint the location, though I knew there was something there. But here…" He eyed me. "It's you, of course. It has to be.

You should come to the Bellagio and show me so I don't go mad."

I grinned, despite feeling like I'd been summoned to the principal's office.

We stepped into the elevator, the four of us—Nikki and Mercault's bodyguard staring each other down. Nikki's Glock was in her Kate Spade bag, and her Hello Kitty nail polish gleamed in the bright lights of the elevator as we shot up far beyond the tip of the Luxor's pyramid.

"While we're at it, you know why we've been called up?" Mercault asked. "I don't mind—I can only count my money for so long each day, eh? But I find the Magician endlessly perplexing. He's spoken to me twice in the last week as if I'm some kind of low-rent waiter, yet today he sends an engraved invitation. It's perplexing."

"He enjoys perplexing people," I said. "And I have no idea. Be prepared to have your mind searched, though."

Mercault lifted a finger—but not his index finger. A nondescript ring set with jade circled his ring finger on his right hand, almost austere. "Again, you forget the power of leading a House. The protection we've been accorded has lasted for millennia. If the Magician had any dominion over me, he would already have exercised it."

My eyes widened, but I was truly impressed. "That's way better than a secret decoder ring."

Nikki's barked laugh rang through the foyer of the Council conference chambers as the doors slid open. Mercault gestured to me to take the lead.

"Sissy," I muttered, but his grin was his only response.

How many times had I entered the inner domain of the Council? It had to be dozens at this point, but today felt different—*was* different, I knew. And not simply because of the sword bumping at my hip, though that was, admittedly a comforting solidity as I walked into the room.

Armaeus stood at the head of the table, practically crackling with energy. The Devil stood beside him. They both turned toward me as I entered, then transferred their gazes to Mercault, who was seeing all this for the first time.

It was something to see.

Eshe and the Emperor sat at the near end of the table, as far away from Kreios and Armaeus as they could reasonably get. Armaeus looked devastating in a perfectly cut black suit with a brilliant white shirt open at the collar, portraying immortal chic down to his platinum cuff links. The Fool and the Hierophant sat at the midpoint of the table, both of them seeming far too entertained. I knew the Hermit would be a no-show, but that didn't account for everyone currently claiming a Council position.

"Where's Death?" I asked. "Or did she give this session a pass?"

"Says it's not her time. I think she doesn't like meetings." Simon stood and walked toward me, his grin echoed in the bounce of his step. "You were *awesome*."

"And you projected me all over Christendom and a few places off the Holy Grid as well." I shifted my attention to Armaeus. "Why?"

The Magician's expression remained unreadable. "Since you insisted on taking the mantle of the House of Swords, if you won, we stood to gain. If you lost, your successor would have been identified and we still stood to gain. Global observation was a simple decision."

I wasn't buying Armaeus's nonchalance, but he had a part to play today. I let it slide. Beside me, Mercault sighed loudly, staring at Eshe. I glanced at him, then rolled my eyes. Not this again.

"Sacredieu," he murmured, stepping forward toward her.

Eshe seemed to notice him in that moment, the Kardashian of the Council ready for her close-up. She turned her head and nodded.

"Another House leader," the High Priestess said with what sounded like grudging admiration. "You've been busy, Armaeus. That's two more than we've known in the past five hundred years."

"Before you ask, we don't know the others," I said flatly. I realized I had set my feet wide, as if I was going to whip out the Honjo Masamune at a moment's notice. I tried to adjust my stance but couldn't. Every nerve was on edge.

"What's the real reason you brought us here?" I asked, ready for anything.

Armaeus quirked his beautiful lips into a smirk. "Gamon has allied herself with SANCTUS."

Okay, I wasn't prepared for that. "I thought SANCTUS was dead in the water."

Armaeus lifted a brow. "In a manner of speaking, they were, but understand the ancient ritual here. As a religious organization dedicated to stamping out magic, SANCTUS purports to be the messengers of the one true deity, the Judeo-Christian God. Though Gamon's methods are significantly more arcane than any Jewish lore would accept, there is common ground there with her history. She could make a convincing argument to gain their trust. She apparently has done so. In return, SANCTUS has opened up its treasury, giving her access to its most arcane artifacts, many items of which they do not know the value. She does."

He turned his attention to me. "In the immediate term, there is little action in the open, but much going on behind the scenes. Accordingly, to preserve the balance, it's imperative for us to identify the other two houses so that we can help build mortal defenses."

"Mortal?" Mercault had regained his senses enough to display some Gallic outrage. "Don't you mean immortal? It seems you're awfully concerned—"

"You misunderstand our role here." Armaeus cut him off. "The purpose of the Council has always been—since its inception—the preservation and balance of magic. Both sides of that coin. Even when we have disagreed." His glare shot to the Emperor, who watched him with distaste marred by his clear fascination with the proceedings. "Especially when we have disagreed, we have known that there is no balance in nothing. There must be magic to balance, or there will be a vacuum that will be filled with something else."

"But Gamon is magic," I protested. "She's Connected."

"She is Connected, yes, but her allegiances go far deeper. SANCTUS believes she will eradicate magic in the world, and she will. At that point, they believe, their mission is achieved. But they are not seeing what lies beyond that victory. We can." He gestured to Eshe.

The High Priestess preened in the spotlight of our attention. "The veil between worlds will fall from the weight of too much external pressure. All who exist outside the barriers of this earth will be granted access."

My guts clenched. I'd seen what lay on the other side. Fought with it. Still had the scars.

"The djinn." Eshe smiled at Viktor. "They will return in droves. The ancient gods will hold sway. Llyr will even break his fiery bonds, returning to earth in whatever form he chooses."

I stared at her, then at Armaeus. "All that because SANCTUS gave Gamon access to the cookie jar?"

"All that because she will gain access to the Houses," Armaeus corrected with a lash to his tone. "Her lieutenant even now prepares to fight Soo's successor. As of today, that seems to be you."

"But that's only one House," I objected.

"Mercault has now betrayed his alliance with you as well—if one of you falls, the other will too," Eshe cooed.

"Alliance?" I snorted. "He's stealing me blind!"

"He won't continue." Eshe smiled at Mercault. "Sorry."

Mercault seemed to be paying no attention to anything but Eshe's face. "Sacredieu," he murmured again.

"The truth is clear," Armaeus said. "Before, our goal was to keep you out of the House of Swords, Miss Wilde. Now, for the moment, you must not only stay, it appears you must defeat all comers."

He met my gaze over the length of the room, and it didn't take Connected abilities to understand what he was thinking. For me to win, it would not be a battle fought solely with the sword…but with the magic that was growing inside me like an angry beast, desperate to break free.

And he was my only hope of controlling it.

Chapter Twenty-Three

The Council meeting shifted immediately to Mercault as I physically stood back, absorbing the blow that Armaeus had dealt me.

"The House of Coins has been in the hands of your family for how long, Monsieur Mercault?" the Magician asked sharply.

Mercault immediately bristled, dropping his hands to his belt. "I don't see how that matters."

Kreios stepped into the breach. "I think we can go about this a different way. First, some introductions, to allow Monsieur Mercault to feel more at home. The Magician you know, of course. And we have met many times, though you've not always known it."

Mercault narrowed his eyes but was distracted as Kreios gestured lazily to Eshe, who was still attempting not to be blatantly flattered by Mercault's obvious adoration. "You have already exchanged words with Eshe, but she is the High Priestess of the Council. She has served as our oracle and guide for—long enough to prove the value of her counsel several times over." Kreios's indolent smile only deepened as Eshe shifted murderous eyes at him. Apparently, even immortals didn't like to be reminded of their age.

"Viktor Dal is the Emperor, and one of the most cunning minds on the Council. His strategic vision is one I think you will appreciate, given your own far-flung enterprises."

Unlike Eshe, Viktor did not appear to be mollified by Mercault's attention. He did bark a few questions at the man, asking mostly about his genealogy, which made sense given his Eastern European upbringing and the fact that he'd lived through the First World War. Mercault didn't know that of course, but he would if he hung around Viktor enough. The Emperor had been…if not in league with the Nazis, then definitely in mutually beneficial collusion with them. Reason number four thousand and sixteen I detested him.

Kreios moved on before Dal turned my way, and I gave him my profile as the Devil introduced Simon. "The Fool is a technological master and can be relied upon for the most innovative of solutions, if not always the most practical ones."

Simon grinned. "You're going to want to get a new phone after you leave here," he said, tapping his computer. "It's been bugged. Not a very good job either. My bet is someone in your operation, if only to keep tabs on you."

Mercault reached for the device, squinting at it. "What do you mean?"

"The bug's got no audio," Simon said. "Which means the tracking is intended only to LoJack you, but it's more souped up than a typical tracker and doesn't rely on the phone being on or within cell range. Plastic disk, no larger than a pinhead. Not fancy but effective." He flashed a grin. "Maybe it's nothing. Maybe someone is worried about you, doesn't want you to go paws up without anyone noticing. If that's cool, then cool. If not—"

"No one plants tracers on me without my knowledge." Mercault scowled. He turned back to his goon, who stared at him with deceptive impassivity. Nikki, on the man's other side, watched with a smile playing around her face. She saw what the man saw. Her eyes connected with mine, and I nodded.

"I'd start with your girlfriend," Nikki said, and her grin widened as Mercault's attention whipped to her. His guard, meanwhile, stiffened only a hair's breadth, not even noticeable unless you were looking at him, which I was. "Your man here doesn't trust her farther than he can throw her, and my hunch is he's on target."

Mercault's eyes widened, first at Nikki, then at his own man. "Charles-Jerome, you warned me."

"Yeah, well, don't let her show up in the Seine," Nikki said. "Better to use her nosiness against her." She shrugged and leaned back against the wall, tipping an imaginary hat as the bodyguard scowled at her. "Good instincts," she said to him, and he turned back to Mercault, shaking his head.

"And I am Michael," the Hierophant said, foregoing Kreios's introduction, and using the far shorter version of his name, perhaps thinking the addition of his Archangel title might make the Frenchman's head spin. Given the man's religious icons in most of the homes I'd visited, he wouldn't be wrong. "The Hierophant, at least for this time on earth. It is a pleasure to make your acquaintance."

"Sir—" Mercault caught himself from genuflecting, and I grinned. Michael had that effect. Though he'd begun assimilating into life in Las Vegas—and kept his wings from manifesting, which was a blessing all around—he still carried the ethereal expression of a being truly meant for worlds beyond our understanding. The longer you looked at him, the happier you got, if only because he was proof that such brilliance, such perfect joy did exist in this world. Or at least it existed for the moment, which was more than we probably deserved.

"We shall have to discuss your homes in France, Monsieur Mercault," the Hierophant said, his eyes glazed with a look of faraway satisfaction. "You've done much to keep them true to the goals of their original builders. That much patience is a rarity among men, even those who are Connected."

"It is a trait common to the House of Coins as well," Kreios put in, bringing the conversation back to him. "In all its numerous incarnations."

"You are still asking questions to which there are no answers," Mercault said stiffly. "The heritage of the House of Coins begins and ends in my line, I'm afraid. It was a gift conferred, not unlike the transfer of the House of Swords by Annika Soo. Nothing was left of the original House—it had been destroyed for centuries. The gift consisted of a small amount of money and a promise of riches untold if we kept the secret of the House."

"Five hundred guilders and a ring of pure diamonds of unparalleled worth, yes?" Kreios said, and Mercault turned to him with wide eyes. "That ring has been a source of mystery. I see now the mystery has been right in front of us all this time."

"Five hundred guilders," Mercault echoed. "How do you know such a thing?"

Kreios nodded to the Hierophant, whose blush turned his pale skin almost rosy. "I confess I was a student of the Houses for a time," Michael said. "I do not know the modern history, I'm afraid, but I had made quite a record of their earlier trials. Before you, the House of Coins had been held by another prominent family, one with whom you do business even to this day." His smile deepened. "I should not, were I you, discuss this passage of leadership. I knew only that a lone wanderer set off in search of an enterprising household, far away from the corruption of his own. I did not know where he landed, but, ah…he was of German descent, if that is helpful."

Mercault frowned as he stared at the Hierophant, then understanding lit his face. "Oh…" he said, startled laughter spilling from him. "Oh…oh my. No, I should think the Fuggeren family would not be amused to find so precious a prize slipped from their fingers all those centuries ago."

Fuggeren? I grimaced. I'd met the current patriarch of that clan more than enough times to know Mercault would have his hands full keeping anything secret from them for long.

Mercault tilted his head, rocking back on his heels, a student of history meeting a like mind. "Did you know that amid the five hundred guilders were ten keys in the form of small disks?" he asked Michael. "And that those keys unlocked treasuries that bore no mark or seal?"

The Hierophant nodded. "The lines of House leadership begin, flourish for a time—a century, sometimes more, sometimes much less—then die out. It is a pattern we have traced through millennia. But of all the Houses, that of Coins has been, if you'll excuse the characterization, the least steeped in mysticism and the occult. It has been the province of Connected, yes, but the Connecteds run by intuition and intelligence, less by the arcane. Therefore, it has held a clearer line."

Mercault shrugged as only a Frenchman could. "Bien sûr."

"But that is being called into question now, it would seem." The Hierophant's eyes lit. "I should like to trace the history completely, learn whatever you know. For you see, perhaps there are more in your stockrooms than you even realize."

I looked between them, startled by the sudden kinship between two such disparate people, then turned to the Magician. His gaze met mine across the room, his eyes shrewd as mine narrowed. This was a neat trap, and one Mercault was falling into all too willingly. But Mercault was a grown man, capable of making his own decisions—and his own mistakes.

So was I.

The meeting broke up a few minutes later, the objective met. Armaeus had wanted us here, in the sway of the Council. He'd gotten that. Mercault and the Hierophant now sat with Simon and even Viktor at the conference table. Kreios had lured Nikki away to God only knew where. Eshe had flounced off with a need to rest, though it took Mercault at least twenty minutes to let her go.

That left Armaeus and me. We left by separate doors, but I was unsurprised to see my only option as I stepped inside the elevator was "P": Armaeus's penthouse office.

The doors opened on the wide vistas of the entire Strip. I stepped onto the deeply plush carpet, scanning the room. Armaeus stood at his desk, leaning against it, and leveled a menacing glare at me. I stared back and manfully refrained from flipping him off.

"You'll find you won't need the sword," he said, gesturing to the Honjo.

"I'm good so far," I said. I stopped well short of his desk, staring at him across the room. "I think it might be best if you started explaining—oh, I don't know. Anything. Everything."

"We'll start with the first." Armaeus moved sinuously away from the desk and stalked toward me. I didn't want to sit, not with the sword, but standing seemed problematic as well. In a chair, he could merely pull up another chair. Standing, he could step right inside my hula hoop.

He stopped before that, though, about five paces distant. I dimly realized that the configuration of chairs was different than I remembered it, rendering the space more open. Real, or another trick of Armaeus's, to make me think I had more room to escape him?

"You won't need to escape me, Miss Wilde." He lifted a hand, effectively cutting off my words—not by the gesture, but by what he held in his fingers.

Er, above his fingers.

He spoke over my stare. "Furthermore, you won't want to. You've forced my hand with this allegiance you have built with the warriors of the House of Swords. You have introduced true magical ability into that House. Despite the legends that swirl around them, none of the Houses were built for magic, not true magic like this. They were built for mortal ingenuity and instincts."

I frowned at him, though I couldn't stop staring at the prism he held suspended in the air above his palm, crackling with energy. It was the most minor of abilities—suspension and, perhaps more importantly, suspension of disbelief—but it wasn't the prism itself that held me so enthralled as it was the images I glimpsed in the center of it. Places I'd been to—the bolt-hole of the djinn, Atlantis, even Hell—and others I had not. A city of ice. A vast desert. A kaleidoscopic wormhole.

"But you, who are mortal, even if your father was a Council member at the time of your conception, you are becoming what you *should not be.* What you *cannot* be, truly, if you would stay within the confines of your body, held within this plane of reality. You're building a true magical ability within you, and it is beginning to fray you at the seams."

"English, please," I muttered. Armaeus was moving now, pacing around me, and I shifted carefully to pivot with him. Not truly turning in an arc, to avoid getting dizzy, but matching him at the angles.

"When I first met you, you were an accomplished finder of lost articles," he said. He snapped his finger, and the prism blinked from above his hand to over his left shoulder. I tracked it with my gaze, stepping back as Armaeus moved forward. Maintaining the distance between us. "Then you showed an affinity for astral travel."

"That's on you," I said. "That explosion with Llyr set all that in motion."

"Not entirely. It improved your abilities, deepened them, but they were there to be deepened. Still, arguably, it was an extension of your finding skills. Easily explained away."

Without warning, the prism snapped out of its orbit over Armaeus's shoulder and hurtled toward me. I kicked out the guard of the Honjo's hilt with my thumb, then pulled the blade free in a sweeping arc, not even getting it fully out of its scabbard before it connected with the prism. The impact sent the small crystal crashing in the other direction until it shattered in a burst of light against the far wall.

"Now you are doing things that defy explanation." He gestured at the sword, which I now held out between us in defensive posture. "You should not be able to master the Honjo Masamune, certainly not on a level surpassing that of a well-trained samurai. I didn't teach you to do that—no one did, in fact." His lips twisted. "And no, YouTube videos do not count in this regard. You further should not be able to react with the instincts of a warrior, even if you somehow came to know and understand the blade."

I kept my grip firmly on the Honjo's hilt, my gaze never leaving Armaeus. "I'm a very motivated learner."

"Of that I have no doubt. But there is more. I've spoken to Warrick of your time on his plane."

"Warrick!" I squinted at him. "He's a demon, and hardly reliable. Furthermore, I was on his *plane* all of thirty-seven seconds. Long enough to do the job and get the hell out."

"A job that, as you describe it, was quite above your pay grade. You should have returned the djinn to earth as they intended you to, then been left a hollow shell. You were not."

"Well, don't break your arm patting yourself on the back. I know you healed me."

He shook his head, his gaze turning more intense. "It would take a god to heal you, as badly as you were damaged, Miss Wilde."

Armaeus's words were low and resolute. And starting to scare me.

"I didn't tell you that at the time, of course," he said. "There was no value in it. But then you returned again and brought the children back with you." He gestured gracefully with his long-fingered hand. "Do you recall that second journey?"

I didn't appreciate the reminder. There had been fire, fire and rending pain, as if all the stars in the universe had ripped across my skin. "Vaguely," I said.

He nodded, a soft and seductive smile creasing his beautiful face. "The scars on your back from where you were burned were not mere wounds, Miss Wilde. Do you remember receiving them? Specifically?"

"I..." I shook my head, pushing the lingering agony away. "You were there, Armaeus. You were there, and you healed me. I break and...you heal me. That's the one constant between us."

My lips turned down at the corners. That was true in so many ways. Until the time that Armaeus himself had caused me soul-rending pain. Pain that had left a hole that could not be healed by him—or by anyone, really.

He moved again, and I turned instinctively, pace for pace.

"I healed you, yes. And you allowed me to heal you, which is always the price. Your acceptance. Your submission, though I know that is becoming a price that is harder and harder to pay. But the price will grow steeper still."

"Yo, I'm not—"

He overrode my protest. "More is required to understand what is happening to you, Miss Wilde. Your skills are growing too fast, too much. The balls of fire you've generated here and to heal the Sword general tap into wells of ability that you should not be able to plumb. And your back—"

"Enough with my back," I growled, though all I wanted to do was throw down the sword, pull off my shirt, and run to the nearest mirror. "What's on me? What did you find?"

"Nothing anymore. But I didn't remove the scars you received entirely." He lifted a hand, and an image turned before us, an image of me—my back bared to the waist. The skin looked pristine until Armaeus drifted his hand down. "I let them remain beneath your skin."

I stared in horror as the image flickered, and a riot of angry scars surfaced, an interlocking web of pits and bursts and constellations of agony across my back.

"Why did you keep that on me—or in me, whatever?" I managed, my mouth dry at the pain I'd clearly suffered.

Armaeus looked at me with his otherworldly eyes. "Because the scars left behind from the demon realm weren't simply burns," he said. "They were a map."

Chapter Twenty-Four

I couldn't help it. I lowered the sword. "A map," I repeated. "A map to what?"

He shook his head. "I didn't recognize it for what it was until after I returned from the plane of Hell. After I began...meditating more deeply."

I thought of what Eshe had said, of the Magician locking himself up in his fortress, deep in his arcane trance. "Yeah, how's that going?"

"Well enough that I can see and understand many of the secrets of the dark mystics before me. To understand why they eventually turned mad."

"So, dark doesn't sound so great." I sheathed the sword and took a small step toward the door. If the Magician had gone dark, I wouldn't need weaponry, I'd need wings. "I thought you were neutral. Balance. Remember balance? That was kind of your thing. I was a fan of that thing, if you wanted to know. Just putting that out there. Balance is good."

"And I am a fan, as you say, of understanding. Since the moment I found you in Rio, Miss Wilde, you've been impossible to understand."

I hitched a shoulder. "It's a gift."

"One I am ready to open," he purred. "Like this."

The Magician didn't move so much as *became* movement, his hands remaining frozen in place yet simultaneously lifting up, his designer suit unruffled yet suddenly swirling around him, a cloak of fire. I sensed the thrust of power shoot toward me even as I staggered back, but I didn't reach for the sword this time. There *was* no time. Instead, my hands came together to shield me.

The blow of the Magician's magic sent me crashing to the floor.

I lay there, pinned, barely able to breathe, to think. "Quit that!" I gasped, and the ball winked out. The pressure remained, however, like an elephant stepping on my chest.

"Crack through the ice with fissures of fire," Armaeus whispered, his voice was pounding through my head, my bones, my blood. *"Spear the fire with lances of ice."*

I had no idea what he was talking about. I strained back, my sight beginning to dim. "Stop—"

The pressure changed but didn't go away. Now, instead of death by big heavy thing, I was bleeding out, the weight that was crushing me becoming spikes that drove deep, piercing me through and pinning me to the penthouse carpet.

The spikes grew and twisted, ensnaring more of my flesh. This was an illusion, I knew it was an illusion, but that didn't stop it from hurting me in a way that wasn't going to go away anytime soon. That didn't stop it from leaving behind damage that couldn't be undone. "Armaeus," I gasped. "Please—"

He dropped heavily to his knees beside me, glaring at me. *"Fight back."*

The pressure changed again. There was no more physical pain, but it was as if a maw had been opened inside me, yawning with pain, with loss, with betrayal. Every friend dead, every hope destroyed, every belief shattered on the rocks of broken promises and unreached dreams. I gasped and half lifted off the floor, but I couldn't stop this any more than I could halt his other assaults. Worse, this one wormed inside me to that special, secret place, the hidden vault that held the most devastating betrayal I'd ever experienced, and one so fresh, so new that the locks had not yet been tested, the catches never tried.

They were tried now.

"No," I managed, though I might as well have been howling into a hurricane, so fierce was the attack against my will.

"I returned from Hell changed, but so did you, Miss Wilde." Armaeus's voice was once again all around me, this time ringing through the air. "I would know what happened to you. What you saw. What you—"

"No!" I screamed again. My hands came up as if released from the floor by some break in the magnetic force of the planet, the sudden movement too strong for me to check. I pushed Armaeus to the side, sprawling over him. I knew it was wrong, knew it was dangerous to touch this man in any way, but I couldn't react to anything but the agony in my own mind. I needed him out of my thoughts, out of my heart, his leaching hands away from the last vestiges of my sanity that were keeping me upright and separate from him.

Despite that need, I was still mortal, and Armaeus profoundly was not. He was a Magician whose power source consisted of sex and fire, and with the briefest of touches, an entirely different sort of need ripped through me, raging along my nerve endings, twisting in my core.

"This," I demanded—not a prayer, not a plea, not anything but the submission to my desire, a desire I had caged for far too long. To hell with it. Literally.

"This," he growled back.

Some dim portion of my mind realized that here too was a trap that had been neatly sprung. The Magician's process at once forward and back, yielding and attacking, learning where he could learn and manipulating where he could not. He didn't give a crap about my secrets, I realized with sudden clarity. He wanted me to draw on whatever power I possessed—however he could get me to do so.

None of that mattered anymore, though. Because Armaeus's gold-black eyes stared daggers even as his mouth met mine.

The touch of the Magician's lips was never a purely sexual charge. It was too layered for that. But it was powerful.

Instantly, the penthouse went up in a stream of fire and sparks, not metaphorically but actual sparks, lines of power running around the room and tracing geometric patterns as sacred as they were arcane, before diving to the earth. There they intersected with the ancient lines of power—ley lines and their axes, each more powerful than the last.

The conflagration wasn't only outside of me, though.

"You are not yet strong enough to fight Gamon's magic." Armaeus's hands gripped my shoulders, pinning me in place, but not to ravage me with his mouth, his body, the way I wanted him too. Instead he reached for me with his mind, clamping down on the broken places, battering against the strong. *"Gamon's disciples have trodden the darker paths, and you must be prepared."*

"I can't fight that way." I stared into Armaeus's furious gaze, and the world fell away. I peered into a roiling abyss. Black fire twisted and rolled on itself, daggers of red and gold shooting through it. The waves surged and retreated, crashing on a distant bank, revealing the skulls etched in bone and gold and amber beneath. "This isn't what I am."

"It's what is necessary for you to survive," he hissed in my ear. "I cannot give it to you, though, Miss Wilde. You must take it into yourself of your own volition, draw it and contain it so you can use it in your time of greatest need."

"No." I gripped Armaeus's hands, a flailing climber scrabbling against a cliff face, knowing that my grip was weakening but unable to resist the allure of the emptiness below. I stared into the power surging beneath me, and I saw more than fear, more than pain. I saw choices and grays and shadows, confusion and doubt. I saw the true reasons for the petrifying terror of great ability—not that it would consume me out of hand, but that it was so easy to simply *let it* take hold of me, to release myself to its pull, to give sway to its desire and madness instead of fighting the endless battle to stay in control, balanced, on the path.

"Gamon has mastered this battle," Armaeus murmured, his words once again deep in my soul. *"To drink so long and so fully of such power as quickly as she has*

can lead to madness or transcendence, the same transcendence savored by the enlightened. The abyss is an easier place to start—it's so much easier in the shadows. And nearly impossible to survive in the end."

"Then why are you showing it to me?" I moaned, but I couldn't turn away from raw power surging beneath me. It wasn't promise of riches, or the surety of dominance. It was the safety of my friends, the protection of the Connected children. It was the flash of the Honjo Masamune, the vindication of Annika Soo and all she fought for. It was the validation that my own foster mother had not died in vain in her misguided attempt to protect me all those years ago.

And it was deception and insanity too.

"There must be another way," I gasped, and Armaeus's laugh was low and dangerous.

"There is another way, Miss Wilde. There is always another way. But it lies through me."

Alarm bells clanged through every one of my cells, but the Magician's voice kept on, inexorably. *"Should you wish to take part of the fullness of power, to prepare yourself adequately for the battle you will fight in the coming days and the terror you will face on its heels, you need simply to give yourself over to me. To commit to me, body and soul. To join with me in every sense of the word but with no barriers between us, no block to my touch in the deepest reaches of your mind. Then there will be no secrets of yours I do not know, no emotions I have not plundered. Then there will be no you where there is not also me. But you will have power and riches of the spirit untold, an access to the divine power of manifestation unparalleled in any of the mortal realm."*

As he spoke, Armaeus solidified himself beneath me, once again becoming the Magician I knew instead of the portal to an alternate dimension filled with screeching, untamed magic. His fierce eyes searched mine; his grip tightened. I could see the truth of what he was offering me. I would have ultimate power but give up ultimate individuality—and worse, his words had been very carefully chosen. *He* would not be giving up that prize. He would not be sharing all of himself the way I would be sharing. He would still be in control.

"And the power behind Door Number One?" I gritted out, my heart quailing as the overlay of Armaeus's humanity slid off like rainwater, revealing once more the aching maw of power within him. "That's permanent?"

"No," he whispered. "If left unfed, it is spent like a drug. Unlike the magic of the ancients, born of light, darkness cannot sustain itself in isolation. It must have more darkness. Cut off the source, and you cut off the power."

I eyed him. "But you're the source."

"Now and evermore." Armaeus's words were tight, almost desperate, and the roiling field beneath me snapped and hissed. I realized suddenly how close he too was to the edge. "But I can control what I keep—and what I give."

For now, at least, were his unspoken words. I could sense them, hanging between us as I witnessed his struggle.

"You could take me now, couldn't you," I said. "The way you were saying. Plunder everything without stopping."

"This close to you, Miss Wilde, I could do whatever I wish," he said, his dark words ending a sibilant hiss. "But I don't want to take by force what will one day be freely given."

I jerked back from him bodily, the assurance in his voice suddenly more frightening than anything the black well of doom could hold for me.

"No!" I snapped.

Before I could think, before I could question—I dove into the sea of blackness.

The waves reached up to take me and pull me under, hard and sure, and suddenly I was swimming for my life. A problem, since I couldn't swim. But that didn't stop me from flailing out, my limbs churning in all directions. I couldn't breathe, I couldn't see, I couldn't even scream. Then, without warning, the full ocean of darkness didn't simply surround me, it twisted and shuddered, and somehow *I* was drawing *it* in, drinking it even as it gathered me close. As if I was the mouth of the world and it was a cup poured forth, the tide of black fury not banking until the last of it sluiced into my body, over my skin, not splashing away but sinking into every pore, every cell, swamping my ears, my mouth, my eyes.

"Miss Wilde!"

The voice was distant, too distant and wrong, but it was pulling at me nevertheless—no, the voice alone wasn't pulling. There were hands at my shoulders, my arms, yanking me, dragging me bodily forth, but there was no need to rescue me anymore, no need for fear.

Because the whole of the world was in me, and I was strong.

Strong.

"Sara!" This time Armaeus's voice was sharp, a command that even the power now churning within me could respect. My eyes snapped open, and I quailed away from the Magician as he loomed over me, his hands outstretched, his eyes a glittering dark gold that would not let me go.

"As small as a seed held in a child's hand, a single grain of rice," he proclaimed, or at least I think he proclaimed it. There were other words too, in Latin and Greek and tongues even more ancient, languages that had not been spoken since the dawn of the world. His hands reached for mine and held them fast even as my own fingers seemed to explode into flame, the mix of fire and acid scalding me bone-deep. Armaeus folded my hands over on themselves and caged them until the blaze dwindled down, down, down, its flame turning white and hard and cold. Finally, there was nothing left in my hand but the smallest grain of rice nestled against my palm. Armaeus lifted that and held it before my face. It dissolved into a powder so fine, my own breath blew it into nothingness.

I stared at him.

Armaeus leaned back on his heels. He was kneeling before me, and I vaguely remembered him starting out that way, but then...

I cleared my throat. "What just happened, exactly?"

He watched me carefully. "You took a measure of power into yourself to strengthen yourself against Gamon's magic. Dark power. You took it willingly, and you will release it willingly when its work is done."

"Dark power." Carefully, I stretched out my fingers, turning over my hands and scrutinizing them. No scars, no burns. "I don't feel different."

"You won't—you shouldn't, until the need is great. The magic is perfectly warded and sealed within you until you call upon it. And then you will feel..." He blew out a breath, and I felt that breath move through me, as if all my cells were expanding to fill yet further with power. "Very different indeed," he said. His jaw was set in granite. "But you will be safe, I swear it. Now and evermore, you will be *safe*."

The intensity of his words made my vision go white for a moment, and when my eyes cleared, I was staring into thin air.

Armaeus was gone.

Chapter Twenty-Five

I staggered to my feet and looked around. "Armaeus?"

There was no reply.

I padded over to the wall of windows, only partially surprised to see I was still wearing clothes. But the Magician had not touched me, in the end. As usual, he'd done everything with his magic, all of it illusion.

Still… I lifted a sleeve of my shirt, and grimaced as I traced the curve of my arm down to my elbow, seeing what I expected to see. My arms were no longer damaged. I suspected my legs and torso had been healed as well. The slicing and dicing I'd received at the hands of Soo's generals had been burned away in the conflagration of my time with Armaeus. It wasn't the only thing.

The gold ring of the Council no longer remained around my finger.

I stared down at my hand with a mix of confusion and—weirdly—despair. Armaeus had untethered me, sent me spinning off to manage my own battle with only a weird magic bullet inside me. Still, I felt stronger than ever before. Was this yet another trick of the Magician's?

How could it not be?

"Yo, dollface." Nikki appeared in the doorway of the penthouse, and I turned to look at her. Another indication of time's passage was her outfit. Instead of the gorgeous dress Jiao had given her to face the Council, she was back in a similar flat gray ensemble to the one she'd worn earlier in the day, a technical top and cargo pants. However, her boots were a magenta pink, and so were her nails. And her hair, for that matter.

Just how long had she been with Kreios?

Nikki lifted a glass holding a suspicious-looking green liquid. "You've been out for hours. Armaeus said to come get you, that you'd be hungry. Then again, Kreios said you'd be throwing up for days if you ate food-food, and the two of them got into a heated discussion in…Atlantean, I think. He recommended this." She shook the concoction. "I tried it. It's questionable at best, but if it keeps your stomach happy…."

I turned toward her and caught sight of the sword, lying in a position of prominence on the desk. "What time is it?" I asked, my voice little more than a croak.

"Half-past three. All's quiet on the Western Front. Brody's back on the streets again, bitching about not being able to find you, so if that doesn't bring everything back to normal, I don't know what does."

I grabbed my sword and we headed for the elevator. I dutifully took the shake from Nikki. "Do you have any idea what's in it?"

"I don't. According to Kreios, though, you drink that, and you won't harf up your intestines the first time you eat." She eyed me expectantly as I hesitated. "Maybe I wasn't clear. All's quiet on the Western Front, but there *is* a front. A front with sharp, pointy swords that bad people want to stick into you."

"Gamon and the usurpers," I grumbled. "Sounds like a rock group."

"Yeah, it sounds like a big problem, is what it sounds like. You go out there with the twenty-four-hour flu, it's questionable as to whether you'll get to hour twenty-five, you savvy?"

I stared at her a long moment as the elevator doors swished open. Then I started drinking.

The elevator ride seemed to take longer than usual, and I found myself bracing my legs wide, my left hand on the sword as I downed the shake. It tasted of cinnamon and chocolate and a whole lot of something herbal that could have been weed but was probably wheatgrass. Still, by the time we hit the first floor, even Nikki was glancing around nervously.

"Bad enough that we take an actual elevator to a different plane," she said. "But this thing was moving decidedly slow. I don't like it."

I stared at the empty glass as we waited for the elevator doors to open. "How much of this did you drink?"

She shrugged. "Kreios gave me my own sippy cup. I drank maybe half of what you had." She turned to me, her eyes wide. "Dollface, no. That was not supernatural spinach."

"Well then, how do you explain..." The doors shushed open, and Nikki and I remained trapped in the elevator bay for a minute, drawing closer to each other out of sheer self-preservation.

Everything in the lobby of the Luxor Casino...had changed.

It went beyond the simple overlay of Prime Luxe. That was there and bolder than ever, but wasn't the main issue. Instead, it was the *people* who had shifted.

Colorful blobs of light extended from each tourist and worker as if they were being hugged by a technicolor gummy bear. We stepped carefully into the lobby, turning around, and the flow of color from the clanging slot machines in the next room almost blinded us.

"Sweet Baby Jesus on a Tricycle," Nikki whispered. "Are you doing this?"

I could feel the dark twist of magic curl within me. "Let's get to the SUV."

We walked forward, trying not to hold our arms out, to keep everyone at a distance, but it was a near thing. Two cops eyed us suspiciously, their gummy bear auras turning a muddy gray, and we picked up the pace ever so slightly. By the time we'd reached the sliders, another pair of cops was standing at the SUV doors.

"That's ours, officers," Nikki said brightly, blinking quickly. Too quickly. "We'll be on our way now."

I expected them to ask her if she was safe to drive, but instead, their attention slid to me, as if Nikki was part of my identifying cover. Then their gaze dropped to the sword.

"Oh! Oh yeah," I said, lifting my hand away from the blade. "Sorry, I just won the darn thing down at Circus Circus, and I couldn't resist wearing it. It's plastic, they said, nothing scary." I frowned down at the blade, the epitome of the confused tourist. "I mean, I think it's plastic."

"You're Sara Wilde." The question came out more of a statement, but with the second set of cops coming out of the Luxor, it didn't seem worthwhile to deny it. The backup officers stationed themselves at the Luxor's front doors, keeping the gawking tourists away.

"Well, yes— " Then apprehension struck. "Why?"

"We have a few questions we'd like to ask. If you'll step over here?"

"Dollface..."

I didn't need Nikki's warning to realize something was terribly wrong. The men's aura wasn't gray anymore—it was black, and it was uniform. The same dark stain of power I'd seen in the bottom of Armaeus's power pit. Though these men were dressed like Las Vegas's finest, no way were they local cops.

"Ma'am, if you'd step over to the side, please..."

Nikki spotted the movement first, the telltale moment of the angled elbow and downward surging hand.

"Gun!" she yelled, so loud that a car across the carport screeched its wheels, its driver cutting the wheel hard. Nikki body-blocked the first cop into the second, sending both of them sprawling in a bone-crunching pavement skid. She yanked open the passenger door to the SUV, scrambling over the seat to get to the driver's seat.

I pulled the quick release sash of my sword, and both the blade and scabbard came loose from the belt, landing solidly in my hand. Wielding the Honjo Masamune like a bat, I turned hard into the cop nearest me and caught him under the chin. He dropped, gargling, but the second cop wasn't so easily fooled. He brought his gun up and shouted harshly, never mind the bunched-up vehicles and screaming tourists.

"Stop! Police! I will shoot!"

I didn't have time to think, and what happened next showed it. I slid the Honjo Masamune out of its scabbard and leapt forward, attacking the cop head-on. His gun flinched upward, and he fired, the bullet ricocheting harmlessly off the ramparts of the carport, sending the tourists into another round of panic. He leveled the gun again but by then, I was arcing fast, my blade slashing down across his chest—not closely enough to cut him, but I did shred his shirt, slicing through what looked like a Kevlar vest. I whipped the sword up and spun it around, until its butt faced him. I punched the man's forehead with enough force to drop a rhino. Then Nikki revved the engine and swerved onto the sidewalk, bumping into me as I clutched the Honjo and its scabbard against my chest with one hand and scrabbled for the door with the other.

I got the door open just as a real cop car bounced into the Luxor's driveway.

"Get in!" Nikki hollered, and I surged into the backseat as she roared over the median, banking hard and shooting out the front of the Luxor even as the cop car's lights flashed and sirens started wailing.

I screamed unnecessary exhortations to go, to get, to *move* as Nikki peeled around the car park and headed out again, bouncing onto the Strip and speeding toward Mandalay Bay.

"A little direction would probably be a good idea, dollface," she snapped, laying on the horn as she blew through a red light, sending cross traffic skittering into each other. Sirens erupted behind us, a Strip-based symphony that was closing fast.

"Crap!" I hauled myself upright, grabbing the pull bar as I threw the sword and scabbard across the backseat. Nikki hit a corner hard and I thrust my hand into my hoodie, swiping for my deck. She corrected, and the few cards I'd manage to yank out went flying, even as I lurched across the backseat.

"Easy!" I sputtered, pawing for the cards.

"Click it or ticket. We've gotta motor. Half the freaking LVMPD is gonna be on our tail if we don't move it like now. And I'm thinking our little death-by-cop greeting party was just an opening salvo sent by Gamon to let us know she's ready to party, whether or not Usurper Joe gets his act together. We've gotta finish this." She gunned the SUV. "Where'm I headed?"

"I'm working on it!" I spit back. The cards had landed in a scatter, and I scooped them up, knowing there was no way I'd be able to replicate their original order. Still, a lot of times I could figure out which came first or last just by the images, and I fanned the cards out, gripping them so hard, the plastic warped in my hand.

"Okay! Okay—we got two majors and two minors, majors are prolly bookends but hard to say."

"Not helpful," Nikki said. She blew through another light, barely slowing on the side street.

"Chariot—that could be the car or it could also be Luxor. Gotta be Luxor; that's first. That's past."

"Definitely past. What else, what are the other cards?"

"Two wands. A trip of two hours, two days, or a long trip, choices, trip, journey. Two, something," I rattled out. "Then there's also Death and the Five Swords, Death is transformation, change—"

"Or, you know, Death—"

"And Five Swords is a fight, a fight you lose but should've won, or win but maybe don't like the outcome for having done so. I can't think—Death!"

"I got that one already."

"No, the Two of Wands is facing left, toward the setting sun, that's west. Two hours west on a journey to Death."

"Sweet Jesus and an armadillo, Death Valley!" Nikki crowed, and she roared around the next corner, running alongside the highway. As luck and the cards would have it, the interstate was I-95, a quick shot out of Vegas and up through the desolate landscape west of the city, until it jackknifed south onto Nevada-373 and eventually crossed the California border into Death Valley National Park.

She jumped onto the highway, and we started speeding away, and it was only then that I realized there were no more sirens after us. "All's quiet from the city," I said, shoving my cards back into my interior hoodie pocket. "What's that about?"

"You focus on regaining your Zen place of happy fighting," Nikki said, eyeing me from the front seat. "And put your sword back together while you're at it. It looks like a messed-up stack of TinkerToys that way."

I shook my head, pulling the sword toward me and sliding its blade into the scabbard. "I think my Zen happy place is under construction. And if these cards are lining up the way I think they are, it's not opening back up for business anytime soon."

"Yeah, well, that's not the attitude of a warrior—hey!"

The display in front of Nikki as well as a monitor mounted into the ceiling of the vehicle crackled to life, and though Nikki tried to smack the electronics into submission, a second later, Simon's face took up the entire screen, like he was peering down a dark hole.

"This should—excellent, we got 'em," he said to someone off camera. His eyes flickered to the right and back directly above the camera, and a grin split his face. "Sara, my man! You guys have gone viral!"

"What—" Despite myself, I leaned forward, but Simon was distracted again, his fingers apparently flashing over a keyboard. His face was replaced by a camera-shot YouTube video, steadier than usual because of the selfie stick that allowed the angle to pike high above the cars. For a moment, there was nothing visible but Nikki and my head—confronted by the two guys in tan. Then Nikki suddenly heaved herself at the cops and vaulted into the SUV, and screams erupted all around.

"Oh my God, those cops! Those cops have a gun on that—" Pause. "Holy shit! Holy shit did you see that? Look at her go!"

The camera swooped, and then we did get a more direct shot on the action in front of the Luxor's main doors, grainy and indistinct though it was. I saw my arms flash out as I disconnected the Honjo from my belt, then the person on the screen started moving so fast, it was impossible for me to believe it was me performing those moves. I watched myself knock the first cop back and slice the second, but I totally didn't recall me leaping up to rebound off the side of the SUV, nor my spiraling flip in the air. I would have thought I'd have noticed that.

The sound of sirens picked up then, and the camera swung dizzily away, the awed viewer's reaction echoed by another voice. "Oh my God, there's more cops, there's more—hey! She made it into the car! The girl with the sword is in the SUV!"

Another crazy swing, and the camera caught Nikki's swerve to bounce the vehicle over the median, shooting out of the Luxor carport as a cop car with flashing lights barreled in. The phone was apparently hauled back, because the next image we saw was a blonde with bubblegum-pink lips, her eyes alight with excitement and her grin a mile wide.

"That was awesome!" she shrieked, and the image cut away again to Simon.

"See?" he demanded. "You're awesome!"

I scrunched up my face, desperately trying to unsee the video. "Please tell me you're pulling that down."

"Ha! Not a chance. This is the best promotion money can buy. Clearly Gamon is hedging her bets, which has gotta be irritating whoever she's got lined up to kill you. Kind of a vote of no confidence, you ask me."

I winced. "Oh, great."

"Never mind that, girl. You were on fire," Nikki agreed from the front seat. "And I'd like to offer up that that was some sweet-ass driving by the chauffeur as well."

Simon gave Nikki the thumbs-up. "Best driving *ever*. You should also be advised that your current conveyance is one of the premier offerings of the Arcana Council fleet, its dark blue-black finish a total changeup once she gets heated up. By the time you hit ninety miles—whoops, you're there—she'll be a flaming-red inferno."

"No way!" Nikki hunched forward, peering over the hood. "Yup, candy-apple red. Simon, you are a genius."

"You're on the right path too," he said, flipping his gaze back to me. "There's a lot of energy signatures flowing into Death Valley, way more than typical tourist season. Head south on Badwater Road and go all the way to Artist's Drive, then head back to Artist's Palette—road's been closed for the past week, but apparently it's open for Fight Club. There's some sort of jamming system on over the whole area that's giving me fits." His fingers flew over the unseen keyboard again. "I'll punch it into your Nav."

"Thanks," I said, grinning despite myself. "Anything coming behind us?"

Simon gave me another thumbs-up. "Nothing I can't handle, sister," he said. "You go fight the good fight. We'll cover your back."

Chapter Twenty-Six

Death Valley lived up to its name, desolate and bleak as we careened onto Badwater and barreled our way toward Artist's Drive. It was closed, as Simon had indicated, but no one was there to stop us from blowing past the barricades and up into the desolate ridges.

"No one's watching," I said, peering back as Nikki bounced over rocks and sand.

"Neural net, you ask me," she said. I blinked at her, and she waved her hand overhead. "Those heat signatures Simon was talking about, running into the Valley. Those weren't cars, I'm thinking. Those were energy spikes. Gamon probably has some kind of network set up here to blank us from satellites."

I stared at her. "She can do that?"

"I bet there's a ton of shit she's been playing with that straight-up Connecteds haven't even touched. The technoceuticals she's cooking could easily link a dozen or so high-level psychics to make their own Skynet. Especially if she's pulling down additional magic from the other side."

"And she's not even here. I get to fight her lieutenant." I grimaced, wrapping my hand around the hilt. "It's Jiao, isn't it?"

Nikki blew out a breath. "I'm thinking so." She turned off-road at the insistent beep of her GPS. "She acts a good game, but she was there from the beginning. She knew where you'd be at every turn. She was on the inside of Soo's operation for years, and then, what, Soo hands it off to a stranger instead of family? No way she'd put up with that. And if Soo was good with a sword, you can bet Jiao is too. Plus, now she knows how the Honjo works, knows you've got no real skills. She'll be ready for you, even though she's old." She shook her head. "Hopefully she's older than she looks, is all."

"Yeah." I blew out a long breath. Jiao didn't know I'd evened the odds with Armaeus's dark magic, though. That she couldn't have planned for.

After another few minutes of rough driving, the rocky ridges gave way to a box canyon—one way in, and the same way out. A single unfamiliar SUV sat at the far end of the open space, and I craned around, trying to see to the top of the ridge. Nothing.

"This...sucks," Nikki said, eyeing her GPS. "Simon, if you're out there, please tell me there's another way out of this thing, or I'm revoking your navigator's license."

Nothing came back from the console but static, and Nikki turned the volume down. "Jammers still messing with him, gotta be." She glared at the lone SUV. "We go in?"

I sighed. There really wasn't another option. If Jiao truly was in league with Gamon, I couldn't back down. The House of Swords would make Gamon too strong. "We go in."

As we approached the center of the canyon, the other vehicle's lights flared once. Nikki cursed as our SUV went dead.

"Blank zone," she said. "I'm telling you, this is one sweet operation."

"I still don't understand why she's doing it this way." I'd pulled the sword back into position across my body, reattaching the scabbard to my belt. "If she just wants to give the House to Gamon, why not find a way around this ritual, or let Gamon storm in and take the House by force?"

"Depends on the goal," Nikki said. Her eyes were fixed on the far vehicle. "You want to kill a bunch of people, you stage a coup. You want to build a loyal army, you win according to the rules that are already in place. That means no one storms the castle, no one shoots a gun. You win with sword and magic, or not at all." She glanced at me. "That's how I'd do it, anyway. Next time I wanted to play Evil Overlord."

Despite the heavy knot in my gut, I smiled. "You'll warn me before you do that, right?"

"You'll get the first invite to my empire."

"So that's how we're going to do this, then. I beat Jiao with no guns," I said. "Not even to save a life. No storming the castle. No cheating."

Nikki snorted. "Cheating I think is on the table. And you'd better be ready for it. Jiao's gonna be."

The door of the other SUV opened, and a figure stepped out. Before I could lose my nerve, I followed suit. As my feet hit the ground, I could sense the charge Nikki was talking about. The canyon was lit up with it, and my feet practically vibrated. Gamon might not have triggered this energy field with magic, but she definitely had some mechanism in place out here. It was eerie and uplifting at the same time, and I wondered how much it would benefit my opponent.

The SUV door slammed, and only one person stood beside it.

One very familiar person.

But not the one I expected.

"General Som?" Nikki's voice carried through the open SUV window. The woman stepped confidently across the shifting shadows of the valley floor, and with every step I knew it had to be her, that there was no mistake. "But you already beat her ass."

"Did I?" I felt the truth of our first encounter settle into me, as certain as my bones. "If the lines clear up, find out where Jiao is. She was with General Som last we saw her. If she didn't know General Som was the usurper, and tried to stop her…"

"On it," Nikki said, and I reconsidered my fight with General Som at Soo's mansion that morning. General Som had pressed hard, I thought, striking and feinting to test the Honjo, but not trying to win, exactly. Not then. Instead, she'd pushed me to feats I hadn't known the sword or I were capable of. I'd thought it a challenge, but it hadn't been that at all.

It'd been research.

"Stupid," I muttered, but there was no going back now. I strode forward and allowed the magic running through the ground to feel my weight. I didn't think the force field could do much more than resonate, sending a blank reflection into the satellite-filled sky. If it suddenly electrified me mid-fight, that wouldn't serve anyone's purpose. Certainly not General Som's.

The full truth of her bid became clear to me in a moment of startling certainty. Because of the jammed visual feed of this canyon, the rank and file of Soo's

House wouldn't know of the general's betrayal—would never know. Not even the other generals would know. They'd merely be told that I had allowed a second fight, perhaps that I had finally accepted the honor of meeting General Som in a real battle. It wouldn't be a fight of a usurper taking over another's House—it would be a general defending her own people. The fact that I was dead would simply be an unfortunate side note.

The House of Swords would fall to Gamon and never realize it'd been betrayed. It was so big, so far-flung, it could operate for years without the core generals or even Jiao realizing the truth, I suspected.

General Som didn't address me as we reached the center of the valley. Her face was set and unsmiling as she lifted her sword. I was pretty sure there wasn't going to be a referee's whistle signaling play, but I took an extra minute anyway, staring her down.

"You didn't need Gamon's backing to fight me," I said, and Som's coal-black eyes flicked to mine. "You could have done it on your own."

"I didn't ally with her to fight you." Her words were cool, measured. "I allied with her a long time ago. To destroy Soo. You are simply the last piece of that destruction."

Another piece fell into place. "The attack in the Bellagio," I said. "That's how Gamon got in."

General Som didn't respond—she didn't have to, and my own attention was now squarely focused on her as well. It didn't matter how we had both come to this place. It only mattered that we were here. The Honjo transferred from my side to my hands in one smooth movement. I loosed the scabbard and let it drop to the desert floor, then paced to the right as Som stepped left, the two of us measuring the other and finding the opponent wanting.

As I had in the lobby of the Luxor, I could feel the surge of Armaeus's dark magic. Only now I wasn't seeing auras but raw power. The flicker of magic that rippled through me was fanning to a higher flame, and the Honjo twisted, practically shivering in my hands. This was not the kind of magic I knew how to handle. It was the darkest depths that Armaeus had plumbed in his own psyche. Fitting that it should be called upon to combat a warrior who followed the blackest of dark practitioners.

"You have no true skills," General Som said, her gaze tracking me. "The Honjo will not save you twice, because you are not worthy of being saved." Her lips curled. "You're not worthy even of carrying it."

"How much is Gamon giving you?" I asked in return. "Is it money only? Or are you souped up on her technoceuticals too?" I pressed the point as her glare intensified. "Good old General Som, taking out all comers gunning for the House of Swords. Of course you took them out. You wanted all the goodies for yourself." Another truth flared before me, obvious and sure. "You set up your fellow generals in that parking lot at the Palazzo. Anything you could do to level the playing field, huh?"

"It's my House to lead." Som fairly spat the words. "Soo was weak, and she chose yet more weakness to succeed her." She scowled as she shifted to the left, and I moved in concert with her, knowing she was shifting to give her better placement in the sun. "Weakness and lies. I lived for two decades in the shadow of Angkor Wat. You cannot tell me that you found the blade there."

That was an unexpected turn to the conversation, and I blinked rapidly, trying to keep up. "Maybe you didn't look hard enough."

"Or maybe it is not the true sword of Masamune." She waved her blade. "We will see, I think. This *is* a sword of Muramasa, and it is *not* benevolent. It will cut down all comers." She sneered. "Even you.

I pivoted in perfect synchronicity with her, and the darkness within me coiled, ready to strike. "I think you'll find out pretty quickly exactly what my sword is—and isn't," I said.

Her eyes caught and held mine, and once again, as I had first with Ma-Singh, his body riddled with the bullets of Som's snipers, I could see not merely Som's eyes but the mind *behind* those eyes. I could see deep into the soul of General Som and know that there was nothing but darkness there, an empty husk that was neither alive nor dead but something hovering in between, tranqued on technoceuticals and the false promises of a living god.

She sprang.

We crashed together like a single creature, meeting sword against sword. As it had before, the reverberation of Som's sword rattled my arms and almost knocked the Honjo loose in my hands, but I gripped the hilt more firmly and brought it up high again. Som fell back, circling, her expression fierce with exultation.

"We are met on the true battlefield at last," she crowed, her smile not reaching her eyes. I knew she was trying to draw me out, bait me. She was succeeding. "You should have taken Gamon's offer to step aside. It was made in earnest. She did not want you to die." General Som smirked. "Far better for her to be able to harvest your living eyes and heart and spleen, still wrapped in your screams."

"So pretty much this is a lose-lose for you guys. I get it." The Magician's power hissed inside me, curdling my stomach, filling my veins with fire. When our swords crashed again and fell away, something flickered in the general's eyes.

Not yet, a voice whispered in my mind. *Not yet.*

It wasn't the Magician's voice, but it was born of the same darkness he'd stoked. And it was a voice I didn't know if I should trust.

General Som and I turned again and again, clashing, then breaking apart, our thrusts and parries growing longer and fiercer with each turn. She fought hard—driving me to the side and pinning me against a wall, making me defend from every angle until I scrambled back into open territory. She was my superior in all ways, but it still took me by surprise when she lurched forward and thrust again, her sword not taking long sweeping strokes any longer but short jabbing thrusts that set me back on my heels as she half chased me across the canyon floor. I finally ducked beneath her arm and arced the sword around, forcing her to parry and stumble back. She lost her footing momentarily and stumbled to the ground.

I should have struck. I could have. The Honjo fairly sang with the knowledge that this was a fair and worthy opponent, someone who did not need to be spared. The benevolent sword would gladly take its due in the blood and bone of General Som. I simply needed to act.

Not yet, the mocking voice whispered, creeping out of the darkness that shifted and eddied within me, a molten pit. *Not yet.*

And then my chance was lost.

General Som and I battled once more across the canyon floor, but I was flagging—fast it seemed, faster than I should. Now the darkness was lost in laughter, a rich and rolling pleasure that slowed the blood in my veins and weighed down my bones. I could barely lift the sword, and the pleasure of my pain was so bright and full and once again…so strangely familiar that I left my side unguarded, flinching back only at the last moment as General Som's blade raked across my arm, laying open layers of my shirt and drawing blood.

"You fool," the voice in my head sneered. A familiar voice. My voice. *"You were never the fighter you should have been, never strong enough to make your own decisions. And now you will die for it."*

"No!" I gritted out, bringing the Honjo up to strike at General Som, startling her. She'd seen my blood and could taste the win. "I will not die!"

Som's eyes flew wide as I spun, moving faster than I could have imagined. I struck and parried and struck again, and she fell back, her eyes shifting, her face flushed, her arms spinning as her hands darted in and out, the magic in her own sword finally coming to the fore.

But my focus was my undoing as my foot struck hard upon the earth and the unsteady terrain shifted beneath me, distracting my attention from our deadly flashing blades. I flailed forward with an ungainly lunge and clipped General Som's hand, sending her sword flying even as she whipped back at me, a dagger now in her grip, her eyes fierce with loathing.

"You're already dead!" she snarled, and plunged the dagger deep into my gut.

I fell to my knees, stunned, the Honjo loosening in my grip as the pain and blackness of General Som's dagger revealed itself as a magical weapon crafted with deadly cunning. Pure evil leached into my bones, but General Som could've had no idea that pure evil was there waiting to receive its brethren. When her blade nicked the deep wellspring of Armaeus's dark power I flung both arms out and back, consumed with the firestorm of energy as I gave myself over fully to the rage coursing through me.

My own doubt no longer spoke in the madness of that roar, no longer taunted me.

But that didn't mean there wasn't any voice.

"Sara!" Nikki screamed.

Chapter Twenty-Seven

The blade shoved deep within my abdomen twisted sharply as General Som spit a curse at me, and pain exploded in a ball of blue and purple light. I gasped, but there was no more breath within me to cry out, to deny the truth of what was happening. The surge of evil crested, then spilled forth, with nothing left to stem the tide.

Som turned her blade on Nikki, and I realized in a heartbeat that my dearest friend had roared forward with nothing but her fists and the scabbard of my sword—no guns, no storming the castle—against a woman who had no honor, a woman made up more of drugs and hate than magic or sinew and blood.

But I was made of magic, at least for now. I had drawn the darkest power into myself for exactly this reason. I flipped over on my back, agony ripping through me, and reached out my hand toward Nikki as General Som dove at her, pushing everything I had into the burst.

Nikki caught that power full in the stomach, the force of it lifting her off her feet even as she swung the scabbard of the Honjo Masamune at Som. The burst of fire that raced along the scabbard slashed across the general's face, melting her skin and making her scream. Nikki struck again and again, the fire burning through her but not damaging her that I could see, though my own pain lurched and tumbled around in the great dark hole that General Som had rent inside me, a hole that could no longer contain Armaeus's dark magic.

I staggered upright as Nikki spun away from Som, but this was not Nikki's fight to wage. Not her battle to finish.

I held the Honjo Masamune high. "General Som!" I roared.

This time the burst of Armaeus's power swelling inside me was infinitely bigger, stronger. When Som wheeled toward me, I didn't hesitate. I had greater forces behind me, before me and above me, and I willed them all to bend to my command.

This battle, it was over. Magic was here, I was here, and General Som would not live to draw another breath. So was it etched in my black-coated bones; so would it be.

The general leapt, and I leapt with her, but in that same movement, I threw the benevolent sword, the Honjo Masamune. This time, it did not evade its target but sang straight and true toward the heart of its opponent. Som lifted her own sword to protect herself, and the Muramasa blade shattered into a dozen shards. Its violent magic crackled through the broken pieces, galvanizing them and turning them on General Som herself.

She twisted and the benevolent blade shot by her into the bright sun, while the shards of General Som's sword buried themselves into her body…

Stealing even her screams.

I sank to the ground, surrounded by utter silence.

I'd won.

I'd lost.

Everything I had wanted, I had gotten, only nothing was good, nothing was right. Because something dark and dead now hung in my bones, refusing to let go. Armaeus had said the darkness would pass out of me when its need was past. He'd said it would go.

It wasn't leaving, though.

I fell forward, even as the buzzing of a thousand angry hornets filled my ears. In my mind's eye, I saw the Five of Swords, and my heart shriveled in my chest. A lone warrior standing on a rain-swept field, gathering up his swords as those he had destroyed turned and limped away from him. I had won this battle for the House of Swords. I had kept it from Gamon's hands.

But there was no victory here.

Gamon was not defeated, only Som was. Lost, broken General Som, a warrior betrayed by her own thirst for war. She was Gamon's minion, but where one follower failed, another would rise up. And another, and another, until there was only endless battle and endless pain.

"Sara—" A voice cracked over me, and somehow it was Nikki once again. I blinked my eyes open and saw her standing there, her face black with smoke and soot, but there was no blood upon her, no blood. And her mouth was split open into a wild, feral grin.

In her hands, she held the Honjo Masamune—which she brandished toward me. "Get up and take your sword," she whispered. Her words spoke through me and into me, coming not from her but from the Honjo itself.

I climbed to my feet. Nikki gave me the sword, and everything dark within me screamed in torment, as the lightness of the sword raged against the darkness of Armaeus's magic. I had won. But I had lost. I was whole and yet still broken. And only madness lay in wait for me. Madness and endless, aching loss.

Without thinking, I turned the Honjo Masamune upon myself and plunged it into my abdomen.

Magic arced through me, and everything inside went up in a fiery conflagration. The benevolent sword did not resist my action, it did not stop but pierced me swift and sure, seeking and finding all that was dark and miserable that had leached inside my soul, and burning it clean.

An eternity seemed to pass as I sagged forward on that blade, as screams and cries mounted around me. I looked deep into the constellation etched on the blade's surface and saw a path picked out in the stars, as if it was a map.

A map…

"Enough, Sara." The voice that spoke to me across the heavens was high and full, the softest murmur beyond the stars. It was a female voice, but something infinitely more than that, larger than a planet, deeper than a void. I felt the gentle touch of a hand caressing my face, drifting back my hair from where it was plastered against my brow. *"There will always be more to suffer. It is enough."*

The whisper of her touch sent a shiver of sensation through me, rippling through my forehead and curling along my spine. The darkness wrenched within me turned to hoarfrost and light, a brilliant winter's day—

"Sara…" The word floated over me, the softest mist, and I blinked open my eyes.

In front of me were more people than I would have thought possible.

There was Nikki, of course, the closest. She was clutching the Honjo Masamune to her breast. The sword looked as pristine as the day I had found it, and I frowned down at my stomach, confused. There was no blood. I was no longer wounded.

More sounds rushed in around me. The chatter of people, the shouts and calls of official voices over bullhorns, insisting that we stop, that we desist, that we scatter, that force would be used and that this was private property.

Another wave of noise broke through—a siren, as a battered sedan and an emergency vehicle bumped into the canyon, past the ring of black SUVs and the scatter of people standing beside them.

I smiled as Brody shot out of his vehicle and sprinted across the valley. He ignored everyone, pounding directly up to me, only to stagger back when he got within three feet. "Jesus Christ, Sara, what'd you blow up?" he demanded.

I looked down and only then saw the scorch marks in the earth all round me, radiating out from my body like the rays of the sun. I opened my mouth, but speech wouldn't come. I stood, and my clothes fell in hunks and pieces from my body, holes burned in so many places that Brody was barking again, and somehow someone produced a reflective blanket. I took a few wobbly steps toward him and Nikki, and half collapsed into their arms, my feet no longer working right.

Nikki steadied me, then bent and slid the Honjo Masamune into its scabbard, the belt also somehow unmarred by fire or blood or gore. She handed the Honjo to me, and I somehow managed to tie the sword back onto my body. I rested my hand on its hilt, my thumb pressed against the guard. As if I had always worn it, always would wear it.

Jiao stepped away from the knot of police cars, leaving two other generals who stood in respectful attention before the gesticulating cops. She seemed not to notice the scorched earth as she came to stand by me. I looked around but could see nothing of General Som's body.

She followed my gaze and gave me a deferent nod. "We have already created a story that will suit any seeking an explanation, Madam Wilde," she said. "The technology that Gamon had set in place to blank this section of earth from satellite view was attached to General Som's body with a set of transmitters. She was the center, for where she was, you would follow, whether she engaged you here or in another location. The box canyon apparently was not a good choice. The unit overheated, exploding in a highly concentrated blast that disintegrated her body and much of the surrounding earth."

Jiao gestured to the blackened ground, as if I needed any further explanation. "She died instantly."

"She—" I swung my gaze to Jiao, shaking my head. "Her sword," I managed.

"A fierce blade, to not have succumbed to the blast." Jiao held up a hand, and a man stepped forward, proffering the sword. General Som's Muramasa sword—no longer shattered into a dozen pieces, but pure and clean. Jiao touched the hilt with appreciation. "For centuries, a blade has guarded the shrine of Buddha in Angkor Wat, it would seem. It is fitting that a sword crafted for brutal death should seek its rest there, at last. It is our hope that this gift of faith to the temple will benefit both the shrine and the sword, each according to their needs."

She turned back to me. "We came as soon as we could." Her smile faltered. "General Som had given me coordinates for the usurper's attack on the other side of the city. Even in her last act, she deceived me. And there is no telling how much further her deception went."

Except, I already knew that. Knew what Som had done to the house, to Annika.

I stayed silent.

"We need to get you to a hospital," Brody broke in, his words gruff with anger. "And then probably to jail." He scowled over at Nikki. "You attacked four cops, Nikki. Four cops who were wearing regulation LVMPD uniforms."

"They so weren't cops," Nikki said, reaching out for me again, her touch ginger. I pulled the blanket around me, grateful for the barrier between me and the rest of the world. "I bet you haven't found those guys either, have you?"

"We have not. As far as we know, they crawled off and died somewhere, making you both the subject of a homicide investigation."

Still, Brody's voice held no heat, and Nikki pushed him on the shoulder. "You're just mad because you missed the fight."

"A fight on national park lands, utilizing possible illegal weaponry and advanced tech weapons that are going to be lighting up the desks of every law enforcement agency from here to DC? Yeah, I think that's a fight I'm awfully glad I didn't see with my own eyes. Especially since we don't have any bodies."

I winced. There may not have been a body for them to collect, but I knew the truth. I knew the reality behind the spin Jiao had set in place to cover what had happened here.

Nikki's grip firmed on my shoulders. "We've got one body right here, Detective, and that's the important one."

Brody turned, flustered, but I shook gently free of Nikki's hold. "It's not over," I said. "No one saw it. No one saw General Som die." No one had seen the burst of magic that had come out of me, channeled through sword and sky, a dark strength so profound that I would swear it still lurked inside me, though Armaeus had told me it would not … It could not.

Nikki grimaced. "Well, about that—"

"Sara."

I turned, and Jiao was in front of me again. Beyond her, the cops were arguing, but the generals were beginning to disperse toward their vehicles. "There is much to discuss tomorrow, after you are released from medical care." She tilted her head toward Brody as he glowered, effectively negating his argument before he could make it. "If you will come to the mansion, we can formally complete the succession process."

"I will come," I said. "We have much to discuss. And to settle, once and for all."

Jiao blinked at me, but I turned away. She had seen what she thought was a battle fought with swords and fire. But I had fought a different battle these past several days. One that had tested my deepest convictions. One that had brought me to this killing field, where I had so quickly embraced a dark power that I could not control—only barely escaping it in the end. That fell magic was not who I was, not truly. There were other paths I would walk instead, other swords I would lift. I knew my place in this war, finally, though it was not the place I'd thought it to be. I had won, but I had lost.

Then I had won again.

I argued with Brody for another fifteen minutes about going to a hospital. In the end, I gratefully accepted the packets of aspirin and bottled water, as well as another blanket, then at length clambered gratefully back into Nikki's SUV. Brody, apparently having given his keys to another cop, sat in the front.

"You gonna give me radiation poisoning?" he growled as Nikki started up the vehicle.

"Will you lay off?" Nikki protested. "She's double wrapped in heat-reflecting blankets. She can't help it if she's a glow stick."

"I have sunstroke," I grumbled.

"Right. That's what you have."

We cleared the edges of the box canyon and turned on the interstate back to Vegas, Nikki cruising along at a positively sedate eighty miles an hour. She kept grinning at me in the rearview mirror, but I was too tired to object. Brody, however, cracked after the first three miles.

"What is your deal?" he asked, wedging himself into the door of the SUV, glaring at Nikki. "You look like the cat who ate the canary."

"So you know how Gamon had the whole tech net set up to kill observation? And our trucks died convincingly?" At my nod, she grinned over to Brody. "It was a great move and even had me going. But apparently, this particular SUV comes equipped with an onsite generator."

My gaze sharpened on Nikki, but she was reaching to the controls on the multimedia dash.

"You wanna see what really happened out there, Brody? Or would you rather check it out when it starts trending?"

"Nikki," I said warningly, but Brody was leaning forward now too.

"You got it on video?" he asked. "The whole fight?"

"I haven't looked at any of it since I headed out to the fight, but up to that point, it was all systems go." Nikki flipped the video screen on and, for good measure, revved the SUV up another click of the speedometer. "You're really going to love this."

I closed my eyes as Brody started cursing.

Chapter Twenty-Eight

I should have known something was fishy when Jiao contacted Nikki the following morning to reschedule the meeting at Soo's Lake Las Vegas mansion, but I was too busy recovering from Post Traumatic Honjo Disorder. I floated in dreams that found me searching miles of open territory—for what, I didn't know. Armaeus was there, waiting patiently for me to find him, but I could never quite seem to connect with him across the miles that separated us.

Nikki and I spent the day burrowed into Soo's Vegas Summerlin mansion, overlooking the majesty of the Strip. The fact that we started drinking at eleven a.m. did not contribute at all to our reclusive moods. But it wasn't our fault—the Council, most likely Simon or possibly Kreios, had sent over magnums of champagne to ensure we recovered suitably. Such was the life of the warrior.

"Which would you choose for yourself, if you could?" Nikki said now, leaning forward, her elbows on her knees as she gestured to the Strip with her flute of champagne. The sun was setting, and all the world was alight with magic. "You go in for all that stone and glass with Armaeus? Or you like that lava-lamp casino the Devil's got going."

I obligingly turned and frowned at the cascade of glittering towers along the Strip. "I've never been truly explored any of them except for Prime Luxe and Scandal," I said. "I was in Viktor's tower only briefly that one time and ugh—all that black."

Nikki nodded. "And you just know he has mirrors on the ceilings."

I pointed to the Council domain glittering above Bellagio. "No interest in anywhere Simon calls home," I said, then glanced farther down the Strip, almost to the Palazzo, and smiled at the Hierophant's white tower. "I would like to see what Michael is up to in there, though. I mean, what exactly does an archangel do for fun? Stop," I said quickly, lifting my hand. "Don't answer that."

"What?" Nikki protested. "I wasn't going to say anything." But her loopy smile betrayed the quips she had stored up to describe Michael's possible activities. She took another slug of champagne, and her gaze steadied on me. I tensed, knowing what was coming.

"You gotta stop, dollface," she said, rolling what was left of the sparkling liquid in her glass. "It was always about the next job, the next gig. The next way to make a hundred thousand dollars. And all that was bad enough. You got banged up, but you recovered. Armaeus did his thing, and the next day, whammo, you were walking again, or at least you weren't leaking blood from your ears. But this…" She shook her head, sitting back in the plush cushions. "This was bad. Ain't nobody going to be there for Father Jerome like you are, if one day you turn up dead. I think losing you would break him."

I frowned. "Father Jerome was helping people long before I came around."

"Yeah, well, then you did come around, and you stayed, and he could see the value you brought to those kids. Not only with your money, although, sure, that helped. It became the currency of your relationship, the way he knew he'd be able to see you. But even that changed, right? Now you barely get out there every few weeks, and there are always more children to protect, so off you go again."

I stared at her. "You're not seriously asking me to give up helping the children."

"*Helping* them, not at all. I love that you help them. It gives me hope for humanity. But you gotta be a little smarter is all."

She tucked her bunny-slippered feet beneath her beach cover-up, the closest she had gotten to clothing today. "What's up with you and Armaeus?"

I lifted my brows. "How much champagne have you had?"

"Not nearly enough." She kept her gaze steady on me. "He isn't helping you anymore. He should be, but he isn't. I don't get it. And yeah, yeah—I know. He's pissed because of what happened in Hell. But there's gotta be some kind of rule for that. Like if it occurs more than ten thousand miles away or in an alternate dimension, you kinda get a pass."

I almost spoke but ended up shaking my head. It was simply too much.

"See, you're doing it again." She laid her head back on the cushion and closed her eyes, as if she was ready to let the warm sun seep into her bones. "You never give yourself a chance to reach out, to lean on someone else for a while. But you know if you did, you might find that they were there, ready and waiting to stand in the fire for you."

"You stood in the fire for me today," I said, and I watched as the smile curved her lips, her fingers going lax but somehow still managing to keep the champagne glass upright.

"I did, dollface," she said sleepily. "And I'd do it again. I couldn't imagine a better person to toast my marshmallows for."

"Nikki, I—" But I cut off my words as her smile loosened further and her mouth fell open, the softest beginning of a snore drifting out between her lips. I watched her for a long time on that balcony, as the night drew down on the city, and I wondered what I'd ever done to deserve her.

The next morning, I wondered how cheap I could sell her at the circus.

"Coming through, coming through!" Nikki bellowed, sticking her head out the window and pumping the horn. She'd woken miraculously without a hangover, hungry enough to eat a bear—or at least a couple of bear claws, but we'd barely had time to grab coffee before the summons to Soo's home had finally come. Then getting ready had taken all the rest of the morning, and now we were fashionably late to our own party.

Nikki had dressed to impress, but that didn't stop her from screeching again as traffic slowed to a crawl. Her motif today was stilettoed superspy, with her black sheath dress and sharply angled white collar the perfect foil to her glittering silver-toed black heels and deep red hair slicked back into a severe chignon. Since everything at Soo's mansion was available via speed dial, she'd insisted we bring in stylists for further consultation, and her fingers now sported a deep red-black polish that would have made Dracula proud.

By the time we reached the Soo estate by Lake Las Vegas, Nikki'd shut up. But only because it seemed like we were in line for Disney World.

"Did something happen?" Nikki asked, drumming her fingers on the wheel. "Did I somehow miss the jaws of life passing by? I've never seen traffic this bad out here. Swear to God, if it's some sort of fender bender and my mousse gives out, there will be hell to pay."

"I'm sure it'll clear up soon," I said, peering over the dash.

It didn't, though. We'd crept forward another ten minutes when a motorcycle zipped by us going east—then flipped around and changed direction, coming up fast on our left.

"I so am not in the mood to hospitalize someone today," Nikki said as I craned around.

"I think it's one of Soo's," I said. Nikki begrudgingly lowered the window, letting in a blast of desert heat.

The motorcyclist flipped up her helmet, and a serene face I didn't recognize beamed at us from a cocoon of plastic and leather. "Madam Wilde! Get out of line and come on up!" she shouted, gesturing ahead. "We'll block traffic. And one of you should turn on your phone."

She sped ahead, and I pawed for my phone—couldn't find it. Nikki didn't waste any time, however. She pulled out of the line, racing forward. A chorus of beeping horns immediately erupted, and I cringed in my seat as windows rolled down. "Uh-oh, I think we've upset the natives."

"Think again, babe." Nikki grinned. She nodded at the cars farther ahead, and the windows were down, arms sticking out—and hands gripping swords of all descriptions.

"You have got to be kidding me." I stared, and Nikki spent the next ten minutes cackling as we reached the front of the line and darted around the remaining traffic into Soo's home, cars already lining the long and winding drive. A stretch of desert had been converted into a makeshift parking lot, and I stared as we passed it, the workers picking up the jubilation at our passing and waving furiously at me. Dumbstruck, I waved back. "Is Jiao holding an auction or something?"

"I think we now know the reason why she made us wait a day," Nikki said dryly.

We parked directly opposite the front door to Soo's western-style mansion, and Jiao stood in her crisp suit, the young motorcyclist now beside her. They bowed as Nikki and I exited the SUV, my sword secure at my side.

"Your phones?" was Jiao's only rebuke.

"Didn't match our outfits," Nikki said succinctly. "Sorry for the delay, but we didn't realize you'd put out the call for reinforcements."

"We didn't," Jiao said. "It appears that a truncated version of your fight with General Som was beamed directly into the computers of every Sword household that had the technology to support it. And those without the technology received visions, even dreams."

"They what?"

She gazed at me, taking in my startled expression. "Not your doing?"

I frowned. "That would be negative."

Nikki for her part looked equally bemused. "I hope you cut the part of me getting my ass handed to me," she grumbled, and Jiao's face creased in a slight smile.

"You'll be pleased with the outcome, I think," she said. "This"—she waved to the cars behind us, and the steady flow of people walking down the rolling bank—"is the result of that video feed. It would appear your people are here to see you take your rightful position, Madam Wilde."

"About that—" I began, but Jiao lifted a hand.

"No matter what you decide, you have brought great honor to our House," she said. Her eyes were strangely bright, and I blinked, taken aback by the show of emotion. "Madam Soo would have been very proud."

Her attendant lifted her hand to her ear, her gaze fixing on Jiao. "We are almost ready. The grotto has been set up. By the time the ceremony is concluded, all the attendees should be in place. You'll go through the archway to the overlook and can address them there."

"Very well." Jiao gestured us forward.

Nikki and I followed her inside, our heels clicking on the Spanish tile. I'd foregone my usual hoodie and jeans for a black pantsuit and boots, not all that dissimilar from what I had seen Soo wear. It wasn't my choosing, exactly—it had shown up at the Summerlin mansion along with Nikki's clothes, courtesy, I assumed, of the Council. The neckline certainly seemed redolent of Kreios, since it plunged down to my sternum and angled wide. There was no missing the artful beauty of Soo's double pendant necklace across my collarbone, however, and the effect seemed to satisfy Jiao.

We entered the grotto, and once again I was struck by the idyll Soo had created, an oasis in the middle of the desert. Had she known that she would not be around to enjoy it for much longer when she'd purchased this home?

"Madam Wilde." The voice that startled me was Ma-Singh's. He stood in dark fighting gear, but the uniform seemed more formal, almost ceremonial, down to the white Samurai sword at his belt.

The other generals wore similar swords, symbols of their service to the leader of the House. They murmured their greetings to me deferentially. No one mentioned General Som.

I nodded to Ma-Singh and stepped forward into the center of the small gathering of Jiao, the generals and staffers, who stood like silent sentinels in the back of the space. There was no sound but that of the water bubbling in several basins, and I took the sword from my side—not in preparation to do war this time, but to end it.

Eventually.

"I will take the leadership of the House of Swords," I said quietly. "But I am not Annika Soo. Her ways are not my ways. Instead, I choose to ensure our House is strong from Ace to King. I choose Madam Peng to manage its operations." I turned in her direction. "If you would be willing."

"I serve the House of Swords," she said, bowing with her gaze upon the floor. I waited until she straightened, and met her eyes. There was no emotion there, but there didn't need to be. This was the right decision. I had assumed Jiao's guilt since the first time I'd met her, so certain that Soo had passed over her aunt deliberately.

She had, but I didn't realize the reason why. Hadn't realized it until I'd stared into the face of General Som.

"Madam Soo did not want you to die at the head of a warring household. She feared for your safety, after she had already lost so much. You must pledge you will stay safe."

"I will," she murmured, and I nodded. Jiao knew all there was to know about the House's operation, and she would serve Soo's legacy well. I had different battles to fight.

But here again, not the traditional ones.

"General Ma-Singh." I turned to him and held out the Honjo Masamune, smiling to ease the incredible disappointment in his face. "There are swords that are meant for ceremonies and those meant for war. The Honjo is most at home in the hands of a true warrior. I will not damage your ranks by fighting with a blade among you. For that, I call upon the elite generals and their warriors. I choose you to fight as the head of that branch, if you would be willing."

He stared at me, unspeaking for a long moment. "You will not fight for the House," he rumbled, as close to a rebuke as he could manage in such a formal setting.

I shook my head. "I will not fight with a sword of steel and bone, no," I said. "That doesn't mean I will not fight. And it doesn't mean I won't lead you."

I lifted the Honjo Masamune higher, until he reluctantly stepped forward. Then, drawing on Armaeus's pool of dark magic, I sent a crackle of energy along the blade, setting it alight. The entire assembly froze, arrested by the vision.

I looked around the room. "You who have served Soo so long and so well, among you is the future of this House. Your hearts and minds will be tested in the coming battle. To win that battle, we much each do what we do best. Even me."

I lifted my left hand and drew upon the magic that still roiled within me just beneath the surface. This power wasn't mine, truly, but I would draw upon it for this gesture to solidify the House of Swords. Even endless darkness could be used for good…if only for a short while.

A set of crystal blades formed above my fingers. They spun as the generals stiffened, their eyes fixed on the illusion. The blades grew, dipped and lengthened, until a matrix of spinning swords twisted around me. With another flick of my hand, the swords plunged into the ground around our company, twelve black blades with silver hilts. I bowed to the generals' startled stares. "Take all the blades but one, and assign them to your most trusted people, a symbol of what's to come," I said. "We begin to build the army of the House of Swords this day."

I pulled the nearest sword and held it out before me, inspecting the long sliver of white that curled down the black metal weapon, glinting with power. It was so much cooler than what I'd imagined in my mind. Infinitely more badass. I couldn't believe I'd created it at all, but then—the Magician's dark magic was still coursing through me. Of course I could create something so epically beautiful, with power like that.

I nodded, clearing my mind once more. "There's only one thing left now."

Nikki turned first, ready to precede me through the archway to the overlook, but I stopped her. "Nikki," I said. "This is for you."

She stopped, confused, so I took the extra steps forward. "I couldn't imagine going anywhere in this war without knowing you were by my side. If you want to become an Ace, the position is yours. If Nigel is willing to show you the ropes."

The amused, sardonic response with a perfect British inflection was immediate. "I think something can be arranged."

"Sara—" Nikki screwed her face up in confusion, looking from me to the sword. "I don't understand."

"As an Ace, you'll have the right to serve any House, pitching your services to the highest bidder." I gave her a crooked smile. "Naturally, I plan to bid high."

"An Ace." Nikki reached out and took the sword from me, hefting it experimentally. "I could be an Ace." She looked up at me with bright eyes, the tears that stood behind them the first intense emotion I'd ever seen her reveal. "It matches my outfit too. I appreciate that."

"Madam Wilde." Jiao stood at the archway, lifting a hand. "If you are ready."

I nodded, gesturing that the generals and Jiao precede. They filed out, and a roar filled the valley—one that only strengthened as I stepped onto the stone overlook and greeted, for the first time, the combined assemblage of the House of Swords.

I would let Jiao manage the House, and I would let Ma-Singh defend it.

But I would lead the House of Swords, for Soo.

For its people.

And for me.

Chapter Twenty-Nine

"She know you're here?"

I leaned against the countertop, paging through the flash tattoos in one of the enormous books that lined the lobby shelves of Darkworks Ink. The voice didn't belong to Jimmy Shadow, the manager of this place. It was a woman's voice, and it didn't sound like its owner was surprised to see me.

"Nope," I said, not looking up.

"She'll be pissed when she figures it out."

"Maybe." I finally glanced up and took in Death, from her half-shaved white-blonde hair to her shit kicker boots. In between were mile-long legs poured into ripped jeans, a muscle shirt, and one arm completely tatted in a complex tumble of images and designs, so thick and vibrant it made me hurt to look at it. But I eventually couldn't avoid Death's cold blue stare, and I met it steadily. "I doubt she'll figure it out, though, unless I show up when she's not expecting me. And at that point, she'll probably need my help to stay alive more than she'll need to stay mad." Nikki was practical that way.

Death shrugged. "Your funeral."

Which, coming from the incarnation of Death on the Arcana Council, wasn't the most comforting of responses.

Nevertheless, she crooked her finger and directed me to follow her to the back, where the familiar sight of the long, utilitarian hallway greeted me. Death directed me to the third room on the right, the illusion of it being another ordinary tattoo station evaporating as we stepped inside. Instead of the floor-to-ceiling bookcases stuffed with books and magazines and bric-a-brac, there was nothing but cold concrete walls and floor, the chair, and Death's rolling cart of tattoo implements. I grimaced. At least she'd held off on displaying a drain in the floor.

"Where?" she asked, hooking her foot around her rolling stool and bringing it underneath her. As she sat, I got into the chair. I'd been inked twice by Death so far. The first, to find Atlantis. The second, to find my way to an alternate dimension, where demons roamed and the children who'd started me down my shadowed path were trapped. But this mark was different. This was an acknowledgment of a bond I hoped would never be tested, but which I'd never willingly break.

"You tell me," I said. "I have to be able to find Nikki, no matter where she is, in this world or any other. If she's in danger, real danger, the kind she can't get out of, I need to know."

"Left arm," Death said, rolling her chair around to my other side. "The right is rationality. The left is emotion. If you want a link to know her true thoughts, gotta go with left. Of course, the leftward path is open more to interpretation, but probably not something you'll mind. If she's in danger, the nuances of it aren't really so important."

"Then the left it is." I nodded. She poked through the bottles on her cart, the needles, and I busied myself with looking in the opposite direction. When the tattoo gun buzzed and she leaned forward, I gripped the chair with my right hand, forcing my left to stay still.

"You did a good thing with the House," Death said, the quiet words so surprising that I blinked back at her, wincing at the sight of my own blood.

"I didn't think you cared about that."

"Why not? Because I didn't show at Armaeus's meet up?" Death twisted her lips, inking another heavy line into my skin. "He doesn't call us all together for consensus building. The others don't realize it, but I've been around other Magicians like him. I know how he works."

I frowned, remembering again that, unlike Eshe and Viktor and even Kreios, I didn't know when, exactly, Death had joined the Arcana Council. What had been the circumstances of her ascension? And why would she choose Death, of all roles? It seemed rude to ask her, considering she was plunging a needle into my arm, so I went for the safer choice. "And how does he work?"

"Energy—all energy. That's what makes up balance, and that's his stock-in-trade. When all the Council members are assembled, there's a certain amount of energy he can draw from it, the whole being greater than the sum of its parts. That extra bit between the parts and the whole is his playground. That's one part of it."

I couldn't help the sense of rightness I felt at hearing Death's words. Armaeus was energy, and I suspected, he was specifically dark energy. I'd just never known how much…perhaps still didn't truly know.

Death moved to the right to assault my arm from another angle, and I realized I'd been quiet for too long. "And the other part?" I asked.

"The energy of the interconnections," she said. "Armaeus has long suspected Eshe of courting darkness, and her reactions to Viktor are important data points for him to gather. Simon and Michael are pure light incarnate, God love 'em, and so they provide a good balance for the twin pools of stank. Then there's Kreios. Kreios is dark, technically, but he edges toward neutral, which makes him a good buffer."

She slanted me a glance. "I bet Kreios was standing close to the Magician or between him and the others."

I frowned, tilting my head as I tried to remember the scene. "He was," I said. "What's that mean?"

"Like I said, buffer. So Armaeus can figure out the interplay of the others. They can't figure him out. I don't mind him playing his games, but that doesn't mean I want to be a part of them, you know?"

"But you're neutral, right?"

"Can be." Death shrugged. "I'm not great as a buffer, though. Emotion passes through me, but I don't refract it back to mortals the way Kreios does. I don't show them what they want, or what they think they want. I'm more like that drain you keep imagining in the floor of this room. Emotions flow through me, but nothing flows back."

"I think I've dated guys like you before."

She snorted, and for a while, there was nothing between us but the buzz of her gun. It was almost soothing, the same sick sort of way a dentist's drill could be soothing, the overflow of adrenaline eventually whiting everything out. I looked down as Death shifted again and tried to make out the pattern that was emerging on my skin. "What design are you using? Because if it's a Nazi swastika or something, I'm not sure I'm going to forgive you."

"All the good designs, already taken," Death said dryly. "But no, nothing so obvious. It's got to twist fully around your arm, with no beginning and no end. That way you don't simply go find Nikki, you can bring her back as well, home to wherever you've designated as sanctuary."

"Sanctuary," I said, testing the word out. "I like that."

"Yeah, well—this band, it isn't only for Nikki. You can connect to anyone and bring them back, anyone with whom you hold a sacred bond."

The needle bit into me, and I winced. "Sacred bond is good. Like a secret handshake? Because there are a bunch of people I have secret handshakes with."

Death said something unintelligible, then bent back to her task, slowly working her way around my arm. Her focus allowed my thoughts to wander back over her own words, and I frowned.

"Why are you telling me about Armaeus? The way he works?" There had to be a reason. Death was never chatty for the sake of putting people at ease. It was generally to put them on their guard.

"He has many threads he's pulling in the weave of the world. Some he understands, some he only thinks he understands."

"Spoken like someone who's lived in the frat house longer than all the other brothers."

She paused, then quirked me a rare smile. The sight of it was spectacularly beautiful, and heartbreaking as well. I wasn't sure if I'd ever seen Death smile before. What would it be like to live one's existence where so little caused you to smile?

"That's not a bad way of looking at it," she said, "But it's not quite true. Michael outranks me. Though if he gets docked for time he spent off the Council, I have him beat. It's not the time for my story, though. Armaeus came back changed from his experience in Hell. And not in a good way."

"Well, he's more of an asshat, if that's what you mean. Am I missing something else?"

She nodded, and a sour pain settled in my stomach. "He turned to the darkest forms of magic he found there and plumbed their earthly equivalents," she said. "Drawing in all that was powerful without concern for any damage to himself."

I frowned. "I thought he did that to make him stronger. And he is stronger."

"A stronger Magician is not always what is in the best interests of the Council," Death said. "Remember what I told you. The Magician and I are neutral, Viktor dark, Kreios is dark edging to neutral, and Simon and Michael light. Eshe plays at neutral but she's dark at heart."

"And Armaeus is kind of dark too, now," I finished the thought for her. "And that means?"

But my question suddenly morphed into a yelp of pain as Death's needle plunged deep into my skin. She lashed out with a curse. Everything inside me lit up in agony, revolting at the touch of her gun.

"What in—stop it!" Death growled, and I got the impression she wasn't speaking to me. I arched off the chair, and she rose from her stool, lifting her leg to brace me to the surface. "Jimmy!" she roared. Her voice wasn't so much of a shout as a command that rolled through the room and out of it, bursting in all directions. It seemed only a second later that the door crashed open, and Jimmy raced into the room, wild-eyed.

"What!" He took in the scene in a blink and ignored his own question, striding up to the chair and laying heavy hands on my torso.

"This is going to hurt like a bitch, and I'm not going to get it all," bit out Death. "*This* is what I'm talking about."

"No!" I twisted in my seat, but Death didn't let up on the pressure she was exerting on my arm. "I can't let that power go yet—I can't."

"Oh, you've got it all wrong, sweetheart. Your magic will stay in you. Once you flip the switch, it doesn't unflip. But this mess—stay *still*," she ordered, and with another plunge of her needle, I gasped, my mind's eye exploding to reveal a pool of raging darkness that surged round the secret vault of recent memories. Death and Jimmy tipped me, and as my temple pressed to the side of the chair, I squinted and stared at the floor beneath me, not three feet away.

There was a drain, all right, and it was huge. It stood nearly two feet across, the heavy reinforced seal slitted narrowly enough that the chair didn't buckle it, but the slashes were long and cruel—and currently covered over with the black, seeping goo that drained out of my arm. The whispers of a thousand voices fell with the sluicing liquid, and I groaned, turned inside out.

"You don't need the Magician to strengthen your magic, you stupid idiot," Death said, though her voice was heavy with pain, not laced with the rebuke her words should contain. "He'll have you believe it because you're a puzzle he needs to solve. He may even believe it himself, but it's not true. You came from other places, and you are born to live by other rules."

I wanted to follow her words, I truly wanted to. But the voices clamoring in my head were taking on familiar cadences. The plaintive cry of Mirabel, the sneer of Sariah, the hiss of an eons-old dragon trapped behind the veil between the worlds.

"I don't understand," I gasped, and my sight began to dim at the edges, causing Death to curse in a language I'd never heard before.

"Enough," she barked, and as if following her own directive, she pulled the gun free of my arm and twisted away from me, leaving Jimmy to keep me pinned to the table.

"I'm not going to be able to drain anymore. That's on Armaeus. I suspect when you tell him that you've still got that shit in you, he's not going to take it well."

"What?" With Jimmy's help, I straightened on the seat. "He knows I—he knows. He was there."

"He doesn't know. There was a broken binding spell," Death said, turning around. She lifted my arm to inspect it, turning it over. "He probably told you the magic would go poof once you were done with it."

I winced as she scraped a trail of black goo off my arm. I didn't want to look at the floor. "He did," I said. "But I needed the magic still—I had to make a display during the ceremony today, to convince the others that Soo's choice was an honorable one…" I shook my head, regretting nothing. "I still needed it."

"No, you didn't," Death said. "That's what I'm trying to tell you. Your conjuring abilities aren't due to the dark power you allowed into your field. They're due to…something else." She tapped my arm above the newly inked symbol.

"There's more I'd like to do to that, but not today," she said. "Now, you need to go to Armaeus, and tell him to fix what he did to you. Pronto, before we have even bigger problems on our hands."

Chapter Thirty

I stepped into the cool foyer of the Luxor, trying not to look conspicuous. Night had fallen while I'd been under Death's tattoo gun, and the lobby was alight with gold and glitz. I still wore the formal clothes from the ceremony, however, and no one gave me a second glance as I clicked across the floor. The elevator panel brought the doors immediately snicking open, and I stepped into the metal chamber with a sigh of relief.

The elevator shot skyward, but when the doors opened again, I stepped out not into Armaeus's office, but onto a short foyer fronted by large French doors. The space beyond was a large, tiled veranda, partially covered but open to the cooling desert night. The music of the city drifted up even to these lofty heights: traffic, the buzz of electricity, and the endless clatter and chatter of people.

Armaeus stood at the edge of the veranda, leaning against the banister, his back to the city. If the setting for our meet up wasn't telling enough, his fierce glare was.

"Death told you already. That I'm… That this happened." I knew I should be angry—at Armaeus, at myself. But I couldn't seem to harness my emotions. When I drew near the Magician, it was as if my brain was astral traveling again, and I saw him through a million different prisms, the whole somehow infinitely greater than the sum of its parts.

Armaeus scowled at me. "She told me that I exposed you to a dark power that was neither needed nor wise, and that she had not successfully rid you of all of it.

His gaze dropped to my arm, the bandage hidden beneath the sleeve of my shirt. "She said I was to watch you for any signs of residual damage," he said flatly.

"It's fine. I'm fine," I added unnecessarily as he left his perch on the veranda and moved toward me. There was a bottle of wine opened on the short table in front of the conversationally arranged chaises, as well as a bottle of scotch. I went for the scotch.

Armaeus took the bottle out of my hand, a cut crystal glass appearing in one of his that he splashed the drink into before handing it back. Another glass flickered to life, and he plucked it out of the air.

"You're doing that more," I observed. "Using magic for little things."

"It appears I need to shore up my skills."

I frowned as he turned and looked at the expanse of the Strip. "So what's going on? What did she tell you?"

"The same as she told you, I expect. I need to finish purging the darkness from you. In my attempt to learn more than you were willing to reveal, in my need to share the power source I tapped into in Hell, I have set in motion a series of events that can only end in calamity."

"Calamity… Sounds bad." Death had not been this forthcoming, and I could understand why. But instead of the fear, the panic I knew I should be feeling, I could only seem to conjure up…giddiness. Anticipation. Even hope.

What was *wrong* with me?

I tried to re-center. "Look, there can't be that much damage to my system from my little dunk in Hell's swimming pool," I said. "She really drained a lot of it out."

"There shouldn't have been any." The look Armaeus turned on me was tortured and angry at once. "The magic I poured into you was bound. Locked in stasis until you needed it, with an encryption as old as time." He made a dismissive gesture with his hand, jostling his drink. "As impossible as it is for me to believe, Death said the binding spell I'd placed on that dark power had been broken. Only there is no magic I have encountered in this plane that could destroy what I have made." He scowled at me. "And you would not have done so willingly."

"That would be negative," I said. "And if I'd realized how gross the extraction process was, I definitely wouldn't have tried it without a tetanus shot first."

"It should *not* have happened." Armaeus set down his glass. "There is no magic on this earth stronger than mine."

"So fix it," I said. Seeing the Magician off his game was seriously giving me the heebs. "There's not that much gunk left inside me. You gotta have a plunger in your conjuring bag somewhere, right?"

He shook his head, a man at war with himself. Once again, I waited for the anger, the outrage to surface.

He'd infected me with the muck of Hell. He'd fed me poison to vaccinate against an even greater darkness… Only it hadn't been needed!

Yet I didn't feel angry. Or outraged. Or betrayed. Not by this.

I felt…empowered.

Before I could explore that little deviancy too closely, Armaeus spoke again.

"Would you consent to an…experiment, Miss Wilde?" he asked.

"Does it involve electrical shock?"

His lips twisted. "It doesn't." He moved his hand, and two pyramids appeared above his fingers, floating in the air. "It involves you taking these two items into your hands and holding them at an equal height."

"Like, suspended?"

"Nothing so difficult."

"Then I'm game." I held my hands out, and the two pyramids dropped into each of my palms. I weighed them evenly, holding up my hands for Armaeus to see.

"This doesn't seem so—"

The shock of magic sweeping over me was so great that I staggered back, my knees buckling as my hands exploded in a fiery conflagration, one white-hot with magic, the other black with death. I struggled to keep my right hand from shooting up in the air and my left from sinking down, but the strain was unbearable, the combatting forces of heat and cold leaching into my bones.

"I can't!" I gasped, and no sooner had I spit the words than the pyramids winked out, and Armaeus was there to catch me before I completely fell to the veranda. Catch me—and cradle me close to him.

I didn't care. I sagged into him, too tired to object. He pulled me to the long couch and sat with me half draped over his body, his lips on my hair, murmuring words that were a quiet incantation. With each line, my body felt lighter, my skin looser, the cells in my body expanding far beyond their normal size. It was almost like I was floating above Armaeus, and I sighed, willing to let him finish whatever it was he started.

"That wasn't an experiment, was it?" I asked, and his chuckle rolled over me, still containing that curious note of sadness.

"It was, of a sort. I needed you to accept magic onto your person, and this seemed the most expedient way."

"You know, ordinary people simply ask. They don't make a game out of it."

"No one has ever accused me of being ordinary."

"And now?" I asked, as my feet also left the couch to hover slightly above his body. "What's this part?"

"This, I'm afraid, is all you, Miss Wilde."

I opened my eyes and turned my head, then grasped at Armaeus's shirt. Both of us were floating at least three feet off the couch on his veranda, like Aladdin without the magic carpet. "Armaeus!" I hissed, pulling him closer. "This isn't funny!"

His smile was lopsided. "It's kind of funny."

"It's not remotely funny. Put us down!"

In response, our bodies dropped like lead, and we sprawled over the couch, our arms and legs entangled in each other's. As the Magician watched me intently, I struggled upright on the couch.

"I wasn't doing that, Armaeus. I can't."

"You couldn't before," he corrected me. "You can now. To take Death's explanation, the evil you accepted into your body didn't make you stronger, not in the conventional way. But the seal was broken immediately, long before you actually called on the strength of the darkness. To withstand its force all this time, you had to draw upon your inner reserves. Reserves you didn't even know you were tapping."

"Because it was poisoning me."

"Would have poisoned you," Armaeus said. "Would have eaten you alive from the inside out. That's what I subjected you to. That's what you had to overcome."

"You sound like a CrossFit instructor."

"And you did overcome it—immediately. I never even noticed the battle you were undertaking before my own eyes. A battle you continued to fight. A strength you continued to build."

"And now?"

"Now we can eradicate what was put within you, but your strength isn't going away. What you have become isn't going to change, not easily." He sighed. "But let us at least do that much. If I..."

He leaned forward, and I nodded, surrendering myself to his embrace. I'd been skewered, burned, frozen, and exploded. Being kissed wasn't going to break me.

Of course, this was no ordinary kiss.

Armaeus bent forward and smoothed my hair from my face, staring into my eyes. His own eyes seemed—more golden now, less dark, but before I could comment, he dropped his lips to mine.

The kiss started out gently enough, and I arched beneath him, happy for the touch of his mouth, so warm and vibrant against mine. I knew I needed this healing touch, and I told myself my reaction to Armaeus was only a reflection of that need. It was practical. Logical.

Only there was nothing logical about the pull Armaeus had on me. When he moved his lips and spoke the words of another incantation, I could feel true magic leap within me. I didn't know if that magic was born of my Connected abilities or if it existed simply because of the need I had for Armaeus, a need that trumped reason. Trumped sanity.

Rationally, I understood I was simply a puzzle to the Magician, a mortal he could not command. My every experience on this earth with him was a give and take of power, requiring me to be constantly on my guard, constantly protecting my heart, my mind, my very soul from his never-ending thirst for knowledge.

But I hadn't only interacted with Armaeus on earth. I'd thought I'd known him in another place…truly known him. Truly touched his heart. I'd thought we'd shared a deep and transcendent love, one that erased all that had come before, and superseded all that could come after.

Only we hadn't shared anything, in the end. It had all been an illusion. I'd been left holding the broken shards of a perfect, precious dream that only I had dreamed. I wasn't sure I could come back from that, no matter how much fury I built up between us.

Oblivious to my thoughts, Armaeus shifted his hold on me from a soft embrace to an iron grip.

"This will hurt," he said, the words flowing through my mind.

I grimaced. *Oh, you have no idea.*

The dark power gave up its hold violently. It crashed and roared, ripping through my every cell, searing my nerves and scalding my veins, a crackling rush of darkness that screamed out of me in waves that seemed to go on forever, leaving me limp in its wake.

I crumbled beneath that bellowing storm, shattered and remade myself.

Over and over again.

Finally, however, Armaeus gathered me close, and heaved a deep sigh. "This is unplanned territory for me. If Death is to be believed, it's unexplored territory for all of us."

"What are you talking about?" I peered up at him, too exhausted to make out his cryptic gloom, too pathetically glad to be in his arms for another few moments, before I had to pull on the mantle of my own defiance once more. "I thought you fixed me."

"I fixed the last vestiges of dark magic within you, cauterized the last of those wounds," he said, drifting a kiss over my hair. "But there remains one small matter to attend to."

"Mmmhmm." If this was a come-on, I had to say, Armaeus was upping his game. My defiance could wait a bit longer. "And what is that matter exactly?"

His kiss was whisper soft, touching down on one eyelid and then the other. "I'm afraid you've become immortal, Miss Wilde."

Forever Wilde

In December, 2016, rejoin the war on magic as Sara and Armaeus go toe to toe with an intoxicating rush of immortal power and attraction that neither can control. Meanwhile, Sara learns more about the mysterious Houses of magic that have remained hidden for centuries—and isn't so certain she likes what she discovers. With enemies old and new taking aim, Sara is charged with locating the Hanged Man of the Arcana Council. His identity comes as…something of a shock.

Want more Immortal Vegas? Sign up for my newsletter at www.jennstark.com/newsletter to receive all the latest updates, enter special giveaways, and receive a sneak peak of Forever Wilde!

A Note From Jenn

Sara's reading in the opening chapter of Aces Wilde provides clues to how she can find some (literally) buried treasure. The cards' general interpretations are below, which fit most situations…unless you're looking for an ancient artifact. In that case, pay more attention to the pictures than the symbology of the cards!

The Four of Swords

The Four of Swords is the quintessential "let's take a break" card. It features a soldier at rest, apparently recovering from a battle and possibly doing so on holy ground (note the stained glass above him.) It's likely that you've drawn this card in advance of some enforced down time. You may not want to take a time out, but before you chafe too much over delays/lack of progress, consider the advantages of rest. Sometimes things need to happen behind the scenes and if you're constantly pushing, you may miss out on an opportunity that needs time to develop. Also, rest helps the body (and mind) recover from stress and taxing experiences, which is never a bad thing. Another interpretation of this card is that you simply need to "sleep on it"—take another night to consider a challenging problem or question, and you might wake up with the answer!

The Two of Pentacles

Balance is everything. The Two of Pentacles is the card of managing multiple and sometimes conflicting obligations, weighing two seemingly equal choices or facing the reality of having to go down one path while leaving another one unexplored. As a Pentacle card, often this choice can have to do with money, security or health. Sometimes it's not a question of one-or-the-other, but how you truly can have your cake and eat it too—if you choose to accept multiple obligations, however, you'll need to take on the aspect of the figure in this card. He's not standing still, but in motion, almost dancing. In other words, if you're going to try and do it all, you'll want to stay light on your feet!

The Three of Swords

This card simply looks sad, and for good reason. It's the card of grief, loneliness, literally feeling that your heart has been pricked by swords. It's also, however, the card of necessary cutting—such as a surgery or the removal of that which is no longer needed. It could mean that it's time to clear out the old to make way for the new, and for authors it could be a sign that editing is needed to improve a work. Feeling grumpy or whiny? This card could literally be advising you to "cut it out." In any event, when you draw the Three of Swords, prepare to open yourself up to pain but also to improvement that such pain might bring, and know that you'll be stronger for whatever you're going through now.

Acknowledgments

Aces Wilde was one of those books that makes you nervous to write. Once I started working on it, it wouldn't let me go—and it's my deepest hope I got close to the vision I had for this tale. My sincere thanks to readers all over the world who asked for another book in the Immortal Vegas series by sharing Sara's story with their friends and encouraging sales and reviews. It means more than you can ever know! I remain forever grateful to Elizabeth Bemis for your friendship and mad formatting/design abilities. Gene Mollica once again created a stunning cover for Aces Wilde, exactly capturing the feel of the book, and my editorial team of Linda Ingmanson and Toni Lee kept me (and the story) sane. Any mistakes in the manuscript are, of course, my own. I am also indebted to Kristine Krantz for your patient and thorough read—the book would not be the same without you! And as always, sincere thanks go to Geoffrey—for your vision, insight and guidance, even when you don't realize you're giving it. It's been a *Wilde* ride.

About Jenn Stark

Jenn Stark is an award-winning author of paranormal romance and urban fantasy. She lives and writes in Ohio. . . and she definitely loves to write. In addition to her new "Immortal Vegas" urban fantasy series, she is also author Jennifer McGowan, whose Maids of Honor series of Young Adult Elizabethan spy romances are published by Simon & Schuster, and author Jennifer Chance, whose Rule Breakers series of New Adult contemporary romances are published by Random House/LoveSwept and whose modern royals series, Gowns & Crowns, is now available.

You can find her online at jennstark.com, follow her on Twitter @jennstark, and visit her on Facebook at facebook.com/authorjennstark